# SMASHED
# SQUASHED
# SPLATTERED
# CHEWED
# CHUNKED
# AND
# SPEWED

# lance carbuncle

vicious galoot books, co.
tampa, florida

# Praise for
## *Smashed, Squashed, Splattered, Chewed, Chunked and Spewed*

"My favorite read in a long time. It's real good that you done that, Son. It's a real good thing that you wrote that book."

*Enid Carbuncle,*
*mother of the author*

"Riveting . . . "

*National Sheet Metal Worker's Newsletter*

"Probing . . . "

*Journal of the South American Academy of Proctology*

"Mr. Carbuncle must be a good writer. He manages to work words like defenestration and Pneumonoultramicroscopicovolcaniosis into the story without sounding awkward."

*Annabelle Sootikins,*
*Professor of Literature and*
*Editor of Most Important and Influential New Authors Quarterly*

For Sister Mary Catherine of
Superfecundation.
You make everything groovy.

# PREFACE

Hi. I'm Lance Carbuncle, sort of. If you're reading this, you are probably a relative, one of my few friends, or (most likely) somebody who has humored me and accepted a free copy of my book. This piece of shit that you are holding actually required a great deal of effort on my part. I know that it is hard to read and poorly written. It is probably cliqued, derivative, and in poor taste. Some might say it's offensive, juvenile, and unworthy of being used as ass-wipe (thanks, Uncle Hank). Fuck them and fuck you too.

If you haven't already realized it, this book is self-published. I don't have the drive, desire, or ability to try to sell somebody on publishing my little story. However, thanks to a slippery tile floor at a national restaurant chain (that shall remain unnamed) and a nasty head wound, I have recently found self-publishing to be within my means. So, in the grand tradition of such creative greats as Mrs. Miller[1] and Lord Timothy Dexter[2], I have decided to

---

[1] Mrs. Elva Ruby Connes recorded cover tunes under the name Mrs. Miller. Her voice sounded something like a dying coyote being anally mistreated. It was beautiful. Worth checking out are her versions of *Under the Boardwalk*, *Sweet Pea*, and

foot the costs of distributing my art to the public. If I have changed just one life with my efforts here, then it has been worth it.

You may notice as you read that I am somewhat fond of footnotes. They are sprinkled throughout the book at the bottoms of some of the pages. I do not like footnotes that are placed at the back of books. I never look at them and neither will you. Also, they are usually boring, seldom used in fiction, and can break up the flow of the writing. Nevertheless, I have footnoted random passages in the book and referred to information that I find interesting, funny, stupid, or at least somehow relevant. If the footnotes detract from your attention to the tale, then just ignore them and stick with the story. On the other hand, if you have a third grade reading level or above, you may wish to check out the footnotes. They won't take too much of your time and may give you something to use for small talk at a party or church function.

Anyway, this is the story of an individual who gets involved in some funny situations, experiences some dilemmas, has disturbing feelings for a basset hound, and then it is all resolved within the half-hour format allowed for a television sitcom. The story contains situations in which I have found myself involved. It contains situations in which I have never been involved. It contains situations which, even if I had been involved, I would never admit to in a book where tens of people would be reading it.

The protagonist in this book has made reference to real people, places, and occurrences. Please keep in mind that this is a work of fiction and none of the information is submitted as actual fact. For

---

*These Boots are Made for Walking.*
[2] Author of literary classic *A Pickle for the Knowing Ones.*

example, there really is a place called South of the Border, in Dillon, South Carolina. All of the occurrences in this tale relating to South of the Border are purely the product of the author's sick mind and probably bear no resemblance to anything that has ever occurred there. Likewise, references to an event with an unlucky pachyderm has been somewhat embellished for the purposes of the story. And some of the story relating to the scatological fascination of one of the characters in relation to certain celebrities is certainly only something that occurred in the author's tiny brain. Take it all for what it is. Mostly it's just good twisted fun. Don't take it too seriously. Read it and laugh, or scoff, or grimace, or write your congressman, or whatever it is you might do.

Finally, it is always difficult for me to share my creative output with others. There is the fear that the reader will not understand or simply not enjoy the writing. It feels like I have taken a big dump on a platter and set it out at a party for people to view. I hope you like the way it looks and smells. If you like it, please contact me at my website[3] and let me know. If you don't enjoy my writing, it's probably because you are jealous of me and have self-esteem issues due to your pendulous man-boobs. Learn to deal with it. Buy a bra. Loosen up. Go pour yourself a nice glass of wine and sit down beside the fire. Relax, read, and enjoy.

LANCE CARBUNCLE

---

[3] www.lancecarbuncle.com

1

Renowned historian, philosopher, and musician, Bruce Dickinson once wrote a song about a guy who pushed his luck too far. Daedalus built a pair of wings by stitching feathers together with string and sealing the wings with wax. When the wings were finished, Daedalus warned his son, Icarus, not to fly too near the water or the sun. Like a dipshit-moron, Icarus didn't listen to his father. He wanted to see how high he could fly. He flew higher and higher, nearer and nearer to the sun. As he approached too close to the sun, the wings made of wax melted and Icarus plummeted to his death in the ocean. I too have flown too close to the sun and been burned.

The metaphoric sun that burned my allegorical wings was a chemical called MDMA. I took it on a whim in San Francisco. When I graduated from high school Mom sent me to visit my brother Frank in California. Frank lived in a cramped apartment above a head shop in the Haight-Ashbury district. A cloud of stench hovered several feet off of the dirty floor, reeking of stale bong water, dirty feet, and patchouli. When I arrived Frank handed me a 40-ounce bottle of Olde English 800, five ten-dollar bills and a matchbook with his phone number scribbled on the inside cover.

"Go out and have some fun tonight," Frank told me. "I've gotta work. But, if you have any problems, get into any trouble, you know ... call me." Frank was always watching out for me like that. He gave me my first dirty magazine, my first cigarette, my first hit off a joint. I was six years old when Frank handed me a badly abused issue of *Playboy*. He made me promise not to say where it came from if I got caught. Even at the age of six I was fascinated by female flesh. Some people might say it's not possible, but I remember getting throbbing boners over the soft-core porn in those tattered pages. It didn't take long for Mom to find the nudie magazine stashed under my bed. I would like to say that I was brave in the face of the third-degree Mom gave me over the incident. I would like to say that I held out and fell on the sword, saving Frank from punishment for corrupting me. I wish I could say I stood tight-lipped and gave no information. The truth of the matter is that I sold Frank out faster than I could unfold a centerfold. "Frank gave it to me!" I blurted out. The look on Mom's face was a disturbing mixture of emotions, loving, surprised and even a maybe a little bit of disappointment that I flipped on my own brother so quickly.

Frank took the heat for the magazine and never gave me a bit of grief about it. That's the kind of guy he was. That's the kind of guy he is. I knew that if I had trouble in San Francisco, Frank would bail me out.

Me and Frank left his apartment at the same time. Frank wore a work shirt that said *Earl* on the nametag. He said that

Earl used to have his job but he died or something tragic like that. The boss was going to make Frank pay for his own work shirt if he wanted one with his name on it. Frank opted instead to use the dirty shirt Earl left behind in his locker.

We split up on a street corner where a crowd had gathered. "Stay out of the Castro District," Frank warned me, "unless you're craving some hot man-love." And he was off. I stayed on the corner to see what was going on. A scurvy looking band of musicians were playing a kick-ass version of *Crosstown Traffic.* The guitar player looked kind of like Jimi Hendrix. Well, he was black, he wore a lot of silk scarves, and he had a dazed look on his face. If you used your imagination, squinted and looked at him from the side, he maybe kind of resembled Jimi. The man played a faded and chipped Stratocaster through a tinny, battery powered practice amp. The drummer was pounding out rhythm on a set of various sized pickle buckets, really tearing it up. The other *member* of the band, a disheveled homeless man with untreated psychological maladies, lurched in front of the crowd holding out a hat for donations. Each time there was a pause in the music his face would break out in a rapid twitching fit and he would yell out "EGGTIMERRR," much to the consternation of some of the audience. After a couple of surprisingly rocking versions of Hendrix tunes a black dude approached me, his eyes darting side to side.

"Hey man," said the shifty-eyed black man. "You wanna buy some reefer? Want some rolls? Doses? What you want, Shorty can get it for you?" I'm leery about spur of the moment street deals ever since Frank and I bought some parsley in Ontario from a hustler who could have been Shorty's twin brother. I think one of Shorty's cousins ripped us off for acid in a similar transaction while on a family vacation in Kentucky.

"How much for the X?" I asked.

"Ten dollars for two rolls. It's good shit man. Shorty only sell the best. This shit is made in a U.S. government lab. Top of the line."

Despite Shorty's dubious claims about the product, I slipped him a ten spot and he pressed a rolled up cellophane wrapper into my palm. As I walked away from the crowd I snuck a quick look to make sure I wasn't getting ripped off. Shorty appeared to be an ethical businessman as there were two small pink pills with the inscription *U.S.* on the faces. I inconspicuously extracted one pill, popped it in my mouth and kept walking.

The city was completely unfamiliar to me. I didn't know where I was going. I didn't really care. A street car stopped. I hopped on and hung from the side, feeling a harsh breeze on my face. When I hopped off the cable car I was in an area that appeared to be an entertainment district of the city. Scanning the skyline, my eyes were drawn to an immense skyscraper designed to look like a pyramid. The street had bars, restaurants, shops and, like everywhere else in the city, homeless people. I ducked into a bar called Vesuvius because I liked the name.

Making myself comfortable at the bar, I caught the barmaid's good eye. The other had a mind of its own and seemed to favor snuggling up right next to her nose, giving her a dopey, half-cross-eyed look. "Hi," she said as she approached. "We have a two-for-one special on Heineken bottles. You wanna do that?"

"Heineken?" I growled. "Fuck that shit! Pabst Blue Ribbon!"

The barmaid's name was Kristi. Her good eye gave me a stern

look while the other flitted about, seemingly checking out the room. She brought me a bottle of Pabst without comment and quickly tended to other customers. No sense of humor. Shit, I was just goofing. "Look at me," I told her and she looked my way. "Don't fucking look at me," I growled. She looked away without so much as a smile. Some people just don't get my humor.

It had been at least an hour since I took the X and nothing was happening. *Damn*, I thought, *ripped off again. Or maybe the shit Shorty sold me just wasn't very strong.* I figured I might as well take the other pill just in case. Chugging what was left of my beer, I stood up and headed down the stairs for the bathroom. The bathroom was empty, but I wanted to make sure no one saw me putting a pill in my mouth. I ducked into one of the shitters and listened. Nobody. The stall had an advertising board on the wall that promoted tanning beds, a dating service, and liposuction. God damn it, you can't even drop mud without being bombarded with commercials. I pulled out the cellophane and studied the remaining pill. Why not take it? I had nothing to lose. Maybe I needed two of them to really get off. I gently set the pill on my tongue and swallowed. *Down the rabbit hole*, I thought.

Back at the bar I caught Kristi's good eye and ordered another Pabst Blue Ribbon. A Tom Petty song was playing. I never really liked his stuff, but DAMN, this song sounded really good. I'd heard it loads of times before and never realized how great it was. It was as if I was becoming a part of the song. I decided that I needed to buy some Tom Petty albums when I got a chance. *Refugee* wound down and *The Safety Dance* followed. WOW, I never realized before how FUCKING COOL *The Safety*

*Dance* is. "Your friends don't dance and if they don't dance, well they're no friends of mine." Men Without Hats also went on my new list of records to purchase.

And then . . . it hit me. I was starting to roll. Shorty done me right. Hmmm, maybe that second pill wasn't really necessary. I downed the rest of my beer, slapped a ten-dollar bill on the counter and yelled at Kristi: "I can't stand warm fucking beer. It makes me want to fucking puke." She half stared at me, perplexed. I winked at her good eye and made for the door.

Stepping back onto the street, I noticed that everybody was better dressed than me. I felt out of place. People were watching me, evaluating, judging me. I just knew it. It seemed prudent to move along. Not knowing where I was or where I was going, I just started walking. I was driven. My feet needed to move. My legs were twitchy. Teeth: grinding. My legs were my guides and the rest of me was along for the ride. The pyramid stayed in my line of vision while my legs worked the spasms out.

The cheesy notes from a Casiotone keyboard caught my attention. On the corner, a street busker was churning out serious emotions on a little electronic organ. The sign hanging on the front of his instrument read: The Outrageous Neal Stevens. Eight or nine people were digging on his stuff. Somehow the rhythm track on the keyboard didn't sound cheesy. The lush tones penetrated me. I felt the song, sensed where it was going, it penetrated me. An older homeless lady (it came to me that her name was probably Crazy Mary) was standing beside me, swaying, not quite in time, to the music. She was dirty, toothless, deranged. We made eye contact. I knew we felt the same about The Outrageous Neal's music. I swayed next to my new friend and shared her emotions. "Trails," I said to her as I saw a greenish-yellow streak weave through the air.

Crazy Mary smiled a horrible, toothless grin and nodded. "Trails," she agreed.

I noticed a cop on the sidewalk studying me and decided it was time to beat it. "So long, Crazy Mary," I said as I ducked around the corner and up the street. "Happy trails."

"Trails," said Mary, "trails."

Halfway up the street, the urge to vomit overwhelmed me. It wasn't a sickening sensation. It wasn't unpleasant. I just knew it was going to happen and rode the wave. "Hrr-phlaggghhhh ... " A warm flow of bile, Pabst Blue Ribbon, and clam chowder (when the hell did I eat that?) spewed from my face. I projectile-vomited a comforting stream of my stomach contents onto the side of a building. Then it was done. Not a drop on me. I continued my journey.

Now that my stomach was empty it seemed that maybe food would be a good idea. I found myself in front of a restaurant. The glaring red, yellow and pink neon sign beckoned. *"The Stinking Rose, a garlic restaurant"* it screamed at me. The maitre d' seated me at a small table near the front door. Everything on the menu had garlic in it. I ordered marinated garlic olives and the Gilroy Famous Garlic Ice Cream with caramel molé sauce. I had to ask my waiter, Angel, what the hell molé was (as if anybody ordering garlic ice cream has any room to be picky about the sauce). Angel explained, "Oh, it's a spicy Mexican sauce made with chilies, chocolate, tomatoes and other spices. It's yum."

"Sounds great," I said. "And I'll have a garlic martini while I'm waiting."

Angel eyed me as if trying to decide whether or not to card me. I was ready with an expired moped license of Frank's just in case I needed I.D. I looked enough like the picture to pass. "Okay. Super," answered Angel, apparently deciding that I appeared to be legal.

The other customers kept shooting me irritated glances while I waited for my food. I had so much nervous energy. The only way I could vent it was to tap my feet and drum on the table with my fingertips. It seems that the manic tapping made some people uncomfortable. I felt like I needed to explode from my seat. *Control yourself*, I admonished. *Take a sip of your garlic martini, take a deep breath and stop that ridiculous tapping of your left foot.*

The couple at the table to my left continued to give me the hairy eyeball. Opening my eyes as wide as I could and biting the insides of my cheeks, I concentrated intensely, focusing all of my will on stopping the tapping. *God, I wish they would play some Tom Petty or Safety Dance,* I thought. That would've calmed me down.

Then an Angel appeared at my side. Not the cherubic, winged and haloed type of Angel. No, it was the dark-skinned, brown-eyed, gay Mexican waiter variety of Angel. "Enjoy," he advised as he set my olives and ice cream on the table.

*Urgggh.* My stomach was rebelling again. The sight of the food made me want to hurl. Why in the fuck was I ordering food? I couldn't eat. The sudden urge to run from the food was overwhelming. "I can't eat that fucking garlic shit," I urgently explained to the appalled couple at the table beside me. I jumped out of my seat and bolted out of the front door without paying my bill. The old dine and dash. I just couldn't eat; the food would have been like broken glass and acid in my stomach. Running down the street I could hear Angel yelling behind me from the front door of the Stinking Rose.

My feet carried me to a park. I stomped around the perimeter of the grounds ten, twenty, thirty times. My legs pumped and burned. There was a heavy hum and ticking inside my head. Pyramid skyscraper, looming, always in sight. My left eye went cold, something in my head hurt, like a rubber band snapping inside my brain. Cold numbness spread slowly along my left side. I went limp. Dizziness, loss of vision, trails, blackness . . .

The rest is lost on me. Somehow I crossed the Golden Gate Bridge because I was found facedown in the middle of a forest of coastal redwoods. A group of junior rangers happened upon what they assumed to be a dead body draped across the trail. It was just me passed out. After a poking with sticks failed to revive me an official park ranger was summoned. The ranger, Rick, was also unable to get me to stir. He hefted my nearly lifeless shell to the ranger station and called an ambulance. Rick inventoried the contents of my pockets and found an expired moped license bearing the name *Frank Gurkin* and a matchbook with a phone number scrawled on the inside cover. Frank was contacted and met the ambulance at the hospital.

I stayed in that hospital for two weeks. Upon regaining consciousness I discovered tubes inserted in almost every orifice: my nose, my throat, my prick. The only one that didn't have something jammed in it was my asshole, and that was sore for some reason. Tests were run on me: MRI, STD, CAT scan, PET scan, Pap smear, Hamster Egg Penetration Test, Testicular Torsion exams, brain swabs, and Pinworm Popsicle Surprise. You name it, I had it done on me. My balls were squeezed, my asshole poked, my nipples pinched. I don't know why all of this was done, but my orderly, Ramone, claimed it was doctor's orders. I became suspicious when Ramone said it was hospital policy that he lock the door during the medically necessary poking and prodding. "Oh yeah," Ramone explained, "it's also doctor's orders that you don't tell anybody that I have been performing these tests on you." Despite my misgivings, I grudgingly continued to endure Ramone's nipple pinching, ball squeezing and ass-spelunking tests. I needed to know if permanent damage had been done by the MDMA.

All of the tests came back and my doctor said he detected no long-term damage. He said I had something called a Transient Ischemic Attack, a mini- stroke. There was nothing else they could do for me. I was released to Frank's care. I don't know why, but Ramone gave me a beautiful bouquet of flowers when I was discharged and told me to keep in touch. Frank had already heard an earful from Mom about my situation. Like always, he took the blame for me. "He didn't do it on purpose," Frank told Mom. "Somebody slipped something in his drink at a club. I never should have taken him there. It's my fault." Frank tried to make me feel better and said that Shorty messed him up bad too when he first came out here. Once after sampling some of Shorty's product, Frank woke up at the pier on a floating dock. The fishy stank of seal shit and an overly friendly sea lion bull shook him from his slumber. Frank wouldn't say a whole lot more about the experience other than to mention that he sometimes goes back to the pier and throws fish out to the seals. Big brother dropped me off at the San Francisco International Airport, gave me a loaf of sourdough bread for Mom and a Muir Woods T-shirt for me. "Good luck, Fuckface," he said, pushing me out of the car and shipping me back home to Mom.

**2**

The way I see things, you take what life hands you and you deal with it. Some people piss and moan all along the way and make themselves miserable. It's like life drags them along ass-backwards, always looking at the past, bemoaning injustices, fretting about the could'ves and should'ves. Not me, I can't live life like that. I wanna enjoy the ride, however short it may be.

If anybody has a legitimate grievance, it's me. I don't know what happened to my head fifteen years ago in San Francisco, but I ain't been right since. My doctors inspect me, scan my head, stick me with needles, and smear my dookey on microscope slides. Hell, they practically give me the old Flaky Dust Poison Torture. Then they say things like: "there is no conclusive determination of abnormality," or "possible impaired perceptual functioning and phobic anxiety." I don't know what the fuck they are talking about. All I know is that I have a constant ticking sound in my head and I sometimes black out when confronted with stressful situations. And something else happened to my head in California. I don't know exactly how to explain it. It's like I have powers or something. I'm not talking crazy shit like I can fly like Superman or anything like that. It's more like magic. Not like Samantha Stevens on *Bewitched*. I don't wiggle my nose and items materialize from out of nowhere. Although I did used to fantasize that I had the power to stop time and I could do whatever I wanted while everyone else was frozen: in that fantasy world I would walk into a bank and take all the money I needed, and if one of the bank tellers was hot, maybe I would bend her over the counter and give her the old inny-outy and she would never even know what happened when I unfroze time. She would just wake up with a warm feeling between her legs and a smile on her face. I wish I had those powers, but that would be crazy if I thought I could do that. My powers are more psychic, I guess. It's almost like I can read people's minds. I can tell when they like me; I can tell when they don't. Sometimes a vague feeling comes over me and I sense what *THEY* are thinking. Not word for word or anything. It's more of a feeling. But I know when somebody's out to get me and I know when to do a preemptive strike against someone who's thinking bad thoughts about me.

Some may think I'm a loser. It's easy to judge me just because I'm 35, unmarried, unemployed, and live in my mom's basement. I can't be too hard on myself, though. I've got a disability. I hear the ticking, I get the blackouts, I lose concentration. People who don't know me well enough might say I'm delusional and paranoid, but they're just out to get me. I don't know what happened to my brain. My doctors can't tell me. All I know is that I'm different. Sometimes it seems that my shit's fucked up, but I don't know how. I've heard that Ecstasy eats holes in your brain. Maybe that's what happened to me. Maybe the holes were filled in with crazy. But like I said, I can't bitch. Me and Mom are moving to Florida. Mom's cool, I have a bad-ass CD collection, and my dog is my best friend.

Idjit Galoot is a velvet-eared, paddle-pawed basset hound. He has lived in my basement with me for the past fifteen years. I've had him ever since he was a puppy. Idjit's old for a basset hound (they have a life expectancy of about twelve years). I guess in dog years he's about a hundred and five. You wouldn't know it, though. He still acts like a puppy sometimes. That old dog has a zest for life. Maybe it's the daily beer and deviled egg that I give him. Maybe it's the fact that I never had him fixed.

The Galoot's frequent farts stink of cheap beer with an undertone of rotting vegetation. This I forgive him as he pretends he doesn't notice it when I cut the cheese.[4] The soulful brown eyes, the loose, droopy dog lips, the pronounced dewlap—I love all of these things about him. When we watch TV, Idjit rests his weighty head in my lap and lets me stroke the loose-fitted skin-folds. It's therapeutic; relaxing for us both. I don't mind my hound's aroma. In his youth he would roll in any pile of scat or smashed roadkill available. Frank told me that dogs do that to attract the attention of the opposite sex. "It's like wearing an orange coat," he explained, "it draws your attention." Idjit

---

[4] **The Great Fart Survey**, a survey of 1,000 Australians found that 39% of those surveyed enjoyed the scent of their own farts. 15% of those surveyed gave no answer to the question. If it can be properly inferred that the refusal to answer amounts to an admission, then the survey can be interpreted to show that over 50% of Australians enjoy huffing their own flatulence.

stopped rolling in rotting filth years ago. He still has developed his own musky odor with age, though. Part of it is from his oily, patchy coat. His odor, like the metallic smell of nickels, clings to my hand when I pet him.

My vet says I need to express The Galoot's anal glands and the musky odor will go away. According to Dr. Dean, I'm supposed to put my fingers on each side of Idjit's rectum and press until liquid seeps out of his butt ("it will look like coffee but taste different," he joked). This will rid my dog of the scent and his favorite pastime of dragging his butt on the carpeting. As far as I am concerned, I can stand his odor and I'm not planning on eating off of the floor anytime soon. So I really see no reason to go putting constant pressure on the perimeter of my dog's butthole. It's a matter of mutual respect. Idjit doesn't go complaining about my musky odor and he doesn't try to express my anal gland. I will reciprocate with the same courtesy.

Sometimes I wish I could wave a magic wand and turn Idjit into a beautiful lady. He has all of the qualities I'm looking for in a woman. He doesn't expect anything from me but to cuddle up while we watch movies or mixed-martial arts fighting. He only really needs a daily ration of Pabst Blue Ribbon, deviled eggs, and snuggling. I've never had a woman who gave me the loving looks that I get from that dog. The Galoot doesn't judge me just because I live with Mom and don't have a steady job. He has never put me down for my fondness for heavy metal. If I don't bathe for a couple of days, he seems to kind of like it. He's never called me a pervert or a retard or told me to grow up. Idjit loved Black Sabbath when they had Ozzy but can't stand them with Ronnie James Dio. Never has that dog told me I'm not sensitive or tried to make me watch a romantic comedy starring an ugly dame with a big nose. If he could assume the form of a beautiful female, he would be perfect.

He's not a beautiful woman. He's a stinky old fleabag. He ain't never caught a rabbit. With age Idjit is amassing an impressive collection of fatty lumps about his body. This is in large part the reason that I stroke his head and not the body. People might say he's gross. I wouldn't trade him for anything.

When I told Idjit we were moving to Florida he stared at me for a while, wagging his tail slowly, unsure, and let out a small sulfuric belch. As always, he was cautiously optimistic.

**3**

Have you ever seen a dog that has broken his chains, jumped his fence, slipped his collar, or otherwise shed his shackles? You will not see a purer form of happiness. A canine unfettered by human restraints experiences joy that man rarely knows—the freedom to chase squirrels, tear into a bag of rancid garbage, crap in the neighbor's front yard, to dig up a flower bed for no particular reason. These are the simple pleasures that make life worth living for a dog. The next time you see a dog running down the street by himself, look at his face. He will be smiling—a big dumb, dopey smile. Unadulterated, ignorant glee. And wouldn't you know it, on the day I'm supposed to leave for Florida, Idjit most likely has that look on his old mug. He's gone AWOL. I can picture him running free, his giant ears flopping, a big moronic grin, seeking out fresh garbage or a bitch in heat.

"The truck is packed and ready," Mom tells me. "You and Cousin Denny need to hit the road. Idjit will get hungry and come home. It's what he does. I'll bring him down with me when I leave."

Cousin Denny and I are supposed to share driving duties on the moving truck Mom rented. Denny is my age and, like me, has never held down a regular job. Even though his hairline is rapidly retreating from his forehead, Denny insists on keeping it long in back. A modified mullet, or skullet as I like to call it. Denny says that his haircut is business in front, party in back. "Did you strap your Daddy in?" he asks me, smirking, always smirking.

"He's tethered," I answer, not appreciating Denny's tone. I never really knew Daddy too well while he was alive. My memories of him are foggy—nothing specific, just a comfortable feeling. I know he was nice to me and I feel a sense of security and warmth when I try to dredge his memory up in my addled brain. The only real memory I have is playing marbles with the glass eyeballs Daddy always kept in his pocket.

All I know about Daddy I learned from Mom, picture books and Daddy's writings. He taught philosophy at various universities and community colleges. According to Mom, Daddy was fascinated by a man named Jeremy Bentham. This Bentham guy advocated the dissection of cadavers during a time when such a belief was controversial. Gravediggers were robbing cemeteries in order to get corpses for medical students. Mr. Bentham wrote a will that provided that upon death his body be used for scientific study and, when done, his remains were to be stuffed and displayed in a glass cabinet at University College in London. Bentham's body has been on display in one form or another since his death sometime in the 1800's. His face was grossly disfigured, though, and a wax head was placed on the body for display purposes. It's rumored that Bentham's *auto icon* is still wheeled out and seated at a table for meetings of the College Board.

Upon his death, Daddy wanted his body to be stuffed and displayed just like Bentham. In his will Daddy asked Mom to make him an auto icon and have him placed on display at the university where he was teaching. Daddy died when I was three. Mom reluctantly honored his wishes, took him to a taxidermist and had Daddy preserved and stuffed.[5] The university balked at putting Daddy on display. Daddy came home with Mom and has sat in his favorite reclining chair ever since, his gaping rictus reflecting apparent amusement at his situation. Mom says that Daddy loved the holidays so we always dress him appropriately for the time of the year: at Christmas Daddy wears a Santa suit; for Easter it's rabbit ears and a strap-on bunny snout; there's the #1 Dad shirt for Father's Day. Heck, sometimes we even put on a colorful yarmulke for Jewish holidays. Denny enjoys ridiculing Daddy's festive attire. But I think it's kind of cool.

"Well if you ask me," Denny offers, "I think it's kind of God-damned creepy that you guys keep him in that chair. Why don't you give the man a proper burial? I don't know how I stand living with you guys." Denny is always full of advice. In his small mind he is all-knowing and all-wise. If you're doing something,

---

[5] Plastination is a technique that is now available to preserve human bodies or body parts. The fat and water in body tissues can be replaced with plastics, thus depriving bacteria of the conditions they need to survive. A plasticated specimen does not smell or decay. Several large displays of real human plastinates have been exhibited around the world. One such exhibit is located in Orlando, Florida. One can imagine a family on vacation in the world's happiest place, stopping in for an interesting science lesson and being horrified by real human bodies with skin sliced away, muscles filleted, and openly exposed genitals.

Denny will tell you how you should do it. If you bought some-thing, he'll tell you ten reasons why you shouldn't have gotten that one. He's sometimes the kind of guy that would crap on your birthday cake and tell you that he's doing you a favor.

"Maybe you just don't understand," I shoot back. "Your dad's still alive and all you ever do is fight with him. Shit, I have a bet-ter relationship with Daddy then you and Uncle Doug ever had."

"Aw, jeez man, I'm just offering some constructive criticism. You don't need to get your fallopian tubes all twisted up. Have some tea. We have a long drive, and we should probably go straight through." Denny brewed a gallon of something he calls Mormon Tea. For a while he had been living in a ghost town in Utah called Cisco. When he came to stay with us Denny brought a big garbage bag packed with a tangle of dusty, green, leafless stems. In anticipation of the long drive Denny crushed up the stems and cooked them in a big pot of water over night. This morning the tea was strained out. Denny hands me a travel mug full of greenish murky liquid. "Bottoms up."

Never one to turn away from a new experience, I down the bitter potion. "What's this do?" I ask.

"It'll keep you awake. Might make you a little jittery. Could give you mud-butt," Denny explains.

The road passes under us—mile markers, fence posts and exit signs whizzing by and disappearing into the past.

*Lima . . . Dayton . . . Cincinnati . . .*

"You know, you should take some courses in community col-lege. You're a smart guy who is wasting time living in his mother's basement. You should do something with your life." More helpful advice from Denny.

Thoughts of Idjit cross my mind. I already miss that big Galoot. I hope he has returned home. When he gets down to Florida we are going to party.

I need to pee. It's unbearable. I bleed the lizard into an empty Snapple bottle so that we don't have to stop. We want to make good time. I almost completely fill the bottle and then throw it out the window. Warm, clear, piss spills all over my hand. There's the bad karma for littering.

*Lexington . . . Richmond . . . Berea . . . Renfro Valley Bluegrass Festival . . .*

"Hey, did you ever notice that babies' clothes have pockets in them?" I ask.

"What in the fuck are you talking about? What do you know about babies' clothes?" Denny forgets that my sister, Kelli, is popping out a new baby almost annually and then dropping them off for Mom to take care of.

"Oh, I know babies' clothes. And I'm serious. Babies' clothes all have pockets. Little, bitty pockets. And I'm wondering: what the fuck does a baby need pockets for? What's he going to put in there? And those pockets are so small, the only thing they can put in the pockets anyway would be a choking hazard."

"You're right," says Denny, kind of dreamy-like. "Pockets, hmmm? You know what does need pockets?"

"What?"

"Underwear!" I can see Denny's wheels turning. Or maybe it is more like his gears grinding. A dim light bulb flickers weakly above his head.

"Underwear?"

"Yeah, skivvies, BVD's, Fruit of the Looms, boxers, briefs, boxer-briefs." Denny likes to say the same thing in as many different ways as he can sometimes. He thinks it makes him sound smart or witty or something. "But not butt-floss or banana-hammocks. You could only put small pockets on them, which of course could only hold choking hazards. And if you have to worry about infant choking hazards in people's underwear...well...we really wouldn't want those people as customers. Hey..." he's smiling.

"Yeah?" I ask, afraid that the Mormon Tea has flipped on a monologue switch in Denny's brain that will not shut off for the rest of the trip.

"I've got a choking hazard for you in my underwear." He reaches over and punches me in the arm. "Seriously, though, underwear with pockets. You can keep whatever you want protected from pickpockets. Ain't no Mr. Slippyfingers going to get down in your pants to take your wallet without your knowing it. And if you're sitting around your basement in your underwear, as is typical for you, you can keep a tube of Jergen's lotion in your pocket so you can lube yourself up for the five-knuckle-shuffle, burpin' the worm, ya know, the tug of war with Cyclops."

Having heard enough of Denny's genius and knowing that our trip is a straight shot down I-75 I nod off for a while (a whole heck of a lot of good the Mormon Tea did me).

*Jellico... Clinton... Knoxville...*

"And who wouldn't want one of those things in his bathtub? Three quick squirts and you're good to go." Denny is still talking as I ease into wakefulness. "Hey, do you believe in love at first sight?"

"Umm, ahh, I don't know," I mumble and wipe slobbery moisture from my chin.

"Or better yet, do you believe each person has a soul mate?"

"I dunno." I'm barely even conscious and Denny wants to engage me in a philosophical discussion of love and soul mates. Jesus. I'm 35 years old and I have only slept with a handful of women in my life. Haven't had a relationship that's lasted over three weeks and I'm supposed to have answers about love and soul mates. If anything, Idjit Galoot is probably my soul mate.

"I have a soul mate," Denny announces proudly. "Her name is Marie. She's still in Utah."

"Izzat so?"

"She's a Mormon, though. They've banned her from seeing me. Sent her away somewhere. But our souls are one. She says our beings are inextricably intertwined. Marie has guaranteed that I will get into heaven, no matter what."

"She can't do that. She's not God."

"No. But she *is* a devout Mormon," Denny defends, "and she's taking me with her when she goes to heaven."

"What is a devout Mormon girl doing sleeping with you?" I ask.

"I ain't never slept with her. Our connection is different. I think she sort of pities me for some reason—feels a need to nurture. She told me that there is a Mormon ritual that binds her soul to mine. I don't understand it all; she was kind of vague. But, what it amounts to is that she will drag me up to heaven with her when she goes. I've got a get-into-heaven-free ticket."

"How in the hell does that work?" I am genuinely curious.

"Don't know. Don't care. I'm going to heaven." Denny tilts his travel mug up and chugs the remainder of his tea. Some spills down his chin and leave a green stain on his shirt.

"What if she dies before you?" I ask. Finally the conversation is getting interesting and I'm starting to wake up. I think the tea is working. The back of my neck is tingling. "I mean, say she dies before you. Do you die at the exact same time and get dragged right up to heaven? Or does your soul just get yanked but your body goes on living, moving, shitting, eating and sleeping, but thoughtless, kind of like you are already I guess."

Worry lines form on Denny's brow. "I dunno. She never explained that to me . . . "

"It is interesting. Do you die or does your body just wander the earth as an empty shell, like a zombie?"

"She never explained any of that shit. She just told me I could go to heaven and I went along with it." His voice rises in pitch. He's freaking. Just for shits and giggles I needle him a little bit more.

"What if Marie commits a mortal sin? What if she somehow falls out of grace with God? If she fucks up and goes to hell, does her soul suck yours down into the depths of Hades right along with hers?"

"I never thought of any of that." I've never seen Denny shaking like that before. It's not a pretty sight to see a slightly balding man with a mullet crying. It's like something straight out of an episode of *Cops*. "She just said I could get into heaven so I said 'great.' It was more like she was sneaking me into the movies through the side door or something."

"Hey, Nancy, I'm just busting your balls. Calm down. I'm sure that Marie is just some wackadoo, probably has no more inside connections with the big man than you or me." I may have gone too far. Despite the fact that Denny's kind of an asshole... and a bumbling idiot... and has a really bad haircut... well, I do kind of like him anyway. He is kin. "By the way, you've already managed to get us lost."

The sign up ahead greets us: "Welcome to Erwin, Tennessee. Population 5610." Somehow we ended up in an area of Tennessee with town names like Bumpus and Dry Hump Cove.

4

Dusk approaches and Denny's despondent over the hereto-fore-unconsidered ramifications of the binding of his eternal soul to someone else. A blinking green neon bull lights up the front of a cinder block building, beckoning us. "There's a bar right over there," I tell Denny. "Pull over and let's get a drink."

Denny wheels the moving truck into the gravel parking lot of the Brahman Bar and Package Store. The once transparent glass door to the bar is smudged with smoke residue and oily handprints. By concentrating real hard and looking at the door from an angle, it appears that there are faces trapped in the smut on the door, as if the spirits of the customers, or parts of them, remain stuck in the bar forever (or at least until the door is introduced to a clean rag and some Windex). A patron exits—smoke and the strains of bad karaoke roll out, trailing him. Denny gives me a shoulder-shrugging question of a look, as if to say *Are you sure you want to go in here?*

"Let's do it," I say as we enter the Brahman. The room is dimly lit and thick with the smog of burning tobacco. We sit down at the bar beside a scruffy-faced, scraggle-toothed customer.

The barmaid approaches. She has red hair, a black eye, and yellow teeth. "What can I do ya for, honey?" She asks, surprisingly without a trace of a southern drawl or twang. And smiling.

"Two PBR's." I smile back, evaluating her. I get a feeling about her—my senses, ESP, mind-reading, whatever you want to call it. I know about her already. She's good-natured. She was pretty once, but time, Pall Malls, ethyl alcohol, and a string of abusive relationships took care of that. Ramona is her given name, but she goes by Annie. *Ramona is a nice name*, I think to myself. She's not from here, maybe up north judging from her speech pattern.

"I can have her," I tell Denny when Ramona walks away.

He squinches up his face, as if I just held a tiny, pungent, nugget of a dog turd directly under his nose. "You'd better drink a bit more first, buddy. You're gonna need some beer goggles for that one." More than anything I know that Denny is striking out because he's still upset about that soul-binding business. He's certainly not the picky type with women.

"What, you wouldn't do her?" I ask defensively.

"I'm lonely, but I ain't that lonely yet."

"I'm serious. I have a feeling. I can have this woman," I tell Denny. "I'm no ladies-man like you. What do I do?"

"I don't know. Tell her a dirty joke. If she laughs, you're in. It always works for me." It's true, too. Denny is way more experienced with women than me. He claims that he "gets more ass than a park bench." My cousin is really more of a quantity over quality kind of guy. White ones, black ones, skinny broads, fat dames, bad complexions, yeast infections, mob connections, he doesn't care. If it has a warm wet hole and is vaguely feminine, Denny will fuck it. He doesn't care what they look like. It is his firm belief that the light switch was invented so that he could enjoy sex with women whose beauty is not readily apparent to the eyes. Aside from the self-serving aspect of his philosophy, Denny truly believes that he is doing a public service by porking the women that most men with vision and the sense of smell would reject.

I don't have Denny's suave and debonair manner. Sometimes just making small talk with people I don't know is like exercise. That's why I enjoy people like Denny. They do all of the talking and I will add something when it's relevant or important. I am pitiful when I try out my skills on women. The few who have slept with me have done so as a result of intoxication, pity, financial incentive or all of the above.

No matter where you go, Karaoke night always brings out at least one person hoping to be discovered singing Patsy Cline's *Crazy*, or maybe *Lady in Red*. As we wait for our beers, a big-haired, mule-faced hopeful sings some fucked-up country song. She's cleaned-up and dressed in her thrift store best. Sequins sewn across her ample bosom spell out her stage name— *Peaches*. I'd bet dollars to donuts there are no Nashville talent scouts in the Brahman scraping the bottom of the karaoke barrel for their next big star. Nevertheless, the big-toothed girl is singing her heart out and rigidly performing her choreographed moves.

The scruffy little man beside me at the bar introduces himself as Crash. "Peaches performs that song every night," he tells me. "I'll be goddamned if my girl don't get better each time. That girl has *IT*. She will be famous, one day, you watch." I suggest to

Crash that he might want to change his name to Herb if Peaches ever does hit the big-time, and he looks at me like I'm speaking Japanese.

Two Pabsts arrive and I take Denny's advice. "Hey Ramona," I venture, "what's black and white and red and doesn't like sex very much?"

Her eyes widen. Shock? I'm not sure. She relaxes, looks at me apprehensively. "I don't know. What?"

"The nun I have tied up in my basement," I answer and wait for a reaction. It's like time stops. Ramona just stares. I think I blew my one shot. Then the corner of her mouth starts to move. A full-blown grin breaks out, followed by a good natured, genuine laugh.

"You're a sick little puppy, aintcha?" She laughs. "I like you."

In my peripheral vision I see Denny give me a slight nod that says "You're in." We hang around, listening to Karaoke and drinking more beer. Denny's mood never really lifts. He still frets. I decide to do something to cheer him up. Borrowing a pen from behind the bar, I write on a napkin and hand it to Ramona.

"This says you're selling me your soul to pay for your bar-tab tonight,"[6] she says. "What am I gonna do with your soul?"

"Well, if you ever get in a jam, you could sell it to the Devil for something and you will still be squeaky clean, no eternal damnation for you," I tell her.

"We usually prefer U.S. currency. But you seem like a nice

---

[6] In the third episode of the seventh season of *The Simpsons*, Bart Simpson sold his soul to Millhouse for five dollars in the form of a piece of paper saying "Bart Simpson's soul." Millhouse traded the soul to the comic book storeowner, Jeff "Comic Book Guy" Albertson, for a set of *Alf* pogs.

enough guy... Probably relatively low mileage and only a few dents and dings on this model," she says, eying me as if I were a used car. "You've got a deal. But you have to let me buy you breakfast at the Egg Hut after I close up."

The black clouds hanging over Denny lift. The possibility of my eternal damnation makes us comrades in the same foxhole. Misery loves company, I guess.

Closing time approaches and Crash explains the origins of his nickname. "I crashed my TransAm into a tree. Flew out, through the windshield, and my forehead smacked into a big old oak tree. My head's been all fucked up ever since." Pulling off his sweat-stained ball cap, Crash shows me a scoop of negative space where much of his forehead used to be. "Go ahead, feel it," he tells me, indicating the large dent in his forehead. I oblige, pushing on the spongy indentation. There is no skull there.

"Ow, you're poking right into my frontal lobe," he yelps. "Pushing too hard on me! I told you to feel it. I didn't say jam your finger through my brain to the back of my head, did I?"

"I–I–I–I..." I stammer, a bit in shock. "I'm sorry. Jesus. I didn't realize..."

"Aw, it's okay. I was just fuckin' with ya anyway," he laughs. "That was my brain you were pushin' on, though. Pretty weird, huh?"

"Alright," the cheesy DJ-wannabe voice of the Karaoke MC says, "next we have Crash singing a little ditty." The music to Kiss's *Beth* begins but Crash has written his own words, a love song about Peaches. I think to myself that he's not so fucking great. If I had a couple more beers I might get up and sing some Iron Maiden, or maybe *The Safety Dance*.

**5**

The plan was to drive straight through to the Sunshine State. The possibility of a sleazy, meaningless, perhaps demeaning, one-night-stand changed everything. Guys (real guys) will help each other out with stuff like that. Denny didn't mind the delay. He even gave me some advice before Ramona and I went up to her apartment above the Brahman: "Don't tell her your real name."

The Egg Hut was closed for renovations. That sucks because their sign advertised a smashed, squashed, splattered, chewed, chunked and spewed bucket of griddle-taters for $1.99. I don't know what they do to those grittle-taters but they sure sound good. Ramona offered to cook us breakfast at her place. Denny declined and stayed in the moving truck with a six-pack of Red, White and Blue to keep him company while Ramona and I went upstairs. Her apartment was small, wood paneled, dirty and warm. Scooping up a pile of dirty clothes from a threadbare chair she told me to sit down while she cooked up some eggs and corned beef hash. The greasy smell of breakfast food gradually and partially edges out the odor of stale tobacco smoke and cat urine.

Emptying an overflowing ashtray and lighting up a fresh Pall Mall, Ramona asks, "How did you know my name? Everybody calls me Annie. Nobody here knows me as Ramona."

"I have powers," I tell her in a spooky voice, wiggling my fingers in front of me as if casting a spell.

"You're weird. I like it. Listen . . . I don't usually bring random guys up to my place . . . " (she lies) " . . . and you haven't even told me your name. But I just have a good feeling about you."

"My name is Larry Mondello . . . " (I lie)

"That's not what you signed on the napkin when you bartered your soul to cover your bar-tab."

"Yeah, I'm lying. I'm not very good at this kind of thing . . . " (I'm truthful)

"You didn't seem like a player. Just relax, Mr. Mondello. We'll hang out and see what happens."

A grey and white, large-footed cat tries to move me off of my seat, its nose an ineffectual bulldozer on my leg. Recognizing defeat, the cat instead decides to make itself comfortable on my lap, purring and nudging my belly with its face. The kitty's name is Earnest.

"He is a poly-dak-tul," Ramona says. "That means he has more toes than a normal cat. It really just means he has more claws to tear up my carpeting and furniture."

We drink beer, eat an early breakfast/late dinner, and talk. Ramona tells me about her adopted town.

Erwin's most famous character was Murderous Mary. Mary was a circus elephant, originally dubbed Mighty Mary. One day, in the early 1900's, while parading through the adjacent city of Johnsonville and thrilling the local townspeople, Mary put on her greatest show to date. She took umbrage at her handler's ungentlemanly manner. In a perfect example of the *Peter Principle*[7], Walter "Red" Eldrige (Mary's wholly unqualified handler) began to hit her with a bull-hook. The long stick with a hook on the end generally irritated Mary, and, specifically, tore into her thick, elephantine, hide and made her as pissed off as...well...as pissed off as an elephant whose skin is being torn apart by a stick with a hook on the end of it.

All that Miss Mary wanted was to enjoy a tasty looking watermelon rind that was left on the street by one of the gawkers. But she was being put down by *The Man*. Walter "Red" Edridge being *The Man* in this case. In front of the entire town, Mary picked up Red with her trunk and bounced his body off of Charlie Morgan's sausage stand. The five-ton bad-ass-mother-fucker of an elephant then crushed Red's head, smashing it amongst a scattering of sausages, onions and peppers and ruining the townspeople's appetite for ground, encased meat for some time to come. Mary's enormous round feet ground Red's large square head into the dirt street, making a muddy, messy, spiced meat, pepper and brain haggis on the ground.

The villagers' original shock quickly turned to anger, giving them reason to form an angry mob (as villagers are always happy to do). They quickly gathered pitchforks, torches and

---

[7] In a hierarchy, every employee rises to his level of incompetence.

random implements of destruction and began to chant in unison: "Kill the elephant. Kill the elephant. Kill the elephant." Mary was promptly arrested by the Johnsonville chief of police and chained to a stake in the ground outside of the police department. Mary's owner, Charlie Sparks, decided he had to do something before the townspeople took things into their own hands. Charlie transported Mary and the rest of his traveling circus to the Clinchfield Railroad yard in Erwin. Sparks's show performed that morning in Erwin without Mary. The real show was to come later that day. After the circus, Mary was taken to the rail yard. The elephant-hating fervor of the Johnsonville angry mob had spread to Erwin like a virulent strain of gonorrhea. Thousands of Erwin's citizens, hungry for blood, crowded the rail yard to watch the execution[8] of Murderous Mary.

Mary's legs were chained to the rails to keep her still while she awaited her fate. Another chain was thrown around her neck and hooked up to the 100-pound derrick that was usually used to unload lumber from freight cars. The signal was given. The derrick operator set the winch in motion. Mary's feet were lifted off of the ground while her back legs remained chained to the tracks. Those close to her cringed as they heard tendons ripping, Mary being in the middle of a tug-of-war between the mighty derrick and the rails. As her body was lifted off of the ground, the chain broke and she thumped back down to earth,

---

[8] Mary is not the only elephant to be executed. Topsy the elephant killed three men (including her abusive keeper who attempted to feed her a lit cigarette). Topsy's owner decided she was a danger and needed to be put down. Thomas Edison suggested that electrocution would be a humane way to execute the animal. Topsy was put to death via electrocution on January 4, 1903. Thomas Edison filmed the event and released it for viewing under the title *Electrocuting an Elephant.*

still alive, scattering the townspeople for fear that they would also be crushed by the dangerous pachyderm. Mary just lay on the ground, stunned and injured. The roustabouts from the circus unchained her back legs from the rails (as they should have done in the first place) and fastened a thicker chain around the wounded elephant's neck. This time the chain held and the crowd watched for several minutes as Mary dangled from the giant crane until the life was choked out of her.[9] The five-ton mammal's corpse was buried at a now unknown location in Erwin.

We drink more, eat more, and talk more. Ramona tells me she's from Alaska. She's homesick but won't go back, for some reason or other. She doesn't want to talk about it. Childbirth almost killed her when she gave birth to triplets—identical twin girls and a boy. Her babies, as she calls them, are still in Alaska with an aunt. Ramona misses them horribly, she weeps. I hold her until she cries it out. I ask: "why don't you visit them?" She doesn't want to talk about it.

We drink more Red, White and Blue and eat more eggs. Ramona wants to know about me. "Not like it really matters, I'll never see you again after tomorrow. But tell me what makes

---

[9] The tale of Murderous Mary was somewhat embellished by Ramona. However, she was telling a variation of the truth. Mighty Mary was lynched in the town of Erwin. Typing the terms "Mighty Mary" or "Murderous Mary" into an Internet search engine will bring up numerous web pages on the subject. Photos were taken of her dangling from the crane and are easily found on the Internet.

Larry Mondello tic," she says.

I'm not a deep guy. Not a big thinker. I try to come up with something interesting about myself. I tell her that I really like music—Heavy Metal music. In my opinion nothing worth listening to has come out since 1987. "Judas Priest," I say, "now there's a band. Rob Halford can scream better than any of those NuMetal pussies." And who would've even suspected that Halford was gay. I just thought that his leather biker outfit was tough. I never realized that he could have easily fit in just as well as one of the Village People. And what's this shit about Kurt Cobain being a genius and the voice of a generation. Bullshit. Give me Bruce Dickinson and Iron Maiden any time. They can rock your ass off and don't make you want to commit suicide in the process.

Ramona yawns. She doesn't care about my theories on heavy metal. I realize that I probably sound pretty immature, like some fifteen-year-old gaywad or something. It's no wonder that I never seem to connect with females. Idjit always is happy to hear my opinions on such matters. I guess he is my soul mate. "Tell me about this soul that you traded for a night's worth of cheap beer and bad karaoke. I really want to know, who the fuck are you?" She really wants to make me work hard for a one-night stand.

"I really don't know who I am," I tell her. "I live with my mom and can't stay focused long enough to keep a normal job. My dog is my best friend and my dead dad hogs the most comfortable seat in our house." I tell her that Daddy comes to me in my dreams and tries to give guidance sometimes. "I'm really quite pathetic." Beer goggles and beer muscles atrophy and alcohol soaked emotions take over the self-loathing center of my brain. I have my own brief and ridiculous bout of weeping as Ramona holds me.

"You're probably a better person than you realize," she tells me. "I too can sense things." She tells me to get up. "Let's go into my bedroom and do what you came up here for."

In the bedroom she turns the light off, insisting on darkness as a condition for her nakedness. "My body looks much better in the pitch black," she half-jokes.

Nakedness . . . warm flesh on flesh . . . the smell of cigarettes, beer breath, cheap perfume, and butt. *Who smells?* I wonder. Me? Her? Who cares? Neither of us is complaining about the smell of ass permeating the room. We are desperate people, seeking release. Seeking something more and pretending that it's not a one-night stand. I spoon with her afterwards and we fall asleep. I like this feeling. It's comfortable. I want it with someone . . . not her . . . but it's okay to pretend for a little while.

In my dreams, Daddy comes to me, walking Idjit on a heavy, thick, chain, like the one used on Mighty Mary. I've never seen Idjit in my dreams. He looks good, happy, as he sits down and lounges at Daddy's feet.

"Listen Boy, you gotta beat it," Daddy tells me. "This city's bad. Go before there's trouble. And don't leave anything behind except for Denny. He'll be okay."

"Hey, while I'm here, I've got a couple of things I'd like to say," says Idjit in a Scottish brogue. I didn't know Idjit could talk and I certainly didn't suspect him of having any sort of accent. "Listen, time is short," the Scottish basset hound continues, "but this is important. Don't ever get me high again. I know you think it's funny, but it freaks me out. Sometimes when you shotgun weed in my face I start thinking strange thoughts. Last time I found myself checking out the neighbor's cat. She was looking pretty fine to me, and if I would have been able to get under that fence, I would have known her intimately. She is easy and would have accommodated me. Hell, who knows what I might have caught from her. That slut has done half of the raccoons and possums in the neighborhood. I heard through the rumor mill that she did an armadillo once. Do you know what that would do to me? I would have trouble living with myself. Just stick to the beer and deviled eggs and everything will be fine. Otherwise I will hump your pillow to climax the next time I get a chance."

"Alright, ya big Galoot," I tell him. "By the way, am I the only person who can understand you or can you talk to others too?"

"I could talk to others if it were necessary," he tells me with a knowing grin on his floppy dogface.

"But you wouldn't tell them anything about what you've seen in the basement, right?" Goddamn, I always knew that I shouldn't have been beating off in front of that dog. He always looked at me strangely, smugly. And one time I took a shit in a garbage bag because I was too lazy and stoned to walk to the bathroom. Idjit had a look of shock and amazement on his face as if he couldn't believe what I was doing. "I mean, there's no reason to go telling tall tales about my behavior if you know what I mean . . . "

"Just remember what I said about getting me stoned," Idjit answers. "Oh and another thing, and this is extremely important for you to keep in mind on this trip down to Florida. In fact it may be the most important advice of your life. The one thing that you should not do is . . . "

. . . Before Idjit Galoot can give me the most crucial counsel of my life, my palaver with Daddy and my dog is interrupted, and I am awakened by the urgent screaming of Denny outside of Ramona's.

**6**

Swirling red police lights sweep the early-morning Brahman parking lot, reflecting off of the discarded cans and bottles that litter the gravel. My head throbs from the aftershock of cheap beer. Coming down the steps from Ramona's apartment, I see the back door of the moving truck open and Denny face-down in the gravel with his arms shackled behind him.

"Don't move, Boy, or I'll blow a hole the size of a basketball in your head!" Somebody barks the command out from behind me. The twangy voice orders me to "Put your hands on your head and get down on your knees."

*What the fuck did Denny do?* I wonder as I comply with the orders. Sharp gravel or maybe a piece of shattered glass punctures my knee.

"You guys are some sick-ass weirdoes," the voice says as my arms are cranked up behind me and I'm lifted to my feet. "I mean, I seen some sick when I was in the service. But, my God, Boy, what in the hell did you do to this poor fella?" The body generating the twangy voice steers me toward the back of the moving truck where I see a cop inspecting Daddy's body.

"Sir," I try to explain, "it's okay. He's my Daddy." I inspect the officer. His rank is Major. His last name is Pickles. The chest and biceps of Major Pickles' uniform are adorned with various military-style ribbons and medals. The epaulettes on his shoulders are askew from hoisting me up. *Is this fucking guy really wearing epaulettes?* Pickles shudders, a crimson hue flushes his cheeks, one eye twitches involuntarily.

"Boy, you and your friend done this to your Daddy? You're in for a world-a-hurtin'." And I start to realize how bad things look. When we packed up Daddy, me and Mom just threw all of the holiday costumes on him so that they would stay together, *compartmentalized* as Mom called it. Looking at Daddy, with all of his holiday paraphernalia, I saw festivity, humor, and mirth. Major Pickles, though, sees something entirely different.

Pickles sees a wrinkled, gray, human corpse wearing strapped-on bunny ears and snout, festooned with beads, baubles, and Hawaiian leis. In his right hand Daddy holds a flag asking somebody to kiss him because he's Irish. In his left hand he grasps a bumpy, bright purple, rubber phallus (a prop from one of Mom's adult Passion Parties that she throws for fun and cash). Daddy's other apparel is a mismatched mishmash of lederhosen and an oversized Kwanza dashiki, all partially covered by an open Santa Claus jacket. Daddy would have laughed at his appearance. Pickles failed to see the humor, instead envisioning acts of debauchery that would turn Larry Flynt's stomach. Pickles did not see yuletide jubilation; he saw morbid copulation. He imagined three-way homosexual necrophilia with a little bestiality thrown in for some extra sick. The stuffed groundhog perched on Daddy's lap probably didn't help to convince him otherwise.

Pickles pushes us face-first into his cruiser and, like a highly trained professional, heads straight for a greasy spoon diner called Burke & Howie's. "You boys make me so dadgummed sick I'm gonna have trouble eating my breakfast," he tells us. "I'm goin' in for some chow. Y'all don't go anywhere 'cause we gonna have a talk. If you try to run, I'll shoot ya through your eyes. And I'll do it right from the front window while I'm enjoying my breakfast." Pickles leaves us alone in the car while he eats.

Burk & Howie's looks like the kind of place where the waitresses would be named Polyethylene, Brandine, or Ruby. Despite our predicament, I find myself imagining the repartee that must occur within the walls of the diner. Perhaps Polyethylene is telling a sweaty grill cook to kiss her grits. Maybe a flannel shirt wearing, unshaved customer flirtatiously asks Brandine if she can warm up his flapjacks.

Denny and me talk about our situation. "They think we killed your Daddy and have been sexing up his corpse," Denny says. He tells me that he was waiting in the truck for me and the Mormon Tea started working on his colon. He knocked on Ramona's door but we didn't answer. Desperate for a toilet, having no real options, and ready to foul himself, Denny dug a hole beside the Brahman, just like a stray cat readying himself for a dookie in the dirt. After the initial groundwork, Denny dropped his trousers, squatted and let loose. This was typical of him. As kids we would go for hikes in the woods behind Denny's house. Without fail, Denny would wait until we got far enough into the woods and announce that he had to take a dump. Me and Frank would have to gather up leaves for him to wipe with. We would gather armfuls of them and bring them to our squatting cousin, all the while breathing through our mouths so as not to have to smell his insides. He would actually wipe his ass with whatever ground debris we brought for him. This happened again and again until me and Frank brought Denny some poison ivy bum-wipes. Following his trip to the emergency room that night for a severe allergic reaction and giant ass-hives, Denny seemed to be cured of his outdoors-induced fecal fascination. But I do have to wonder if Denny actually knocked on Ramona's door to look for a bathroom. I think I would have heard him.

The early morning nature call would have gone unnoticed (maybe somebody would have seen the scat and thought that a sick mountain lion was in the area) except for the fact that Major Pickles was patrolling the neighborhood and saw an obviously intoxicated Denny squatting beside the Brahman like a drunken monkey afflicted with the rotavirus. Pickles let Denny finish his duty and then arrested him for public intoxication, indecent exposure, and generally just being icky. Upon conducting the routine post-arrest search of Denny and inventorying the moving truck, Pickles discovered Daddy. Since that time, Pickles took on a hostile position against us.

"We're going to need to get a lawyer. This is not a good place to be in trouble." I tell Denny about Murderous Mary and the town's bloodlust. "If they think we did Daddy in and have been humping his corpse, we're goners. We'll be lucky to make it to court. I'm gonna use my phone call to contact my Mom and have her get us an attorney."

"Yeah, but don't they have to appoint one for us?" Denny asks.

"Sure, if you want a public defender who is just out of law school and sprouting his first pubes. But I'm gonna get the best."

"Who? Roy Black?"

"Nope."

"Johnny Cochran?"

"Dead."

"F. Lee Bailey."

"Shit, he's disbarred and dead."

"Who, then?"

"I'm getting Loren Rhoton. That handsome motherfucker ain't cheap but he could walk Hitler out of Hell if he wanted to."

At the station me and Denny are placed in separate rooms. My room is bare except for me, Pickles, three chairs, a beat up card table and a two-way mirror on the wall. The maple syrupy smell of urine turns my already churning stomach.

"Don't I get a phone call?" I ask Pickles.

"Not yet, Boy. We need to talk," he says as he turns a chair backwards and straddles it.

"I want a lawyer before I say anything," I protest, thinking that my request will show him I'm not messing around.

"Whatcha want a lawyer for, Son, if you don't have nothin' to hide, hmm?" Pickles asks me with a big, fake, friendly smile on his face. "I'm sure you didn't do anything wrong. We know that it was your buddy that done it. We just want you tell us the facts. Then we'll let you go."

"I didn't do anything wrong. Neither did Denny," I try to explain. "That's my Daddy in the truck..."

"Look, Champ, I don't care if he's Jeffrey Dahmer. Y'all can't go around killing people and anally raping their dead bodies. We have laws against that kind of stuff.[10] Now just tell me what happened to that old boy in your truck," Pickles asks, once again trying to assume a sincere tone of concern.

"That's what I'm trying to do but you keep interrupting me and..."

"Listen up, Chief," Pickles cut me off again, "I know your buddy done it. He has the look of a cadaver humpin' freak. You don't look like that type. Maybe you'd play with yourself a little while watching your boyfriend pump away on a corpse. But you're not a sicko like him. I can tell these things."

"Hey man, that's my Daddy in the truck. I love him..."

"Aha, so you made love to him!" Pickles jumps out of his seat, excited about the apparent break in the case. "I knew it, you sick little bastard. Why, I oughta..."

"No! No! No! You are not listening to me," I shout. My frustration is pushing my already challenged brain towards shutdown.

"Lookee here, Scooter," Pickles calms down again, trying to get a hold on the situation. His red face has an oily sweat sheen. "We know you and your boyfriend killed that poor son-m-bitch and had illicit relations with him. We have irrefutable proof.

---

[10] The Tennessee Code does not specifically prohibit anally raping a dead body. However, Tennessee Code Section 39-17-312(A)(1) does make it a class E felony, punishable by up to six years imprisonment, for somebody who physically mistreats a corpse in a manner offensive to the sensibilities of a normal person. It would be a question for a jury, then, whether anally penetrating a corpse is offensive to the sensibilities of a normal person.

And we're performing DNA tests right now. I'm going to need blood, urine, sperm, and fecal samples from you. Why don't you just give me your underwear and that should take care of all of the specimens I need?"

"I want my phone call! I want my lawyer!" I scream. My left eye throbs. It feels like my head is going to explode and blood will start shooting from my eye sockets.

"Phone's broken, Chief. Listen, all we want is to know what happened. You boys are caught. You're guilty. You know it. We know it. Just tell me what happened."

"I want my phone call! I want my lawyer! I want my phone call! I want my lawyer! I want my phone call! I want my lawyer..." I begin to chant, partially as a mantra to keep my brain from exploding, partially to drown out Pickles.

"Listen, I just want to know why you boys did this," Pickles takes on a concerned tone, like a father asking his son why he tried smoking. "Did you have a bad family life? Unhappy childhood? Did Ozzy Osbourne tell you to do it in one of his devil songs? I'm not going to judge you. Hey, it's not like you're the only person who has ever thought about having sex with a dead body. Heck Boy, I've thought about it myself a few times when I've shown up at a scene and there's a pretty little girl whose life's been cut short too soon. We've all seen a fine looking man and thought, 'hey, why not strangle him and then anally rape his lifeless corpse?' You just lost control and acted on it. I'm not going to judge you for that. I just want to know what happened."

"I want my phone call! I want my lawyer! I want my phone call! I want my lawyer! I want my phone call! I want my lawyer..."

"Maybe this fellow led you on. You had too much to drink and he was waving around his big purple dildo and *Kiss Me I'm Irish flag*. I mean, just look at the way that ol' boy was dressed. Boy Howdy, if that ain't just begging for murder and sodomy, then I don't know what is. He was practically asking you for it. You just gave him what he had coming, right?"

"I want my phone call! I want my lawyer! I want my phone call! I want my lawyer! I want my phone call! I want my lawyer..."

"Like I said, I'm not judging you, Champ. Sometimes we do things that aren't right and we're not responsible. I mean, you were drinking, right? And he was asking for it? Things got a little crazy. Who's gonna condemn you for that? Not me. I just need the details. Now tell me what happened."

I focus on my mantra: "I want my phone call! I want my lawyer! I want my phone call! I want my lawyer! I want my phone call! I want my lawyer..." The throbbing in my left eye worsens.

Major Pickles is unrelenting: "Maybe this guy tried to do something to you and you were just defending yourself. Is that what happened? Come on, you might as well just tell me what went on. Your buddy is already telling us everything in the other room."

"I want my phone call! I want my lawyer! I want my phone call! I want my lawyer! I want my phone call! I want my lawyer..."

Pickles sighs. "Please stop it with that silly chanting, okay? You do have the right to remain silent. That's your privilege. I'm not even going to try to take that away from you. If you don't want to talk...well...okay. But put yourself in my position..." he leans in toward me as if we are close buddies sharing a secret "...suppose you found a dead body, already killed and raped, and you had to call me in and ask me about it. And suppose I start whining about lawyers and rights and saying I don't want to talk to you. You'd think I was hiding something. And you'd probably be right. That's precisely what I think about you and your friend. And so will everybody else. So..." he rolls his eyes, sighing "...I'm here, you're here. Let's just talk about this a little. And, hey, if you're innocent like you say, why would you need a lawyer anyway? Why don't you save yourself the money a lawyer would cost? All I'm looking for is the truth. And if you're innocent and telling me the truth...then you can handle this by yourself and there's no need for an attorney to be involved."[11]

"I..." (the vein on my forehead twitches like a snake biting down on a live wire) "...want..." (my left eye is pulsing with almost unbearable pressure) "...my..." (OUCH! a rubber band snapping sensation in my brain) "...lawyer."

Half a foot in front of my face I awake to a large sweaty man. As I regain consciousness I note that his tie is wrapped far too snugly around his floppy, fleshy neck, like a shoestring tied around a bratwurst, as tight as is possible without breaking the casing. I imagine myself snipping the tie with a pair of shears

---

[11] If the reader should doubt that Pickles' interrogation techniques are realistic, a perusal of the U.S. Supreme Court case of *Miranda v. Arizona*, 384 U.S. 436 (1966), is recommended for an interesting and entertaining read.

and watching his neck expand to the width of his thick head. The man fastens a Velcro strap around my arm, makes sure it's secure, and stands up. He has a black eye, more deep purplish really, and a chipped tooth, as if he'd recently been involved in fisticuffs. Contrary to my normally peaceful nature, I feel the urge to deal him a vicious beating. I want to finish the job that somebody else started on him.

The Velcro strap around my arm has blue and black and yellow wires attached which run to a large piece of electronic equipment. The big fellow nods at me and exits the room.

"Who was that?" I ask Major Pickles.

"His name is Robert Paulson. He's our polygrapher," Pickles explains. "You are now hooked up to a polygraph machine, a lie detector. I'm going to ask you some questions and this here machine will tell me if you are being honest."

"I don't want to speak with you. I just want my lawyer."

"No you don't," says Pickles, smiling as he waives a piece of paper in front of my face. "You signed this here waiver of rights form. You already agreed to talk to us. Now let's stop farting around and get down to business." I don't even have enough time to read the paper that I supposedly signed. I see the word *waiver* at the top of the page and a signature scrawled out at the bottom that is *not* in my handwriting.

"First I'm gonna ask you some preliminary questions to make sure that the levels are set right. This here's a very sensitive piece of equipment," Pickles explains, patting the machine with his fat little hand. "Now what's your name, Boy?"

"Puddin' Tane, ask me again I'll tell you the same," I answer, trying my best to be uncooperative.

"Alright, Mr. Tane, and what's your address?"

"2525 Fuck You Lane, Findlay, Ohio."

"Great," says Pickles, almost as if he isn't hearing my answers. "And, what's your date of birth?"

"I want to pop your eye out and skull-fuck your empty head, you fat bloated hunk of goat shit," I answer, hoping to get a rise out of him.

"Perfect," Pickles says as he fiddles with buttons on the polygraph machine. "It looks like our levels are set and we're ready to go. I'm going to ask you a series of questions. You are going to give me answers. If you're lying, the machine will tell me with one-hundred-and-twenty percent certainty." He looks down at the clipboard in his hand, takes a deep breath, and wipes his sweaty forehead with a handkerchief. "Now who is the man in the back of your truck?"

"He's my Daddy," I try to explain again.

"Well let's just see what the machine says." Pickles pushes a button on top of the machine. It starts grinding and beeping, lights on the side rapidly flash, and a standard eight-and-a-half by eleven piece of white paper pops out of the side. "Uh, I'm sorry, but I think somebody isn't being honest here." He shows me the paper with large, 72-font, bold black letters which declare *HE'S LYEING.*

"What the fuck is that?" I ask, incredulous. "What kind of sensitive piece of equipment is this? Lying isn't even spelled right."

"It is spelled correctly," Pickles mutters. "That's the European spelling. You know, like how they put a *U* in color. Same thing. Now . . . why did you kill that man, who obviously isn't your Daddy?"

"I didn't kill him!" I shout.

Pickles pushes a button on the machine again and out shoots another piece of paper: *HE'S LYEING.*

"Uh, Uh, Uh," Pickles grins. "It seems that you did kill him. The machine doesn't make mistakes. Now was this poor sucker your first victim?"

"Once I shot a man in Reno, just to watch him die," I answer, doing my damnedest to be a smart-ass.

Pickles pushes the button on the machine and inspects the paper it spat out. He crumples the sheet up, throws it at the trash, missing the can by a good two feet. "Well, at least you're starting to be honest with me now. We'll talk more about your Nevada victim later. Have there been any others?"

"I once killed an Arab on a beach and didn't feel a bit re-morseful."

Pickles reads another sheet of paper from the polygraph, crumples it up and throws it at the trash, missing the can. "Good, now we are really getting somewhere," Pickles en-thuses. "I'm glad you're getting this off of your chest. We'll have you make out a list later. Let's talk about that feller in the back of your truck though. How did you do him in?"

"I'm not going to answer any more of your questions," I tell Pickles. "This is bullshit! I didn't kill anybody. I was just yanking your chain. That machine is a piece of shit; it's probably not even a polygraph."

"Oh, now that's not so, Boy. This is an advanced piece of lie detection equipment, cutting edge and state of the art, on loan from a well-respected European university."

"No, it's not," I argue, raising from my chair, rounding the table and inspecting the machine. "It's a fucking all-in-one copy/printer/fax machine." I lift the lid of the machine and see a piece of paper sitting on the glass copying plate. The paper reads: *HE'S LYEING.* "You just keep hitting copy and it copies this piece of paper."

"No, no, no," Pickles counters. "This is an all-in-one machine, but it also has an integrated lie detector."

I pick up one of the wads of paper near the trashcan and un-crumple it. Not surprisingly, the wrinkled piece of paper reads: *HE'S LYEING.* I raise my bushy eyebrows at Pickles, saying nothing further.

"Alright, Buddy, you caught me." He laughs a big dumb coun-try-boy laugh. "Listen, I'm just trying to find out what's going on. Are you going to talk to me or not?"

It dawns on me that Pickles will believe nothing but that Denny and I killed Daddy. Daddy's advice comes back to me: "This city's bad. Go before there's trouble. And don't leave any-thing behind except for Denny, he'll be okay." I can see clearly what I have to do. I promise myself that I will come back for Denny as soon as I can.

"Okay. Alright. I'm going to level with you," I tell Pickles, doing my best to sound deflated. "I didn't kill that man. But I do know what happened. That fellow that you have in there, he's my cousin. He's borderline retarded, obsessive compulsive and de-ranged. I was taking him to a clinic in Georgia for treatment. He did that man in a couple of days ago. And . . . yes, he did have sex with the corpse several times. He threatened me. Said that if I reported him to the police he would do the same to me. I was so damned scared, even in here, that I didn't want to talk. I'm willing to give a sworn statement, testify against that monster, whatever you need."

"Now we're getting somewhere, Boy. Now don't it feel good to get all of that out. Let me get a tape recorder so that we can memorialize all of this." Pickles starts for the door . . .

"Wait just a minute though," I stop him. "I am more than willing to help. But you have to get me out of here and grant me immunity. I want a new identity, and some funds for starting over."

"Let me talk to the chief and see what I can do," Pickles tells me as I watch his lumpy ass go out the door.

Me and Pickles walk to the back of the police station and he directs me to a window. A sign that says *Discharge* hangs askew over the window. Pickles smiles at me. "Thanks a lot, Champ. With your help we should be able to put this sicko pervert away for life, at the very least. I want you to stick around here until we make sure we have the case put together against your cousin." A slight twinge of guilt pulls at me for selling Denny out. I know Denny would not have done the same thing to me. And that's the problem. We would both be in the Erwin jail for who knows how long. At least this way I can get out, get us attorneys, and change my testimony against Denny later. Perhaps I went overboard with the information that I gave Pickles, but I wanted to be convincing. Maybe I shouldn't have said that Denny has a refrigerator full of severed heads that he likes to pleasure himself with. Perhaps the tales of him running through public places wearing nothing but a banana-hammock and knitted leggings were ir-relevant. Maybe I didn't need to make up the part about eels, PVC pipe and electric tape. But I needed to be convincing. And Pickles bought it. I'm getting out. I can make it up to Denny later.

"Here's one hundred dollars for you to live on here for a little bit while we work up the case against that . . . that . . . monster. Go get yourself a hotel and make yourself available because we are going to have a lot of questions for you," Pickles tells me. "I have already contacted the prosecutor and he has granted you immu-nity. But you are going to have to cooperate one-hundred-and-thirty percent. Now I have to go get myself some lunch over at the Egg Hut; they are opening back up for lunch. Why don't you come back to the station for more questioning in a couple of hours?"

"Thank you very much, Major Pickles," I say, mustering up all of the false sincerity that I can. "I feel a lot better since I came clean with you. I think that something needs to be done about Denny. He's a predator and a menace to society. I'll see you back here in a little bit."

Me and Pickles part ways, him headed to the Egg Hut and me turning around the corner of the police station and walking to-ward what I assume is the downtown area of Erwin.

"Hey!" I look up at the side of the building to see who's calling me. Denny's face is smashed in between the bars on a second floor window. "Hey, how did you get out?" He yells down at me. "They told me that you said I killed your daddy."

"Shhhhh," I whisper up at him. "I've got things worked out," I say as softly as possible, sort of a shouted whisper. "I'm split-ting, man. I'm getting out of here and getting us attorneys. I will be back for you with help."

"Hey, don't leave me here!" Denny starts shouting. "They fucking execute elephants in this town. What do you think they're going to do to me? Get me the fuck out of here before I end up dangling by my neck from a crane. Don't leave me man."

Denny's panic touches me. I feel great pangs of guilt and shame for selling him out the way that I did. But Daddy said it would be all right. And I don't see any other way. "I'll be back for you with a lawyer," I tell him as I duck around the corner of the station.

There is nobody behind the police station. The only thing back there is... great googley-moogley... it's beautiful, almost unbelievable. I see it in a different light. It's the moving truck— just sitting there, smiling at me, welcoming me. They must have used Denny's keys to take the truck to the station. It's a good thing that Mom gave us each a set of keys. She figured that we were both so irresponsible that at least one set of the keys would get lost. My keys were in my pants pocket when I was arrested. And, lo and behold, my keys were returned to me with my other belongings at the discharge window.

Nobody is around. I open the back door of the truck. Everything is there. Everything. Daddy said not to leave anything but Denny behind. He must have known this would happen. It's like it was predestined. I shut the back door and look around. Not a soul in sight. The entire police force is probably over at the grand reopening of the Egg Hut, gobbling down hash browns that I imagine to be slathered in bacon grease, mayonnaise, melted cheese, ham chunks and topped with ranch dressing. This is almost too easy. I unlock the front door of the car. Everything is in order. Quicker than you can say *Mayberry,* I turn the ignition, glance around once more to make sure the coast is clear and drive in the opposite direction of the Brahman and the Egg Hut. With the sun in the west behind me, I steer the truck out of town and weave my way up and down the meandering mountain roads, not exactly sure where it is that I am going but knowing that it is out of Erwin. I must be heading east. Without a map in the car the best I can do is move forward, towards the east coast until I hit Interstate 95 and then head south for Florida. *I'll get Denny that badass lawyer from Tampa*, I tell myself, trying to suppress my feelings of disgrace for ditching him.

I see things clearly as Erwin fades away behind me. Denny will be all right. I call Mom on the pay-per-use cell phone she gave me for my birthday. By the time I reach her, she is already in Florida, waiting for Denny and me. Mom flew down so that she could get the new house ready before all of our belongings arrived. Mom says she will get on the phone with the Tampa attorney and take care of things for me and Denny.

"How's Idjit?" I ask, figuring everything is okay.

"Well...Baby..." (hesitation) "...he's fine. Just get on down here with the truck, okay."

"What's up, Mom? I can tell something's wrong. Do you have Idjit with you?" I begin to shake. Panic floods my system at the thought that something may be wrong with my best buddy.

"Baby, he's here, I just had to...uh...board him while I'm getting the house set up."

"Mom! You know he doesn't do well in jail. You need to spring him and have him there ready to greet me when I show up." I can't believe that Mom would do such a thing. I knew that she had other things going on, things that she feels are important. But to put the Galoot in a kennel is not like her.

"Baby," Mom pleads in her gravelly, lifetime-smoker voice. "You know that I need to focus on Barney's parole hearing right now. Idjit will be alright. Just come on down with the truck. I'll take care of everything else. Okay?"

Barney is the reason that we are moving down to Florida. Ever since Daddy passed on, Mom has been true to him. Until recently, that is. I guess that after a while the loneliness was more than she could bear. Sure she had me and Idjit around to keep her company. But we mostly hung out in the basement, drinking beer, smoking whatever we could get our hands on, and eating deviled eggs. I guess she needed more. Mom started dating local men a couple of years ago and found that she just wasn't connecting. Everybody she saw was either divorced and brought along all of the issues from previous marriages, widowed and still in the grieving process, or lifetime bachelors (which she says actually meant closet gays). Nothing worked out for her until she became pen pals with Barney Obusek, Florida Department of Corrections number 104988. Mom and Barney hit things off immediately and are now engaged.

Barney's serving a life sentence for armed robbery. Mom says that he isn't a bad guy. He realizes the error of his ways. He's found Jesus Christ while incarcerated. Specifically, he found Jesus somewhere within the walls of Everglades Correctional Institution in South Florida. That's what Mom says anyway. She met Barney on a prison pen pal website. I looked up his posting on the website and couldn't believe Mom would fall for his shit. His ad looked something like this:

*Hi there, sexy. How are you? Fine I most certainly hope. Please allow me to introduce miself. I am Barney. I have a loving Body that ripples with sinewy mussles. I am single, available and looking for sexy friends and pen pals. I am willing to try anything once and expect the same of my lady friends.*

*I am an inosent man who was wrongfully coherced into entering a guilty plea to a criminal act. My attorney told me that adjudification would be witheld and I would get probation. Instead I am in prisen for life. I am looking for someone to share beautiful thoughts and experiences with. Age and race unimportant. I care about what is inside.*

Barney wrapped up his posting with a flowery poem about birds flying free, caterpillars turning into beautiful butterflies, and something about the breeding habits of the Florida Panther that I really didn't understand.

Mom told me that Barney used to have a drug problem before he found God in prison. Barney was addicted to crack and was brought up in a broken family. In the midst of the mother of all drug binges, Barney and a cohort of his used a BB gun pistol to rob a Girl Scout cookie stand outside of a Piggly Wiggly supermarket. After snatching up a cash box containing $56.84 and an armload of Peanut Butter Patty boxes, Barney and his accomplice attempted to carjack a minivan. Unfortunately for Barney and his friend, the van had a manual transmission and neither of them knew how to use a stick shift. The van convulsed and jumped a couple of times as Barney popped the clutch, trying to drive away. A gang of Piggly Wiggly bag boys converged on the sputtering minivan, dragged Barney and his friend out, and beat them soundly, holding them down until security arrived to take them into custody.

I tell Mom that if Barney ever gets out and comes to live with us he better treat us good. He writes me and signs the letters "Dad." The letters have yellowish stains and give off a vapor of cheap cologne. He's not my Dad and I don't want him to be. I tell Mom that if he ever hurts her he better watch out because I have a Kaiser blade[12] and I will whack him smack-dab in the forehead with it if I need to. Momma says not to talk like that. She says Barney is a changed man and she hasn't met anybody as sweet as him since Daddy. I tell her maybe he's so sweet to her because Mom keeps replenishing his canteen account and sending him care packages. Mom says that's nonsense. She loves him and she would do that for anybody she loves, including me.

At least Barney isn't a child molester or something like that. Mom was corresponding with one of his friends named Gabe. She says that those people are lonely and need contact with the outside world. This guy was in there for performing medical services without a license. He was a deputy with the Broward County Sheriff's Office and told his colleagues that he was training to be a registered nurse. He also told them that he had to perform so many hernia examinations to qualify for his certification. Gabe offered different men within his department $50.00 to be

---

[12] Some people call it a Slingblade.

the subjects of his "examinations." Gabe would have a coworker meet him at a hotel, and then he would fondle his bare, droopy, balls, and say things like: "hmmm," "uh-huh," and "okay." Some of his "patients" also volunteered for the prostate exam for an extra $10.00. During the prostate exam Gabe would probe the rectum with a gloved and lubricated finger or two, wiggling his digits around a little while uttering concerned phrases like: "Oh! Very interesting!" "Eureka!" "ah-ha," and "um-hm." Eventually, after repeated "tests" on the subjects, it was discovered that Gabe was in fact not in training to become a registered nurse, he was not even in school, he just liked touching guys' balls and butt holes. Gabe is currently doing time for performing unlicensed medical exams and sexual battery. When it comes down to it, I guess I'll take Barney over Gabe for my new stepdaddy.

Mom told me that when I make it to I-95 I should stop off to rest at a town called Dillon in North Carolina. Buddy Hinton, an old neighborhood kid, lives in Dillon and is the assistant night manager at a hotel just off of the interstate. Buddy could probably get me a good rate on a room for the night, according to Mom. She says she'll try to call ahead for me and set something up with Buddy.

The serpentine mountainous roads have a soothing, hypnotic effect on me. Denny's Mormon Tea is still in the truck so I drink some more of it, hoping to keep myself awake. As darkness craps away another day, my head involuntarily nods, my heavy eyelids droop, I am on auto-pilot, not really paying attention to my driving but managing to keep the truck on the road. Without Denny to talk to, it's hard to keep myself awake. If I weren't on the run from Major Pickles, I would probably pull over on the side of the road and sleep for a while.

In order to stay awake I pick up a hitchhiker. His name is Rudy Erikson. Rudy has a backpack, a face full of bushy black beard, and the aroma of something like a cross between B.O. and moose piss. His intense eyes burn passionately. He doesn't blink. Rudy rants about stem cell research causing the destruction of innocent lives. He rails about abortionists being the instruments of Satan. I play devil's advocate and suggest that perhaps there are people who should be killed. I tell Rudy that maybe we have too many people on the planet who just use up air and space and contribute nothing but excrement, foul fluids, and a burden for the rest of us. Rudy shouts, he weeps about the beauty of human life and taking all necessary steps to preserve it, including killing others who disagree with him. I don't know what I believe. I just know that Rudy's fanaticism scares me to the point of making me very aware and alert. I'm so fucking spooked by him that I'm not tired anymore and don't need to worry about drifting off while driving.

I drive through the night with Rudy. As I find myself getting tired again, I tell Rudy that I'm thinking about making a financial contribution to Planned Parenthood. Rudy explodes. He tells me that organization is a bunch of whores and whoremongers. I don't exactly know what a whoremonger is, but it sounds bad, and, I suppose, has something to do with whores. Rudy tells me that there is a bomb in his backpack and that he will blow us both up if I really am going to contribute money to their murderous cause. He scares the shit out of me and, in the process, wakes me up. I tell Rudy that he has changed my mind and I see his way of thinking.

"Promise me you won't make any such donation to those godless heathens," Rudy orders. He tells me that if I disagree with him again about the sanctity of human life, I will regret it. Rudy has big plans for the bomb in his backpack. However, he is willing to use it to obliterate the both of us unless I renounce my evil ways and acknowledge the sanctity of human life. I concede that Rudy is right, human life is beautiful and should be protected at all costs. I don't know if he really has a bomb but I do know that the machete-like buck knife hanging from his belt could probably take one of my arms off in one powerful swipe from Rudy. I have a mental vision of wild-eyed, fur-faced Rudy jamming the knife into my ear and twisting it; the vision is all too real and I realize that I don't like Rudy so much. We pull over on the side of the road to take a piss. I finish quickly and jump in the truck. In the moonlight I see the bush branches moving around the area where Rudy is. He takes forever. I lock the door of my truck and decide I've had enough of him. He has kept me awake. He has served his purpose. I am afraid that he will hurt me eventually and it is time for us to part ways. In my side view mirror as I pull away I see Rudy running from the bushes, pulling up his pants and jumping up and down. He screams something that I can't hear with my healthy, unpunctured eardrums.

I drive on through the night, stopping once at an all-night convenience store to get something to eat. I crave deviled eggs. The closest thing they have is massive a jar of pickled pheasant eggs near the register. I ask the cashier to get one for me. She tells me, "Just reach in and grab a couple, honey. We ain't shy around here."

On the road again, I head east, I think, toward Interstate 95. I eat the salty eggs, wishing I had bought something to wash them down with. They taste slightly rotten. I drink more Mormon Tea and manage to stay awake the rest of the drive to the interstate. At I-95 I take a right and head south as the sky to my left takes on the faint glow of dawn.

8

The signs for the South of the Border tourist trap clutter the roadside. Billboards with Pedro, the sombrero and poncho-clad Mexican, pop up every half-mile with a crazy saying. *PEDRO'S WEATHER FORECAST: CHILI TODAY, HOT TAMALE.* In my short time driving the highway I have become fascinated by the extreme billboarding the tourist trap has managed. *What is this place?* I wonder, wishing I had more time to check it out. But I need to get down to Florida so that I can drop off the truck and head back up to Ohio to look for Idjit.

*PEDRO'S FIREWORKS! DOES YOURS?*

The morning sun stains the sky pale magenta. After having been awake since yesterday morning, I am weary and ready for rest. I hope to make it to Dillon, South Carolina, soon so that Buddy can hook me up with a room.

Pedro tells me that South of the Border has *SOMETHEENG DEEFERENT FOR EVERY JUAN.* He counts down the miles to his attraction. According to Pedro, I am only miles away from a spectacular extravaganza of cheesiness. A billboard with a giant,

3-dimensional pink hotdog exclaims: *YOU NEVER SAUSAGE A PLACE! YOU'RE ALWAYS A WEINER AT PEDROS.* And then I realize that Dillon, South Carolina, is South of the Border. And just before the Dillon exit: *KEEP YELLING KIDS! (THEY'LL STOP).* To my left I see what looks like a water tower but it is capped with a gargantuan sombrero. The bright lights of South of the Border are like a Mexican mock up of the Las Vegas strip. I drive my truck between the legs of an enormous neon-lit statue of Pedro that straddles the road leading into the grounds. Scanning from side to side as I drive in, I am in awe of the unabashed tackiness. Almost every square inch of the facility is covered with the gaudy, the garish, loud and lewd, and the outright bizarre. A 25-foot tall Gorilla wearing an orange t-shirt beats its chest at me outside of a t-shirt shop. A large green fiberglass brontosaurus wearing a sombrero seems to watch me as I pass. Ceramic lawn ornaments have overrun the grounds. A loudspeaker somewhere blares out a distorted *Wooly Bully.*

The truck slows and I ease it into the parking lot of the hotel, Pedro's Pleasure Dome. *Christ,* I think, *it sounds like the name of a Mexican brothel.* It's still early in the morning so I figure that Buddy will still be working.

A cute young Asian girl greets me at the front desk. Her nametag says *Pedro.* "Hi, uhh ... Pedro ... is Buddy Hinton around?" I ask Asian Female Pedro.

Asian Female Pedro hits some buttons on her computer keyboard and says: "We don't have any guests by that name staying with us."

"No, he's supposed to be the assistant night manager here. Is he around?"

"Oh, yeah," she says, "that would be Pedro. Let me get him for you."

She picks up the phone, covers her mouth and mumbles something into the receiver. I can't tell what she's saying but it sounds to me like: "Mmmm-gurble-gurble-gurble ... Uh-huh ... Gurble-mamble-momblay ... Uh-uh ... Umphlatmombism flatmo ... Uh-huh ... Okay." Asian Female Pedro sets down the phone and tells me: "Pedro will be right with you."

Almost immediately Buddy parts the green and red strings of beads that block the doorway into the manager's office and homes in on me with his glad-hand. He looks ridiculous with his big goofy grin and multicolored vest. I remember Buddy being the cool guy in the neighborhood. He had a way about him as a kid that seemed to scare the parents and draw the girls. He was a tall kid at six-foot-two and had a full beard by the time he was fourteen. He was a cool guy to be friends with because he looked like he was thirty and could buy beer without ever getting carded. He was very popular around the neighborhood. The last time I saw Buddy was just before he was sent away to juvenile detention or something. People said that he went crazy and started attacking his house with a baseball bat. Others said he beat up a teacher. I even heard he tried to eat his own foot.

"Welcome to *S.O.B.*, ya big S.O.B.?" Buddy greets me. "It's been forever. How are ya, buddy?" Buddy looks different, like life has beaten him down. His beard is gone, replaced by a five o'clock shadow that stops near the top of his cheeks like a facial hair timberline; there is a clear demarcation just before the bags under his eyes. Without the facial hair it looks as if somebody has pushed his chin back into his neck. His hairline has receded to a pointy, black, widow's peak and his S.O.B. vest (complete with Pedro name-tag) rides up noticeably on his bulbous paunch. Buddy is bent over, shoulders hunching up as if he is trying to avoid being hit, his posture making him look like a giant question mark.

"Hey, Buddy. Or is it Pedro?" I joke. "It's good to see you. You look good."

"No I don't. I look like shit. And so do you. We look like a couple of before pictures for some weight loss product. But it's good to see a familiar face down here anyway." Without even looking back, Buddy grabs me by the arm and leads me out the front door. "I'm out of here, Pedro. You're in charge," he tells Asian Female Pedro. "Adios."

We walk over the main strip on a pedestrian overpass and get breakfast at Pedro's Casateria. "Hey, man, this shit's free for us. Those is the perks of being an assistant manager. Get whatever you want," Buddy tells me. I grab a bowl of red gelatin with fruit cubes suspended in it, a plate of some sort of brown meat covered with gravy, three deviled-eggs, and a cup of coffee. Buddy fills his tray up with a mound of glazed donuts and a plate of biscuits and gravy. A blond teenaged white boy with his hat on sideways mans the register. He waves us on by without asking for payment. "Thanks Eminem Pedro."

"No problem, Pedro," Eminem Pedro says.

The deviled eggs are excellent. Buddy catches me up on his life, nonstop-talking with his mouth full of chewed up donuts. It's been decades, but we still feel like friends. Buddy tells me about his disappearance as a teenager. He didn't beat up a teacher, he didn't attack his house with a baseball bat, he didn't eat his own foot. Buddy just liked to get high, a lot. When his parents found his stash of weed and prescription pills, they freaked out and sent him to a drug rehab called Straight, Inc., in Milford, Ohio. Buddy was in the rehab for three years until he turned eighteen and could legally sign himself out. During that time, though, he ran away three or four times, just taking off and hitchhiking around the country until he would get caught and shipped back. One time he was sticking his thumb up on the side of I-75 in Sidney, Ohio, and his mom drove by the other way on the highway. Buddy skedaddled into the woods, was picked up by the sheriff later that day, and was shipped back to the rehab. After he turned 18, Buddy started hitching around the country, working day labor or some dead-end job until he had enough money to hit the road again. He liked being on the move. He really liked it. Then he met Gypsy and settled down.

"Settled down," he chuckles half-heartedly. "Bullshit. She broke me. I ain't got no fight or fire left in me. You know what we do for fun now? She makes me do Tai Chi with her right out in front of the giant sombrero. She says I'm getting fat and un-healthy and need to balance out my ying and my yang. We put on matching jumpsuits and waive our fucking arms around while all of the tourists point and laugh. It's fucking emasculat-ing, Bro. I'm the only man out there. At least it's better than the country line dancing class we were taking last year."

"It can't be that bad," I tell him. "Shit, I wish I had a wife. I would love to have someone to share my time with. I mean, I've got my dog and all but it ain't the same. You guys must have some fun together or you wouldn't stick around, huh?"

"Yeah, on weekends we go shopping for antiques that I can't afford. And for a really hot time, I help her with clipping pictures and shit for her scrapbooking." Buddy has polished off the mound of glazed donuts now and pulls out a pair of SOB souvenir nail clippers. *Sproing,* a thick yellowed crescent from his thumb springs from the clippers and lands on my side of the table. I cover my coffee cup with both hands to keep the high-flying keratin slivers from landing in my cup of Joe.

"Yeah, it sounds like you've got it pretty bad. Maybe I'm kind of lucky not to have to deal with that whole trip. Scrapbooking, huh?" He just nods slowly. "Man, I'm sorry dude."


Buddy set me up with the best room in Pedro's Pleasure Dome, the Honeymoon Suite. "It's heir conditioned," he tells me. That's supposed to be a joke, I guess. After letting myself into my room, I immediately throw myself down on the king-sized waterbed with the sombrero canopy headboard and I'm out.

Idjit Galoot comes to me again in my dreams. I'm on the beach. The ocean breeze blows the salty smell of the Atlantic. Gulls circle overhead and the sandpipers run in and out with the waves, looking for tiny shrimp in the wet sand as the water recedes. Down the beach I see Idjit running to me. Giddy with the excitement of seeing my best buddy again, I run to him with my arms out. We jog toward each other in slow motion. Idjit bounds toward me with his floppy dog lips turned up into a goofy smile, his long velvety ears trailing behind him. The string-quartet playing the soundtrack to my dream crescendos.

At last we reach each other. I embrace Idjit and we roll in the sand, me hugging the Galoot while he affectionately nuzzles me with his muzzle. The waves wash over us.

"Get up out of the water, you damn fool!" It's Daddy, sitting in his easy chair, just above where the sand meets the water. He's wearing a Speedo and an enormous black velvet sombrero. "You're not Dudley Moore or Burt Lancaster, and that stanky dog sure as hell is not Bo Derrick or Deborah Kerr. You've got business to tend to; you can hump your lumpy old hound dog later. Now get a move on."

"He's right," Idjit tells me, without a trace of the Scottish brogue he had in my last dream. "You need to hit the road again and soon, and take that big fella Pedro with you. You need each other."

"What happened to your Scottish accent?" I ask.

"I was just trying that out. It's not me," Idjit explains and shrugs his dog shoulders. "Hey, I've never really spoken before just recently, I've got to figure out what works for me, ya know? Maybe I *chould* try Chicano. You know, like that *leettle* taco eating *chee-wa-wa.* Hand over *thee gor-dee-da.* I don't know. Anyway, it's time to wake up . . . It's time to wake up . . . It's time to wake up . . .

. . . It's time to wake up . . . It's time to wake up . . . It's time to wake up . . .

" . . . Come on dude . . . It's time to wake up," Buddy is pushing down on the foot of the water bed and making waves that gradually rouse me. "God damn. You've slept for like thirty hours now. You've gotta get up. I mean, I don't mind setting you up with a place for the night, but listen up Rumple Foreskin[13], I have a newlywed couple who is going to need this room tonight. Get out of bed, get yourself cleaned up, and then get the fuck outta this room, alright. And then we're gonna party South of the Border."

---

[13] Almost all mammals have foreskins, except for the platypus and echidna (spiny anteater). Echidnas have no nipples; their young sup at milk patches on the mother.

**9**

"Man. I can't fuck around here partying all night," I tell Buddy. "I've already slept way too long. I gotta get moving. Mom boarded my dog. He's gotta be freaking out without me. I gotta hit the road again."

"Whoa, whoa, whoa! You're not just gonna come in here, eat my food, crash in my best room for free, and then skip out again without at least having a couple of drinks with me." During the time that I slept, Buddy's face already sprouted a dark, short stubble of a beard and his posture seems to have perked up somewhat. It may just be the facial hair returning, but it seems as if Buddy's chin is trying to work its way away from his neck. "My old lady's gone to her cousin's house in Asheville for the next couple of days. I'm going stag tonight. We are going to party. Think fast..."

Buddy throws a can of beer at me on the bed. Still groggy from the slumber and lacking my usual ninja-like reflexes, I can only watch and try to fumble my hands out from underneath the covers as the ice cold beverage container hurtles through the air toward my face. *Fwap.* Twelve ounces of cheap beer and metal unsuccessfully (and painfully) attempt to share the exact same space as my right eyeball. "Owwwww, my fucking eye! You stupid fucktard," I shout at Buddy but am unable to focus my anger because I seem to have gone blind in my right eye and can only see bright bursts of pain floating before me.

Buddy helps me to a chair and hands me two more ice cold beers, one for my eye and one for my gut. "Here, hold this on your eye. I'm so sorry. You used to be fast," Buddy tells me. "I've got a fistful of reasons to keep you around here, though. Take a handful of these; they'll take care of the pain." He holds out his hand, palm up, and it is cupping a handful of white tablets. The pills have *222* etched across their face.

"What the fuck are you doing, trying to make me O.D.? I don't even know what this shit is?" I examine the pills with more than a bit of curiosity.

"No, no way. Those are kind of like aspirin, or something. And they have codeine in them. But you have to take a bunch of them to feel anything good. Shit, I've been eating them like peanuts and I haven't O.D.'d." The whites of his eyes are bloodshot and yellow like a pepperoncini.

"Where'd you get these?" I ask as I pop five of the pills in my mouth and wash them down with my beer.

"One of our guests left a big bottle of them in their room. You'd be surprised what we find." Buddy laughs and pops a handful of the 222's, chewing them like they're candy. "I never buy beer, shampoo, or milk. People just leave shit behind when they check out. Weed . . . pornography . . . dildos. Once I found a prosthetic arm in the trash can. Sometimes they'll leave lingerie behind. I'll just have the laundry room wash it for me and I bring it home for Gypsy. She thinks I bought it special for her. Now come on. Get yourself cleaned up, we're going out."

Buddy has an insulated backpack filled with various beers that were abandoned by guests of the Pleasure Dome. He hands me a Blatz and pulls out a Pabst Blue Ribbon for himself. We walk to the gas station and borrow a bag of ice from the icebox for the beer cooler/backpack. "Wait here, I'll be right back," Buddy says and he leaves me in front of the gas station while he goes inside to talk to the cashier. After a minute or two, Buddy comes back, saying "Thanks, Pedro," as he exits.

"Don't you kind of worry that somebody might do something weird to the shit they leave behind in their rooms?" I ask. "I mean, I'm always afraid to use the coffee maker in my hotel room. I always start thinking 'what if somebody pissed in here?' You know, maybe just left a little piss in the bottom so that the next person who made coffee would drink it. Or maybe they could put some sort of poison or something down in the coffee maker and the next person who drinks it will die. I never use the fucking coffee makers in hotels."

"You're messed up." Buddy looks at his beer and scoffs. "Who would do shit like that? What kind of twisted bastard would do that?"

"I have," I answer, just to mess with Buddy. "And I always leave a couple of beers behind in my hotel rooms. But first I spread my butt cheeks and rub the drinking area all over my asshole. Sometimes I fart right on top of the can. So make sure you always wash the tops of these beers before you drink 'em."

"You have always been one of the weirdest mother-fuckers," Buddy laughs and discretely rubs the top of his Blatz can with the bottom of his t-shirt, hoping that I don't notice. "Come on, let's go for a little ride in your big-rig. I have to do something."

"I don't wanna drive. I'm feeling nice, let's just chill," I say. "Or maybe you can drive."

"Gypsy has my ride. Now come on, man. We've gotta pick somebody up and we'll be right back." Buddy hands me a name tag that says *Pedro* on it. "Here, this is for you. You are an honorary Pedro for the evening. Now put that on and be proud to be a Pedro."

"What's up with this Pedro shit? You all call each other Pedro. How do you know if somebody's addressing you when you're in a big group of Pedros?"

"We add describers on the front," Buddy laughs. He looks at my *Iron Maiden* shirt. "Like maybe we'll call you Retarded Heavy Metal Pedro."

"Retarded Heavy Metal Pedro . . . I like it. What do I call you?"

"For the rest of your time here you can address me as Pussy-Whipped Beer-Belly Pedro."

Buddy's conferring Pedro status on me made me feel wanted. A soothing warmth washes over my body. Happy, loving, artificial opiate-flavored warmth. I smile to myself and agree to drive Buddy out to pick up his friends.

We are all packed in the front of the truck—me, Beer-Belly Pedro, Little Gay Pedro and Buck-Toothed Negro Pedro. These guys do not mess around with sensitivity or political correctness when assigning Pedro names. One must have elephant-thick skin to be a member of the Pedro family. Pulling back into the South of the Border grounds, Buddy suggests that we park the truck and hit ladies' night at Club Cancun.

We grab a seat at the back of the room in Club Cancun and Buddy stashes the ice-filled backpack under his seat. When the bartender isn't looking Buddy passes us beers under the table so that we don't get kicked out for not buying the house drinks. I notice that Buddy is now drinking the beer from his cans with a straw[14]. Buddy holds court at his table as various off-duty Pedros approach and pay their respects. Buddy introduces me to Big-Butt Pedro, Stinky Pedro, Peg-Leg Pedro, and a short little guy the call Beer-Bitch Pedro.

"Beer-Bitch Pedro always has to haul our beer around for us." Buddy pats Beer-Bitch Pedro on the head. "I have another backpack full of beer out in Heavy Metal Pedro's truck, behind the passenger seat. Go get it, Beer-Bitch Pedro, and meet us at the top of the tower."

The sombrero tower is a 200-foot high structure capped with a giant sombrero. Buddy tells Elevator Operator Pedro to shut

---

[14] The ancient Sumerians are credited with the invention of the drinking straw. It was used for drinking beer in order to avoid ingesting the solid byproducts of fermentation.

down for the night so that we can hang out in the sombrero. Elevator Operator Pedro smiles at us with half of her teeth, the other half have presumably made the tooth fairy a very happy little sprite. The Pedros gate-off the elevator door and put up an *Out of Order* sign to keep tourists from bothering us. A glass elevator rides us to the top of the tower. We exit the elevator and I see that we are standing on the brim of the giant sombrero.

"This is the Mexican Eiffel Tower of South Carolina," Buddy says as he hands me a Schlitz and pulls out a Milwaukee's Best for himself. His back-pocket is full of paper-wrapped straws that he pilfered from Club Cancun. He uses a clean one for each new beer he opens. "Look around, ain't it a beautiful sight out there?"

Past the rim of the sombrero I see neon lights and highway. Two hundred feet below us the parking lot is teeming with fiberglass animals, lawn ornaments, tourists, tourists and more tourists. Children scream with glee as they enjoy rides with names like *Quadzilla* and *The Wild Sombrero.* The smell of hamburgers and fried food wafts up to the top of the sombrero. I reach deep within and dredge up a mucilaginous lung cookie. Hanging my head over the side, I let the loogey drop and watch it ride the air current all of the way down, one solid green gelatinous glob until it splatters on the top of somebody's car. "Beautiful!" I am amazed by the cohesion of my goober. "Hey, Buddy, give me some more of those 222's." It looks like my one or two drinks with Buddy is going to turn into an all night binge.

Pedros pour out of the elevator and Buddy introduces them one by one. "Here we have Big Titty Pedro and Hatchet

Wound Pedro," Buddy announces as two female Pedros join us on top of the sombrero. They are not unattractive in the sense that I am drunk and they likely have female genitalia. "Ah, and this is Hairlip Pedro and his best friend Obsessive Compulsive Pedro." Hairlip Pedro shakes my hand, his friend just nods, and nods, and nods. "This is Fat Albert Pedro."

"Hey, hey, hey," Fat Albert Pedro greets me.

"And," continues Buddy, "of course you have already met Beer-Bitch Pedro." Beer-Bitch Pedro has two similar looking backpacks that he has brought with him. "What's up with this, Beer-Bitch Pedro? I only had one backpack of beer in the truck?"

"I don't know, I saw two in there so I brought them both up," says Beer-Bitch Pedro handing one backpack to Buddy and one to me.

Buddy's backpack is loaded with cheap beer and ice. I study the backpack in my hands. It's not mine, it's not Buddy's, and it's not Denny's. The heavy knapsack is filled with gamy, gritty clothes and a battery powered radio boombox. It's Rudy Erikson's pack. It dawns on me that when I ditched him I forgot to throw his belongings out of the car.

A short funny looking Mexican teenager exits the elevator and Buddy starts to say something about him.

"Wait, wait, wait," I tell Buddy. "You guys are all so funny with your nicknames. Let me guess." I study the teen's sharp, squarish, facial features and dark brown skin. Giving it a great deal of thought, I proudly theorize: "Hmm...I'm gonna say they probably call you Totem-Pole-Face Pedro or Stankfist Beaner Pedro."

And then I am on my back, fending off wild swings from the boy as he perches on my chest and screams at me: "You fucking racist motherfucker. I'm gonna beat your ass. Who the fuck do you think you are calling me shit like that?" His arms are like little brown buzz saws, inching toward my face.

"Whoaaaa, take it easy there pal . . . " Buddy is pulling the raving Mexican off of me. "He doesn't work here. He's not a Pedro, I don't know how this kid got up here." Buddy wraps his arms around the teen and pulls him away from me, allowing the boy to swing himself out on the empty space in front of him. "Take it easy, guy. Now, what's your name?"

"I'm Chad," gasps the Mexican boy who is not named Totem-Pole-Face Pedro. We give Chad a beer and explain my mistake away. In light of the new information, Chad decides he wants to be an honorary Pedro for the night and gladly accepts the new moniker I bestowed upon him. "Totem-Pole-Face-Pedro. Hey, you know what? I guess I kind of like it. It's a proud name," Totem-Pole-Face Pedro declares after washing down a handful of 222's with a Rolling Rock.

"Okay, Pedros," Buddy shouts, "we're going golfing. Everybody grab a beer and let's go to the Golf of Mexico."

The Golf of Mexico is the one of the schmaltziest putt-putt golf courses I have ever seen, and it's indoors. The Pedro with the most strokes at the end of each hole has to chug a beer from Buddy's backpack. Totem-Pole-Face Pedro is the worst miniature golfer amongst us and has already had to suck down an

Old Dutch, two Little Kings, a Mickey's Big Mouth, a Genesee Cream Ale, and another Rolling Rock.

At the 14th hole Totem Pole Face Pedro is staggering and Goofy Golf Manager Pedro is giving us funny looks. We leave for the giant sombrero before we have to be escorted out. Pedro's Rocket City is right next door. Ass-Crack Baggy Pants Pedro waives us in and discretely slips Buddy a brick of bottle rockets that are the size of soup cans on a stick. We all crunch on the rest of the 222's and start lighting up the rockets.

*"Tres. Dos. Uno. Encender!"* Totem-Pole-Face Pedro chants as we light each rocket. The rockets are some of the most beautiful amateur fireworks that I have seen. I am not sure that they are actually something that is legal and for sale to the general public.

"Watch this, Pedros!" Buddy hoots and hollers as he twists long fuses together and simultaneously ignites half a brick of giant bottle rockets. We watch in awe as the missiles launch from an unused drain pipe sticking out of the ground and trace sparkling arcs of blue across the sky. Some of the rockets blow off prematurely, halfway toward their intended destination and fill the sky with expanding flowering bursts of blue, red and green. Visitors *OOOO* and *AAAAAH* at the pyrotechnics. They think that dangerously out-of-control fireworks are a nightly ritual at the park. Three rockets cross paths just above the top of the giant sombrero and explode, throwing off brilliant multicolored crackling gunpowdered displays. As if part of the show, the sombrero explodes into a fiery ball, scattering flaming chunks of shrapnel and burning the faces of the weary travelers.

*Oooos* and *Aaaaahs* turn to screams of terror and pain.

Panic reigns and tourists scatter. The flaming sombrero melts the girders that support it. Deep green flames lick the iron beams. Everyone backs up, watching in horror as the conflagration causes the two-hundred-foot high steel structure to groan, sway, and collapse in on itself.

"This is bad," I say to the Pedros.

"Yeah. We have to get out of here," says Buddy.

"Sì," agrees Totem-Pole-Face Pedro.

**10**

They say that there's no time like the present. I say that there's no better time to hit the road than when you're blitzed on cheap beer and narcotics and just blew up a giant sombrero on a two-hundred-foot high iron tower and possibly caused numerous casualties. Me and Buddy run for the moving truck with Totem-Pole-Face Pedro right on our heels. I see people pointing at us as we all jump in the cab and take off. I'm on the road again.

Buddy throws the beer backpack behind the front seat and scratches his head. "What are we going to do?"

"I'm going to Florida to spring my dog from jail," I answer. "You guys can do what you want but I'm not sticking around here." The truck barrels down I-95. In my side mirror I see a beautiful ball of fire lighting up the night and fire truck lights flashing back at South of the Border.

"Well, shit." Buddy thoughtfully scratches at the beard that has already taken over his face. "I've had more fun tonight than I have in a long, long time. But, I'm sure I've lost my job. That would mean Gypsy is going to leave me and take everything we own, which ain't much. That means I'm going to be homeless or more likely in jail for what we just done. That means I'm going to have a sore cornhole. That means I won't be happy...Hmmm..." Buddy chuckles to himself "...what the fuck, it was time for a change anyway. Let's go to Florida. What about you Chad?"

"Hey, doan' call me Chad," Totem-Pole-Face Pedro slurs at Buddy. "I like my new name."

"But it's a little bit wordy," Buddy suggests. "How about we just call you Totem."

"Yes. Yes. I like it." Totem closes his eyes and smiles.

"Well, how about it, Totem? You coming with us?" I ask. Totem doesn't answer. It seems that the cheap beer and painkillers have put him in an alcohol-induced slumber, from which we hope he will eventually awake. "Silence is consent. Right?" I ask Buddy. Buddy winks at me and smiles. I have new travel companions.


The moving truck carries us on through the night, almost of its own volition. I do very little to contribute to the effort. After the initial adrenaline rush from exploding Sombrero Tower fades, I hit the cruise control and my mind goes on autopilot. I just steer the truck down I-95, keeping it in the same lane and not allowing us to drift into a ditch or plow somebody from behind. We stop at a rest area just past the Florida border and sleep off the events of the night before. I leave Totem and

Buddy in the cab of the truck and stretch out on a picnic table for some sleep.

"Now you've really made a mess of things," Idjit tells me. He sits on my chest and licks the cheese from my sleep-crusted eyes. "You've managed to get arrested, flee the law, and now you blow up a major interstate landmark. Can't you just drive from point A to point B without wreaking havoc all along the way?"

"*Hello*," I respond in my sarcastic, sing-song, tone. "You can't make an omelet without breaking some eggs."

"What's that supposed to mean?" Idjit asks.

"I don't know. On the road to rock-n-roll there's a lot of wreckage in the ravine."

"Huh?" Idjit eyes me with a befuddled basset hound type of look.

"Some people say that cucumbers taste better pickled."

"Wha . . . "

"This is a dream, right? They never make sense. Just roll with me here," I answer trying to make my confused friend feel better. "Hey, I really miss you pal. I want to see you for real and share a big plate of deviled eggs. Maybe we could watch some *Ultimate Fighting Championships* or something. We could even get a pay-per-view title fight instead of just watching rebroadcasts of old fights. Maybe we can catch the Chuck 'The Iceman' Lidell title match that's coming up."

"Awesome. You know, I miss you, too, big guy." Idjit's big cataract-clouded eyes tear up. As they run down his droopy face each tear rips out a small piece of my heart. "I can't wait. But, for now you need to focus on your journey. You messed up. Your daddy warned you not to leave anything but Denny behind in Tennessee. You didn't listen. You're going to need to go back."

"For what?"

"What you left behind. Now kiss me you fool." Idjit's dog lips morph into luscious, succulent, ruby red, female lips. Real sweet looking DSL's.

"No, I don't think I will kiss you," I tell my dog. "Although, you need kissing badly. That's what's wrong with you. You should be kissed and often. And by somebody who knows how. Now what do you say to that?"

"You had me at *Hello*," Idjit gives me a coy, sideways look. "By the way, you're covered with mosquitoes and fire ants."


In fourth grade I cut in front of Shelby Rubituson in the cafeteria lunch-line. Shelby was a slight red-headed mulatto kid in my class. He was also the regional golden gloves champion in the light flyweight category. My affront to Shelby sent him into a wild fourth-grader rage. He was worried that I would order the last serving of Salisbury steak. In a split second his fists were everywhere on my head and torso at the same time. All I could see was a blur of his mocha hands. The punches didn't hurt, it was like being struck with a lightning fast balsa wood paddle, but they were disorienting. I didn't know how to defend against the rapid and unrelenting pummeling. I stepped back to let Shelby return to his rightful place in line and he immediately let up. And don't you know it, that little piece of shit got the last serving of Salisbury steak. I was stuck having to eat pasty macaroni and cheese and breaded white fish covered in tartar sauce.

The beating that I suffered at the hands of Shelby Rubituson was much like what I awake to in the rest area outside of Jacksonville. Open hands slap my face, my arms, my legs. The entire surface of my body burns, something similar to what it would probably feel like to be attacked by a swarm of killer bees.

"He's covered in fire ants," somebody screams. Leaping from the picnic table I try to outrun the pain. Totem tackles me hard, taking me to the ground. Buddy and somebody else continue to slap at my face and body. Tiny red demons sting my eyes, my ears, and the inside of my nose. I roll on the ground as if on fire and they continue to slap and smack at my body. It feels as if somebody is kicking me in the ribs. Heart thumping in a crazy giggle-jazz syncopated beat. Instead of enduring the thousand burning bites of the red demons, I pass out and my friends tend to me.

Reality rudely rips the bedcovers of unconsciousness from my face. I am on the floor of the rest area men's room, the fog of urinal mints, human effluence, and cleaning fluids snake their way up my chin and nestle in my nostrils. A long, low, mournful fart bellows out from one of the stalls. Buddy, Pedro and a security guard lean in over me. My asshole is sore.

"Hey there, fella," the security guard greets me. "My name's Officer Sleestack. I'm the head of security at this rest stop. You hunkered down on a table that was sitting smack dab in the biggest durn colony of fire ants I ever seent." Sleestack chuckles to himself, his first, second, and third chins all gently jiggle to the rhythm of his laughter. He grabs one arm and Buddy grips the other. They help me stand. "You know, you ain't supposed to sleep overnight in these rest areas. It ain't safe. But I'm guessin' you learnt your lesson."

I look at myself in the smudged piece of polished metal bolted to the bathroom wall. It barely resembles a mirror. A fuzzy reflection of something that looks vaguely like me gazes back. From what I can tell, I look like hell. My eye is blackened from the beer can that Buddy threw at me. The rest of my face is red and swollen with hives. My ribs are sore and each breath feels as if someone is stabbing me in the lungs.

"I'm calling an ambulance. You don't look right," Sleestack tells me. "You're gun'ta need medical intervention. Your lips are swollen ... your eyes ... what you're experiencing looks like an allergic reaction. Durn it! I wouldn't be surprised if your balls ain't swelled up like coconuts."

Shoving my hand down my pants, I grip my right nut. It's heavy and enlarged, easily filling up the palm of my hand. My left nut is even bigger. My scrotum is stretched taut, like a drum skin, over the gargantuan cajones. "I will go to my doctor," I tell Sleestack. I haven't had a regular physician in fifteen years and don't know who I would even see about my condition.

"Where's your doctor?" Sleestack asks. "You need to get to him soon."

"He's in Miami. Doctor Bhanigrath Gupta." I make up a name, figuring that an Indian name sounds good. "He'll get me fixed up in no time flat."

"You can't go to Miami. There's a hurricane watch down that way. Angus is supposed to hit somewhere down that way tomorrow morning. Everybody's evacuating. You won't even be able to drive down the interstate. Both sides are opened up for northbound traffic for people to get out of the path. You will not find your doctor, if you can even get down there."

"We're goimb," I mumble through my swollen lips. My tongue has now puffed up to an enlarged, flapping piece of meat; it offers no help in articulating my position. "You canth thtop us."

Sleestack's eyes narrow to determined slits. He inhales deeply and then exhales a breathy reptilian rasp, a flabby, defiant X of forearms cross over his chest. "You boys are not going anywhere. In fact, I'm gun'ta need to see your identification. You," Sleestack points at Totem, "let me see your greencard and . . . "

*BLAMMO!* Buddy clocks Sleestack across the back of the head with an empty mop bucket from the bathroom. Sleestack crumples, unconscious. We all raise our eyebrows and shrug our shoulders at each other: What do we do now? Collectively we drag him into a stall. Totem pulls Sleestack's pants down and sets the unaware rent-a-cop on the toilet. There is a giant green turd coiled up in the bowl, the tip of the turd breaks the surface of the water and points proudly upward. One lone, completely unstained, square of toilet paper rests near the top of the frightening curlicue.

"Let's leave him here," Totem says. "He'll think he overexerted himself and passed out pushing that *grande* thing out of his *culo.*" Totem shakes his head, "Man, how do you give birth to something like that and have nothing to wipe off of your butt?"

"That's called a Mississippi Mudslide," Buddy explains to Totem. "It's when you lay out a giant turd and have no poop to wipe off of your butt ... wait ... No, I'm sorry. It's not a Mississippi Mudslide. I think it's a Depth Charge ... no ... "

"It's called an Alabama Slider," opines a voice from the abutting stall. Someone has heard our entire episode. "It's an Alabama Slider when there's nothing to wipe. A Mississippi Mudslide is when you have to wipe shit off of your legs all the way down to your knees, and a logjam is when ... "

We all lock eyes. It's time to beat it. Once again, Buddy and I high-step it to the truck with Totem right behind us.


My rig screams out of the rest area. We stop at the next exit to fill up the gas tank. I top off the tank and go inside to pay. A handwritten sign hangs on the swinging door that says: *No shoes, No shirt, No service.* In smaller print, the sign further explains: *The shoes are for your protection. The shirt is for ours. You don't look as good as you think you do.* Inside I present the last of my money to pay for my gas and a pickled hot sausage that calls to me from a big glass jar on the counter. Pedro comes into the store to use the restroom.

Clevis, the gas station attendant, tells me that everybody is heading up I-95 to get away from the storm but I can take A-1A all of the way down the coast to Miami. We head for the edge of the continent and steer the truck south on the coastal highway. Clevis was right. The roadway is eerily vacant. Pedro stole a carton of generic cigarettes from the convenience store. I chug the remainder of Denny's Mormon Tea, feeling the stimulant effect immediately. Obviously all of the ephedra settles to the bottom of the tea. I don't even like cigarettes, neither does Buddy or Totem, but we chain-smoke for the rest of the drive. The gas pedal becomes well-acquainted with the rusted metal floor of the truck.

I am so zipped on the tea and nauseous from the cigarettes. Flames shoot from my fingertips, sparks from my swollen and inflamed eyes, smoke from my ears. The truck and I are like lovers that know each other's moves. The brakes fail and the transmission grinds, engine smoking like an AA meeting. I feel like a long-haul truck driver pushing his oversized transcontinental hobbyhorse across the country, shipping a load of string beans to Utah. Totem and Buddy grip the seat as I ball that jack all the way to Little Cuba. In Miami I jerk the truck to the west on State Road 41 toward Frog City. Windows are boarded up on the green and orange and pink buildings. The truck chokes to a stop as the transmission drops.

We are close to the new house. I want to call Mom, but I have lost my cell phone somewhere along the way. The nicotine and ephedra have me so jacked up. I don't care that it's raining. I don't care that I am in unfamiliar territory. I don't care that the tiny store that I enter slaps me in the face with the funk of half-rotten vegetables and that none of the products are familiar to me. I don't care that the group of men playing dominoes at a table near the front door eye me suspiciously. I don't give a shit that nobody in the store speaks English. Totem is with us. He chatters and jibbas and jabbas with the men in the store. Why is it that when people speak in another language they talk so fast? Totem and the men look at me and Buddy and laugh. I think they are calling us *Gueros*. We laugh back, uncomfortably, sure that us gringos are the butt of some awful joke. They give us something sweet called *platanos* to eat. There is a payphone, and that is all that matters. I pick up the phone handset and place a collect call to Mom. She is coming to get us and the truck.

**11**

"Oh baby, look at you! What happened?" Mom evaluates my condition and looks like she's going to cry.

"Mom, I'm fine. Let's just get out of here and pick up Idjit from the kennel."

"Uh, let's just get you home and out of sight right now." Mom's eyes suspiciously scan the area outside of the little bodega. "We'll talk about Idjit when we get there. You have bigger problems to deal with right now, if you know what I mean."

I don't know exactly what she means, but once we get into her rental car Mom explains. Right now there is a man-hunt up and down the east coast for me, Totem, and Buddy. It turns out that the Sombrero Tower did not explode because of our fireworks. The radio in Rudy Erikson's backpack was packed with C-4 explosives and probably was intended for an abortion clinic. The bomb coincidentally detonated just as the fireworks were bursting overhead. Surveillance video from South of the Border showed me, Buddy, and Totem sprinting for the moving truck with a massive explosion booming behind us.

"Baby, they're saying you boys are confederates of Rudy Erikson." It seems that everybody in the country except me knows who Rudy is. Rudy's a Christian terrorist that has been on the Top 10 Most Wanted list for the past three years. He is wanted for setting off a bomb during what he thought was a gay pride convention in Savannah, Georgia. Due to the speech impediment of a worker at the information desk, Rudy detonated his bomb in the wrong section of the convention center. Instead of a Gay Pride get-together, Rudy blew up a May Bride show. The explosion killed twenty engaged couples who were watching a fashion show of bridesmaid dresses. The men in the audience may have been praying for such an end to the show. Taffeta-wrapped disembodied limbs littered the convention center and Rudy went into hiding in the Blue Ridge Mountains.

Mom tells me that my face has been all over the news. "You look good on television. They keep showing your picture. You're famous."

"How in the hell did they get a picture of me so fast?" I wonder aloud.

"Oh, one of them news stations contacted me," Mom explains. "All they had was a freeze frame of the surveillance video. You looked kind of funny. Not ha-ha funny. More drunk and crazy funny. I didn't want them running that photo so I gave them a copy of your senior picture."

"Mom, that's a picture from twenty years ago. And I look like a fucking dork in it. I had a mullet and braces. And you made me wear that gay pink shirt. You need to get in touch with the news station and give them a more recent picture."

"No. I like that picture of you. You looked so handsome."
Mom gives me that Mom-look that says *don't argue with me,
young man.* "They are keeping that one and that's it."

Mom drives us to the new house, a three bed, two bath, green
stucco dwelling with palm trees in the front yard. Plywood has
already been nailed over the windows in anticipation of the
hurricane. Mom called for a tow truck and it's on its way to
drag the moving truck here.

"Mom, let's go get Idjit Galoot. I want my dog here before the
storm hits."

"Well," Mom hesitates, "we need to talk about that. Idjit's not
here. I wasn't altogether truthful with you when I told you I had
Idjit boarded down here. I couldn't find him before I left. I put
up lost posters and called the pound. I cruised the neighbor-
hoods looking for him. I even paid that nice neighbor boy,
Kevin Emory, to look for him. That dog just disappeared."

"Help yourselves, boys," Mom says in the direction of Totem
and Buddy who have already raided the refrigerator and made
high-piled, Dagwood-styled, processed lunch-meat sandwiches.
Totem takes a swig of milk right from the carton.

"Hey, get a glass you filthy beast," I snap at Totem. He smiles
sheepishly, shrugs his shoulders, and hands the milk jug to
Buddy who also places his mouth right on the jug's opening and
swigs. "Mom! I can't believe you would leave Idjit behind. I'm
going back up to look for him. I need to take your car and I need
some money."

"You're not going anywhere right now, Baby. There's a hurricane coming our way. There are no flights or buses going out of here right now. I'm taking my car out to get more storm supplies and I don't have any cash on me for you right now anyway. Just wait here for the tow truck while I'm gone. After this storm passes you can decide what to do." Mom rubs my back and tries to reassure me. "That nice Kevin Emory promised me that he would continue to look until he finds your dog. Things will work out. Now stay here. I'll be back soon."

Mom was lying about not having any cash. I found $150.00 in her overnight bag. I don't like sneaking around in her stuff and taking money without her permission, but sometimes a man's gotta do what a man's gotta do. It ain't right that she left Idjit behind and I'm the only person who's willing to do something about it.

I don't give a shit about a hurricane, a little wind and rain won't stop me. I'm going for my dog. Mom's not going to stop me. The lack of a car is not going to stop me. God himself isn't going to stop me unless he drops that hurricane down right on top of me.

My skin burns from the fire ant toxins, my eyes hurt, lips and nuts are swollen, and it feels like somebody is stabbing me in the lungs every time I take a breath. Yet still I am determined. I pack one of Mom's duffel bags with canned food and toiletries to get me through on my trip back to Idjit. I don't need no stinking trains, planes, cars or buses. I'm going to hitchhike right out of Florida and then figure out the rest of my trip from that point.

"You're not going out in this shit alone," Buddy tells me. "I'm gonna go with you. You're going to need a traveling partner in case you run into any trouble. Besides, I'm having too much God damn fun and I'm not ready to stop yet." Buddy's beard[15] has grown out to full facial covering and his chin juts out valiantly. His posture is straight as a board and his appetite for adventure is obvious. "Yessir-ree, Gawdammit! We's gwanta have fun!"

It is decided. Buddy and I will go. Totem will stay behind and wait for the moving truck. He can stick around during the storm and then do whatever he wants. As Buddy and I leave, Totem pops his head out from inside of the refrigerator and wishes us luck through a mouth full of chewed up lunch-meat.

Outside of the house, Buddy asks: "Do you trust that guy? I mean, he seems alright, but...you know...you're leaving him at your Mom's house to wait for all of your possessions. You're leaving him alone with your Mom and I think he's been looking her up and down. We barely know anything about him and he's hardly said more than a few words to us."

"He's okay," I tell Buddy. I've got a feeling about him. And we are on the road again.

---

[15] The study of beards is called pogonology.

**12**

With $150.00, a duffle-bag full of canned meat products[16,] and Buddy's half-full beer pack, we are on our way. And oh, sweet providence, two totally rad *BMX* bikes lay abandoned in a neighbor's yard. Obviously the spoiled brats who owned the bikes didn't care if they were left out to rust or blow away in a storm. They were all but abandoned and clearly meant to be there for us.

Not a soul to be seen out on the street. No sounds of dogs barking, kids playing or birds chirping. The dark grey sky and fast moving clouds cast an ominous shadow over the cookie-cutter stucco houses of the Boca Del Vista planned community. Buddy quickly seizes the cooler of the two bikes, hops on, and rides a wheelie down the street. "Come on, Peckerwood!" he

---

[16] Armour Star potted meat product contains the following ingredients: mechanically separated chicken, beef tripe (stomach), partially defatted cooked beef fatty tissue (huh?), beef hearts, water, partially defatted cooked pork fatty tissue. It also contains less than two percent of the following: mustard, natural flavorings, dried garlic, dextrose, sodium erythorbate, and sodium nitrite.

yells back at me. I mount my bike and trail behind him as we pedal our way out of the community.

The main road, Calle Ocho, is mostly unbothered by auto traffic. Homeless people mill about, pushing shopping carts and holding involved conversations with invisible friends. A wild man in a brown bathrobe and a matted gray beard shouts at the clouds, wagging his finger at the charcoal sky. We do the same as we coast by on our bikes.

"That's right, Amigo," shouts the mad monk. "Follow the trails. Watch the clouds, follow the trails." I look up and see a westward flowing trail in the clouds, like a river, the clouds in the current moving faster than the others. Gales of wind pressing on our backs, we speed along on bikes that are too small for our bloated man-bodies. Vegetable stands and grimy gas stations give way to strip malls with nail salons and insurance brokers. Cuban restaurants and dollar stores line the sides of the road—new development, crunching up the tip of the Florida peninsula, encroaching on the swampy Everglades. Buddy throws me a warm beer and pops one open for himself.

In a Piggly Wiggly parking lot sits a giant recreational vehicle shaped like a bratwurst.

"It's the fucking Bratmobile!" Buddy shouts at me and the wind almost carries his voice away before it reaches my ears. He points toward a brown, tubular, simulated-meat behemoth on wheels. "Oh, man, we've gotta fucking stop!" Buddy jumps off of his bike while it is still rolling and lets it do an awkward cartwheel into an overturned shopping cart.

I set my bike down beside the meaty vehicle and we both gaze on with shock and awe. Who hasn't seen the commercials with the Albert Morgan Bratmobile. It's a freakin' pop culture icon. I didn't even really believe it existed, but there it was, just sitting in the grocery store parking lot. I give Buddy a boost so that he can look in through the windshield.

"Oh, my fucking gawd! It's incredible!" Buddy squeals. "It's like a gargantuan penis on wheels."

"Hey, why don't you guys take a picture with your camera phone? It'll last longer." Two teenage boys approach us. One is dressed in jeans and an AC/DC shirt. The other is similarly dressed in ripped up denim shorts and a Led Zeppelin shirt. The youngster in the AC/DC shirt introduces himself as Spencer and explains that he and his friend, Kyle, are driving the Bratmobile across the country as part of a college internship.

"Yeah," giggles Kyle as he tries to give his friend a high-five and misses. "We're marketing majors and we contacted the company to see if we could interview somebody about the Bratmobile ads. Next thing we know, Spencer and I have a job driving the giant dong cross-country and feeding people bratwurst." Kyle wipes his hands on the front of his t-shirt, tugs on his braided belt, and giggles again. "Here, have a couple of these. They're like stress balls, except it's like squeezing a schlong." Kyle hands us foam rubber Albert Morgan bratwurst-shaped stress relievers.

"Can we see the inside of it?" Buddy asks, like a little boy wanting to see the cockpit of a plane.

"I don't know," Spencer winks at Kyle. "Do you think you could do us a favor in return?" Spencer and Kyle are underage college boys and they accidentally left their fake ID's with frat brothers before embarking on their tour of the nation in a giant wiener. "Can you buy us some beer and some Goldschlagger? That douche-bag in the liquor store carded me."

Kyle gives us a fifty-dollar bill, puts in their order for alcohol, and tells us to keep any leftover change. Me and Buddy give the boys the beer pack to keep them busy while we do the shopping. We buy two cases of Old Dutch, a bottle of Mad Dog 20/20 and a bottle of Leadschlager and still have twenty bucks to pocket. When we get back to the Bratmobile Kyle is passed out in the passenger seat.

"He beerbonged the rest of the slop you had in your back pack. I dared him to." Spencer laughs as he draws "*I love boys*" and a crude hairy penis on Kyle's forehead with a permanent marker. "Now it looks like I'm going to have to do all of the driving myself."

"Where are you going?" I smell an easy ride out of here.

"We're supposed to show up at some festival in Sarasota in a couple of days. I guess they're going to have all kinds of crazy crap there: Blue Man, mimes, the Brady Bunch musical, water-skiing squirrels, Elvis impersonators, you name it. It's gonna be glorious," Spencer says in a dreamy gay tone. "We're gonna cruise across the Tamiami trail and ease our way up there, as long as the hurricane doesn't stop us."

"We can help you with the driving since your buddy there seems to be out of commission," I offer.

"You're on, Bro! Hop on in and do a little artwork." Spencer hands me the magic marker as I enter. Buddy follows, wide-eyed and giddy like a little girl.

"Oh, man. I don't know. I don't feel right about drawing on some kid I don't even know just because he's passed out drunk.

He seems like an alright kid. I mean, he's wearing a *Zeppelin* shirt. At the very least the guy has good taste in music, right?"

"Nawww, he couldn't even name one of their songs for you. He's really quite a fucking dork. He just bought that shirt in Dillard's because he heard some of our brothers saying it was retro-cool. He bought a Doors shirt there too and when I mentioned how cool Jim Morrison was, do you know what he said?"

"What?" Buddy and I ask at the same time.

"He said 'Yeah, dude, *Brown Eyed Girl* is the shit.' Can you fucking believe that? He gets Van Morrison and Jim Morrison confused."

"No." I want to kick him in the nuts.

"Yeah. And don't even get me started on his Iron Maiden shirt. I challenged him on that. Asked him to name me one song that he knew. He just looked away and told me he doesn't look at the song names, he just likes their music."

"He's a Maiden poser?" I ask.

"Yep."

"Give me that marker." Spencer is actually pretty cool for a kid. He puts on the *Screaming for Vengeance* CD that I bought for $3.00 in the liquor store, cranks the stereo, and spins the tires of the Bratmobile in the parking lot as we're heading out to the highway. Buddy pops the seal on the Leadschlager and passes it around. I draw a swastika on one of Kyle's cheeks and a dangly venous nutsack on the other.

Like an inquisitive three-year-old discovering his surroundings, Buddy queries Spencer about every aspect of the Bratmobile. Spencer is the obliging tour guide answering all, satisfying Buddy's curiosity. The Bratmobile was originally powered by two motorcycles welded together by steel bars and covered with a painted wooden simulated bratwurst. Albert Morgan, Sr. originally used the Bratmobile to run bootleg liquor during Prohibition. Everyone (including cops) was so fascinated by the large penis on wheels that they completely missed the fact that Albert and his bother, Richard, were hauling bathtub gin to speakeasies. If asked what they were up to, Albert would hand out "samples" of his world famous sausages on hard German rolls and talk about his meat products. He really did make a tasty sausage. All the while, Richard would be standing just behind the side gull wing door with a .45 caliber Tommy gun, ready to blast away if the true use of the Bratmobile was discovered by a nosy copper. After Prohibition ended and bootleg liquor was no longer profitable, the Morgan boys went legit and actually started marketing Albert's sausages. Richard built a fleet of Bratmobiles to drive around the country. The drivers would hand out sausages and meatwhistles to gape-jawed gawkers. Soon everybody knew Albert Morgan Brats. Everybody loved the Bratmobile.

Fueled on Leadschlager and childlike joy, Buddy relentlessly questions Spencer about his job and what it's like to drive the Bratmobile.

"Why don't you see for yourself?" Spencer pulls over outside of an air boat tour business and lets Buddy take the wheel. "Just be careful. Kyle had to put a deposit down on this thing with his mom's credit card."

Salty, alcohol-tinged, liquid happiness leaks from Buddy's eyes as he hauls ass down the Tamiami trail. "This is the best thing since I discovered how to spank the monkey," I hear him mutter to himself under his breath. Rob Halford screams for vengeance, Buddy gently weeps with joy and watches the road through his blurry tears, Spencer reclines in a bucket seat in the back, Kyle lays motionless and clueless, a human canvas ready for more permanent marker artwork, and I pine for Idjit Galoot, unable to enjoy my ride in this incredible meatstick on wheels.

The sky weeps for my lost dog. I find only a dollop of joy in treating Kyle's face like the wall of a gas station bathroom. My thoughts are of my lost best friend. I can see him hungry on the street. Or maybe locked up in the pound, howling all night at the lonely moon. I'm afraid they're gonna give him the gas if I don't get there soon.

I slip away from our motorized bratwurst-shaped fiberglass shell to visit Idjit in my dreams. We are sitting around a chipped and water stained oak table. Cigar smoke rises and forms a blue cloud above the room. I sip at my scotch and water. It burns my throat, warms my belly. I think to myself that I would like a PBR instead.

The red glass of the hanging ceiling light throws soft crimson rays on my cards. *What am I doing?* I think to myself. *I don't know how to play poker.* The Airedale to my right has called out a game of high/low roller coaster with a red-eyed devil. I don't know what any of this shit means. The bulldog with a cigar laughs at me. The collie is so drunk, he drops his cards, laughs, takes another sip of his scotch, and picks up his cards and drops them again[17]. In the middle of the table is a glass jar filled with balled-up pieces of paper.

Behind me a grandfather clock chimes. To my left a familiar voice tells me that it's "two minutes to midnight." I turn and see Idjit sitting beside me, his rubbery dog lips turned up in a smile. He winks at me and kicks me in the leg.

Coolidge, the sad-eyed St. Bernard shifts his eyes back and forth. He chews on a giant burning spliff and asks me: "Well, what's it goin'ta be? You in or out?" Over Coolidge's shoulder I admire a beautiful painting of sailboats cutting through choppy waters, storm clouds looming above. I look at my cards and only see shifting colors and faces. I don't understand the game.

Again I feel Idjit's foot kicking me in the leg. I look down and see an ace of clubs wedged in between his dog toes. The untended curlicue of a dewclaw wraps down and over the top of the card. Idjit raises his eyebrows at me as much as a basset hound can and kicks me again. Beneath the table I take his offering. I slip it into my hand and slam my cards on the table. "What've ya got?" I challenge Coolidge, still not knowing what in the hell I'm doing.

Whines and whimpers rise from the players and mingle above us with the smoke. My poker buddies all cower as if I'm going to hit them with a newspaper or rub their noses in feces. Coolidge grunts and growls to himself. And then he addresses

---

[17] In 2005 two oil paintings of dogs playing poker, painted by C.M. Coolidge, were purchased together at an auction for $590,400.00. It was expected that the paintings would be sold for somewhere between $30,000.00 to $50,000.00. The works, *A Bold Bluff* and *Waterloo*, are part of a sequential narrative of paintings that follows the course of a hand of poker played by a group of dogs.

me: "I think it's time you took your winnings and left. And you should probably take your friend with you."

Under one arm I scoop up the giant jar from the middle of the table. Under the other I pick up the Galoot as if he was a sack of potatoes. We exit the side door of the room and I realize there is no floor underneath me. Idjit embraces me as we fall.

Forceful tropical gales buffet the giant wiener. Raindrops the size of water balloons splatter on the windshield, making it impossible for us to see. Buddy slams on the brakes, swerving and launching me from my seat. Mid-nap I regain consciousness halfway between a seat shaped like a German hard-roll and the sloped windshield of the vehicle. The phrase *land in the lap of God* occurs to me as everything happens in slow motion. The side of my face slams into the back of the driver's seat and my legs hit the console between the front seats. The Bratmobile settles into a ditch on the side of the road.

"Gawwdammit! Did you see that fucking thing in the middle of the road?" Buddy screams. "It looked like a seven-foot tall monkey with a boner."

Kyle is crumpled on top of me, still unconscious. Spencer pulls him off of me. "Is everybody alright?" Spencer asks around.

"My face feels like it's broken. So does my wrist, and my ribs, and my knee." I evaluate myself for more damage. It's getting hard to keep track of the injuries.

"How about you?" Spencer asks Buddy.

"I'm fine, but this Bratmobile won't start. And, uh . . . " Buddy hesitates and shakes his head, "I don't know what that was on the road, but it was huge. I may be kind of fucked up, but I know I ain't seeing shit."

"What about Kyle?" I ask about the unconscious boy in the fetal position beside me. "He's not moving. That can't be good."

"Nah, he's fine," replies Spencer without even looking at his friend. "I've seen him sleep through worse. My question is what do we do now? There's a hurricane headed our way and we don't have the wheels to outrun it."

Through the windshield we see the lights of a pickup truck in front of us. The driver keeps honking.

"Well, maybe he can get us to shelter," Buddy says as he nods toward the truck.

Spencer runs out in the blowing rain to talk to the driver. After a minute or so they start honking the horn, calling us. Me and Buddy shrug our shoulders, what the fuck? Buddy throws Kyle over his shoulder and hands me the beerpack. "Let's see where this takes us, eh?" We run out in the rain. The wind tries to push us back and the fist-sized water drops sting our faces. Within seconds we are soaked through.

Me, Buddy, Spencer and the driver all fit snugly into the cab of the old beat-up Willys Jeep. We throw Kyle on his side in the bed of the pick-up and push him up against the flat spare-tire. Spencer gets out and wedges a rolled up rug behind Kyle's back so that he will stay on his side instead of going face-down and drowning.

"What in tarnation are you boys doing out in this weather? There's a hurricane warning. Everybody's evacuated. Only a durn fool would be out in this mess." The driver reprimands us, apparently forgetting that he too is driving around in the same weather. "My name is Arnette. You boys can come back and ride the storm out with me and my brother Pervis. You'll be safer in our building than in that monstrosity you crashed into the ditch back there." Arnette steers us down a gravel path to a cinder block building. We jump out of the truck and sprint for the building, leaving Kyle in the bed of the truck.

**13**

"Come on in, boys." Arnette invites us into the cement building. The pounding rain outside almost drowns out his voice. "Make yourselves at home. We have a storm to ride out." Hundreds of eyes stare at us as we enter. It seems that the building has been overrun by bizarre fairy tale creatures. Squirrels with horns. Winged fish. Dogs with alligator heads. Three-headed pigs. Monkeys with two butts.

"What the fuck?" Spencer blurts, freaked out by the animals.

"Aww, don't worry about that." Arnette laughs. "Those is stuffed. They ain't real. My brother Pervis is a taxidermy artist. He's not satisfied with just killin' and stuffin' 'em. He makes his own critters."

"Kind of like the jackalope[18], huh?" I remember seeing a jackalope, a stuffed jackrabbit with antlers, in a restaurant once when Mom took us on vacation in the Black Hills. Our waitress

---

[18] It is thought that the myth of the jackalope was inspired by sightings of jackrabbits afflicted with *Shope Papillomavirus*, which causes the growth of horn and antler-like tumors about the rabbits' heads and bodies.

told us that it was a hoax, a creature created by some jokester. "Those are pretty funny."

"Ain't nothing funny about it." At the back of the room, sitting near the fireplace, sits a man who looks just like Arnette. His thick beard covers most of his face. The sad moustache hangs down over his mouth, obscuring it, the opening only apparent because the whiskers blow out slightly with his breath as he talks. "Those jackalopes is some fucked up, mean little critters. You get gored by one and you'll be lucky to tell the tale. They don't just hurt you with their antlers. A wound from a jackalope don't heal. It gets all infected-like and just festers until you cut the whole rotted area out. That is if you're lucky enough to cut it out in time."

"Boys, this is my twin brother, Pervis." Arnette interrupts his brother to introduce us. "He's goin'ta be in charge of enter-tainment and tale spinning while you're here."

"Now that jackalope," Pervis continues, ignoring his brother, "he's tough, but he ain't nothin' compared to a Wolpertinger or the Feejee Mermaid. And don't even get me started on the Skunk Ape ... "

"We ain't goin'ta get you started, Pervis," Arnette interrupts his brother once again. "We need to get these fellas into dry clothes and then hunker down for this little South-Florida rain-storm we're expecting."

Buddy's eyes pop and his jaw drops. "We left college boy out there in the bed of the truck. He could drown or get blown away." Buddy runs out the front door into the stinging rain and Spencer follows. They fish Kyle out of the back of the Willys and drag his waterlogged body back to the building. He's still un-conscious but breathing.

We set Kyle by the fire. Arnette gets everybody towels and dry clothes. We don the camouflage hunting jumpsuits and dry out by the fire. Pervis asks us if we want to get high. "I got some Florida Swamp Bhang Bhang shit that will blow your top. You wanna get Chinese eyes?"

"I don't exactly know what you just said but it sounds pretty good to me," I tell Pervis as he pulls a three-foot long, ceramic, skull-bong out from behind his seat, and places his bearded orifice on the end. Pervis fires up the organic material in the bowl with his confederate flag Zippo. The loud bubbling of the bong water sounds like a public toilet flushing. After a long pull on the water pipe, Pervis sits back and convulses, trying to hold the smoke in. Unable to hold it any longer, Pervis deflates and the smoke is diffused by his beard. His entire face fumes. In the light of the fireplace we watch the lunatic with bloodshot eyes and smoldering facial hair.

We pass the Florida-Cracker peace pipe around, watching in turn as each of our bodies is racked with coughing fits from the harsh fog. The smoke leaves us drooling and hacking. I smile to myself as I consider that we are all willing to place our mouths on the same thing, which we have all drooled in, without any misgivings so that we can get high. I inspect Pervis's beard and note food particles and small amounts of something crusted about the face pelt. If he wiped his beard clean with a napkin and tried to hand it to me I wouldn't touch the filthy thing. But offer me some weed and I'm the first one to put my mouth right where Pervis's crusty beard just was.

With all of the coughing, the room sounds like a tuberculosis ward. Pervis gives himself a blast with an asthma inhaler and passes it around. "Get those air passages opened up wide for more, fellas," he says. We all zip ourselves with the inhaler and the hacking and drooling subsides. I inhale deeply and then let it go. In my head I hear the *wha-whas*. My ears echo with a muted fuzz-tone of *wha-wha wha-wha wha-wha*. Somebody giggles. The Florida Swamp Bhang Bhang shit whacked me in the fucking head like a sledgehammer. Buddy passes around cans of Old Dutch to everybody.

"Heyyyyy," Buddy says, long and drawn out, as if he has something to share, and then pauses. "I like the sound of that. Heyyyy.
Heyyyyyyy."

"Yeah!" I laugh, also liking the sound. "Heyyyyyy. Yeah, that's nice. Heyyyyyyy."

"Heyyyyyy," Spencer joins in and we all break into uncontrollable laughter. Each time the laughter starts to subside, we make eye contact and it starts up again.

"What the devil are you people doin' in here?" Arnette comes back into the room and shakes his head. "Oh, I see. Pervis's been passing the skull bong around. Alright, well you guys are goin'ta be hungry, why don't you give some of this a try?" Arnette sets down a tray with some sort of barbequed meat and eggs the size of ping-pong balls.

We dig into the food. The meat's from something Pervis calls a Hoover Hog. I like pork. I like it a lot. The sweet smoky meat is drowned in a spicy BBQ sauce. The eggs are pickled. Arnette's meal is incredible. We polish off the first platter and Pervis is surprised. "I ain't never seen people scarf down armadillo meat and gopher tortoise eggs so damn fast. You boys want more?"

"Armadillo?" Buddy laughs. "We've been eating fucking armadillo?" I notice that Buddy's facial hair has grown out to a full-on mountain-man beard in a matter of days. In the borrowed camouflage he looks remarkably like Arnette and Pervis. One would be surprised to discover that Buddy is not related to them.

"That's right," Arnette seems to be smiling beneath his mouth-obscuring whiskers. "Possum on the half-shell, Texas bar-bee-que style. It's some pretty tasty shit, huh?"

"You're darn fuckin' tootin' it is!" Buddy hollers. Me and Pervis join in with *yee-haws* and long drawn out *wooooos*. Spencer tries to fade into the wall as paranoia sets in for him. He is whacked on swamp weed and has just realized that he is cooped up with a group of madmen.

Arnette returns with another tray of armadillo and eggs. Buddy hands him a beer and the water pipe. We hoot and holler and laugh and guffaw until our lungs, voices and hearts hurt.

We turn on the television to see what to expect from the storm. At the edge of the Everglades, miles from civilization, these boys have high-definition cable television and a 56-inch plasma set. They don't have air-conditioning. They don't have a dishwasher or a garbage disposal. Obviously they don't have beard trimmers and the washing machine on the back porch doesn't seem to work. But they have cable television and a badass plasma boob-tube.

We turn on the Cable News Channel mid-story. The attractive Asian reporter says with an unwavering smile: "and now Muslims worldwide are protesting and issuing death threats against Mr. Hayman for his commentary in which he stated that

Muslims are easily goaded into protesting and issuing death threats. Back to you, Rusty."

"Thank you, Suchi Punani," says the anchorman. "And now more on the terrorists who blew up a roadside tower in South Carolina. The three fugitives who committed this horrendous act, seen here..." Arnette starts to laugh and Pervis joins in as pictures of me, Buddy, and Totem and our names are posted on the television screen "...appear to be on a crime spree. Security cameras in a Florida rest area captured images of them leaving the men's room where a security guard was later found unconscious in a bathroom stall. The security worker, Officer William Holly Sleestack, has reported that the terrorists seemed to be on some sort of a mission and are determined and dangerous. A manhunt for the suspects has been delayed due to the imminent landfall of Hurricane Angus on the Florida Gulf Coast. We'll keep you updated on these events as they develop. And now to our meteorologist, Lumpy Rutherford, with more on Angus."

"Thank you Rusty," the meteorologist cuts in. "Angus is bearing down on the Gulf Coast of South Florida. Angus is a category four storm. That means wind speeds of up to 155 miles per hour. The eye of Angus is well defined and should make landfall within two hours just below Naples. It's going to be a bad one. Not since Andrew has South Florida seen a storm of this magnitude. The eye is slow moving and that may be problematic as it passes over the bottom tip of the Florida Peninsula. Luckily Angus is going to hit a relatively unpopulated area and most of the residents have evacuated. Hopefully the storm will break up some before it hits the other coast. Otherwise, damages will be extensive. Back to you Rusty."

Hurricane Angus will clear a path through Florida straight toward our little shelter, and we love it. Arnette and Pervis are impressed with the way the Sombrero Tower exploded. They see us as anti-establishment heroes. They ask to see our manifesto, whatever that means. Once the storm passes, the brothers want to take us out into the swamp in their air boat to blow things up and shoot at beautiful animals with automatic weapons.

Pervis brags about his "critters." He walks around the room. I limp on my sore leg and Arnette hands me one of his hand-carved walking sticks. Pervis limps too and uses one of the sticks to help him hobble around. "This 'un here," Pervis points with his staff at a mounted fish with razor sharp teeth and soft white fur, "he's a fur bearing trout. I caught him while ice fishing in a lake in Canada. The water there is so cold that the fish grow thick fur to help keep 'em warm."

I watch in amazement and slight discomfort as Pervis tells the stories of his taxidermied chimeras, not sure if he believes what he is saying or if this is all just a performance. "And this little feller," Pervis picks up a leathery looking beast about the size of Idjit, "is a baby Chupacabra. That means goatsucker in Mexican talk. He was clearing out all of the livestock just west of here. They called me in to trap him." The creature looks like a shriveled dog with tiny forelegs, small ineffectual wings, sharp spines down the back, and enormous jaws. His underbelly was ripped in a zigzag and crudely stitched up with something that looks like a guitar string. "These things used to just be in Puerto Rico, but a mama Chupacabra musta stowed away on a ship and ended up in South Florida 'cuz these nasty little fuckers been showing up and slaughtering livestock all over the place. I was called in to catch this little guy. I pretty much vaporized one of his friends with a load of buckshot and then was lucky enough to lay this ole' boy out with a tranquilizer dart full a Special K. Shit," Pervis sighs, "even tranquilized, the little feller ripped right through two leather duffle bags."

"Why would somebody call you to catch these guys?" I ask, halfway taken in by Pervis's creatures. Maybe I'm high. Maybe the creatures look real. Maybe they are real. "I mean, why would you be the one to hunt down the chooba-choppa?"

"Chupacabra," Pervis and Arnette correct me simultaneously.

"Chupacabra," I correct myself. "Chupacabra. Anyway, are you some sort of hunter of bigfoots and mythological creatures?"

"Well," Pervis slips his thumbs under his suspenders and stretches them in front of his substantial belly, "as a matter a fact, I am, and the best one in this state prob'alee."

"Umm-Humm," Arnette grunts in agreement.

"No shit!" I laugh and light up another toke. "Those little choopa-choppas . . . "

"Chupacabras . . . "

"Chupacabras," I correct myself, "look like some mean little fuckers. I wouldn't want to mess with 'em."

Buddy has been drifting in and out of sleep. The current conversation catches his interest. "If you know so much about these crazy-ass creatures," Buddy says to Pervis, "why don't you tell me a little about that fucked up thing I saw out on the road?"

"What'd you see?" Pervis swings around to look at Buddy, his eyes lit up, large and beaming.

"I don't know," Buddy tries to explain. "It was tall and lanky like. It looked like a big, hairy monkey with an erection."

"Hot damn!" Arnette and Pervis share the words.

"That could be one of two things," Pervis explains. "Either it's that politician lady that used to be a prosecutor wanderin' around naked again ... I think her name is Remo or sum'thn ... or it's the fucking skunk ape. Chances are good that it's the skunk ape 'cuz we ain't seen Ms. Remo in some time."

"What the fuck is the skunk ape?" Spencer materializes from his crack in the wall.

"It's the meanest motherfucker south of the Mason-Dixon Line, that's all, says Pervis. "Ya ever hear of Bigfoot?"

"Yeah," we answer.

"He's a pussy!" shouts Arnette.

"Ya ever hear of the Yeti?" asks Pervis.

"Yep."

"A Goddamn pussy!" shouts Arnette.

"That's right," says Pervis, dropping his voice. "The Skunk Ape smells like a bag of ass soaked in cat piss. It has a perpetual hard-on and will use it on gators, stumps, buzzards, tourists, you name it. You see one coming and you best cover your bunghole and run as fast as you can. To the best of my knowledge there are sumwares between ten and twenty of those bad mothers in this area, and most of 'em are males with big forearm penises."

"Yeah, that's what I saw," Buddy agrees. "It looked like a forearm with a big fist on the end."

"Yep," answers Buddy, "the scarcity of females makes 'em fuckin' crazy 'n horny. And the fact that the males smell so damn bad, well it scares off the females that are around. They're crazy-ass bat-shit insane for any kind of female attention. Couple a-years back, some French-Canadian women were carried off by a group of horny males. We sent out a rescue team and found the ladies. They didn't want to come back, sent us away. Since then we ain't seen the Skunk Apes."

"Yeah," agrees Arnette, "and we ain't been allowed to hunt for them big hairy bitches, and I mean the Skunk Apes, not the Canadian ladies, any further because our government won't let us."

Arnette nods his head sadly. "Yep, I don't know what's goin' on. But we ain't even allowed to get out in the swamps anymore. You know the Everglades restoration program?"

"Uhhh . . ." Buddy answers, unwilling to say he doesn't know what Pervis is talking about.

"Yep," says Pervis, "the restoration program. Uncle Sam is spending two-hunert-fifty-billion dollars to close off big tracts of the Everglades. They's closing off big portions of a swampy, mucky mess. Why in tarnation would they do that? Huh?" Pervis's face stretches tight with consternation.

"It's them big smelly monkeys," chimes in Arnette.

"Bingo!" shouts Pervis. "The big smelly monkeys! And do you know why they smells so God-awful shitty? They sleeps in the airpockets under alligator dens. All that is down there is lizard shit and rot. What do you think? A big sweaty, hairy monkey living in those conditions. No wonder they stink." The big bong is passed to Pervis and he hits hard on it, coughing, choking, and clearing himself up with the asthma inhaler. "Goddamn monkey. I'm gonna get me one a them and hang his head over the door." It turns out that Pervis and Arnette have been hunting the Skunk Ape most of their lives. As children they would go in kayaks with their father, searching the saw grass for traces of the elusive beasts, occasionally finding large heaps of scat and knots in tree trunks that had been bored out. Arnette claims that he caught one on some grainy video from hundreds of yards away and shows us the film. To me it looks much like Oprah Winfrey in a bath-towel, lumbering through a campground in search of the bathhouse. To Arnette and Pervis it was, so far, the most exciting experience of their lives. "I'm gonna get me one a-those smelly monkeys," promises Pervis as we all settle in around the fire and carry on with talk of Skunk Apes.

14

Sleep evades me. I nod off, in and out of consciousness, but not in a full slumber. I want to see Idjit. Every time I find myself slipping toward dreamland, Pervis or Buddy will break into a death-rattle coughing spasm from the swamp weed and drag me back to consciousness. I hear snippets of their conversation. Pervis asks why we were traveling right into the face of a hurricane. Buddy explains about Idjit as best as he can. He says Idjit is like my girlfriend, except there's no sexual relationship or romantic love (as far as he can tell). In that space between awake and asleep I sit and listen. Pervis is impressed; he understands the sweet platonic love of a good hound. He's lost several of them to skunk apes, he says. I feel comfortably numb thanks to the big bong and several shots of leadschlager. Eventually my high blood alcohol content and general road weariness prevails.

Presleep visions of Idjit flash before me, warmth emanating hypnagogic hallucinations. Idjit invites me to sit down on a cushy red velvet loveseat. He sits in front of me at a small table lit by an accountant's lamp. The green glass lampshade throws a soothing emerald glow onto the table. Idjit holds the glass jar that I won in the poker game of my last dream. Putting on a pair of reading glasses and a green celluloid visor, Idjit sits and pulls out the wadded up papers out to read them.

"Shopping list. Things to do before you die. I notice that none of these are checked off. By the way, is intercourse with Marie Osmond a realistic goal?" Idjit continues to review the papers and look at me judgmentally over the edge of his glasses. "Hmm, order form for something called a pulsating pocket-pal ... a list of Spanish curse-words. Oh," the sad basset hound eyes light up, "a recipe for beer-infused bacon-stuffed deviled eggs. We need to try those."

"That's right, *Pendejo*," I tell him.

"Ah, here we go," the soulful hound looks at me over the top of his reading glasses, "one contract for the purchase of beer in exchange for your soul. You need to get this back."

"But that was a joke. I've got more important things to do than chase down a piece of worthless paper. I've got to get back to you."

"This was not a joke. Ramona is a succubus, a spiritual parasite."

"She didn't seem all that bad. A succubus? Like a demon you mean?"

"She is not malevolent," Idjit explains, "not like that. She's a pranic vampire—an energy leech. She's like a ... a soul-collector. She has the ability to entrap the spirits of others and she does so to fulfill some sort of emptiness, a void in her own soul. And that crazy bitch has your soul in a mason jar on her kitchen counter."

"What are you talking about?" I ask, confounded by my dog's outrageous claims.

"Ramona was a soul guide." Idjit explains that Ramona is supposed to help lost souls find their way to their final destination, whether it be heaven, hell, or Hazard County, Kentucky. Somewhere along the line she changed. Instead of helping lost spirits, Ramona began collecting the essence of the living and keeping them like betas in fish bowls for her own fulfillment. "You're her favorite. She keeps your soul on her kitchen counter like a prized gold fish and feeds it a pinch of collard greens, black-eyed peas and hoghead cheese[19] each morning. It is doing well under her care, but you need to retrieve it."

"This can't be," I argue. "That was just a joke. I do not believe that my soul is gone. What? Am I just a husk of flesh walking around with no spiritual essence? Has she robbed me of that?"

"She didn't rob you. You sold your soul to her in an arm's length contractual agreement. It has all of the legal requirements to make it legit." Idjit holds up the wrinkled paper and studies it under the green light. "Let's see: offer, consideration, acceptance. Yep, she got your soul fair and square. In fact, she probably overpaid."

"Can't be!"

"It's true. Have you noticed that your body is falling apart? More and more injuries that aren't healing?"

I scan my beaten and bruised person. "Yeah, I guess it does

---

[19] Traditionally made by simmering the cleaned head of a hog (with the organs removed) to produce a gelatin from the bone marrow, and mixed with any incidental meat which comes off of the head, such as snout, lips and ears. Should be served cold or at room temperature, perhaps spread on a cracker.

kind of seem as if I am disintegrating. Why?" I grab an eyetooth between my pointer-finger and thumb and wiggle it back and forth, feeling it loosen even further.

"You cannot heal yourself. Your spirit is a well of healing power. Although it was a weak flicker when you actually did own it, at least you could draw upon that power to cure yourself. Now it's like your body is running on a battery that cannot recharge itself. Eventually, and maybe even soon, it's just going to go *ka-put*. Your energy source will be gone for good. You're running on fumes right now. What it boils down to is that you are dying on the inside, but your physical being doesn't realize it yet. It just keeps going and sustaining more damage until you fall apart, literally. Just get up to see Ramona and get that soul back. Then you can come to get me. By the way, I think I love you." Idjit pulls the chain on his green lamp and all goes dark.

My eyelids slowly raise, like a garage door opening to the early morning. I'm seeing double. No, triple. Three bearded redneck, camouflage jumpsuit-clad lunatics are inches from my face. I smell their armadillo-barbeque-morning-breath. I vomit just a little bit into my mouth and swallow back the sour bile. Buddy is virtually indistinguishable from Arnette and Pervis.

"Hey dude," Buddy greets me. "It's passed us by. Angus has blown through and we're still here. Get up, you've got to get moving. You know, dogs to catch, people to do and things to see. Miles to go before you sleep, yadda yadda yadda." Buddy's beard has grown out to what would be two month's worth of facial hair for most men. "Get up. I've got some shit to show you."

"Yeah, come on," says Pervis, or maybe Arnette. I can't tell. "You need to get moving. Buddy here has told us about your hound dog. You need to get back to that old fleabag." The brothers each grab an arm and haul me up. "Here you go," one of them says as he pushes a pistol into my hand. "This is a Luger 9-millimeter. Our granddaddy pried it from the hands of a kraut he killed during World War Two. He passed this down to our daddy and he passed it to us. Ain't nothing that handles better than one a-these bad boys. You're gonna need this as you pass through hoards of looters and other desperate folks on your way up."

"What are you talking about?" I look at the gun. It's so cool. I had a Luger cap gun as a kid. Not one of those plastic pieces of shit they make now with the orange tips on the end of the barrel. My cap gun was a heavy, metal, full sized replica of the real thing. It was solid and weighty. And so is the Luger these old boys have given me. "Why are you giving me a firearm?"

"You need to get moving," Buddy says. "I don't know why, but you need to get to your dog now. We all agree. And Pervis and Arnette here ... well, they're gonna give you everything you need. You've got the gun. Take this." Buddy helps me strap on a heavy backpack. "It's filled with provisions. And you're gonna be able to travel better than anybody else, come on." He tugs at my arm, dragging me outside. I tuck the Luger into the waistband of my pants.

Palm trees, gnarly messes of something Arnette calls melaleucas, and uprooted palmettos litter the front yard. A small circle has been cleared and in the middle of it sits a Honda 350SX. The thing is a fucking brute. A three-wheeled monster with nubbed balloon tires, several feet of ground clearance, and suspension that looks like it would soak up all forms of rough terrain.

"Weren't those things outlawed because they are so dangerous?" I ask, itching to try it out anyway.

"Yep," mumbles Pervis.

"And weren't people tipping them over, rolling them, wrecking them and dying in every way possible?"

"Um-humm," says Arnette.

"And is that the baddest looking motor-scooter you've ever seen, or what?"

"Fucking-A right it is!" Buddy pats me on the back and flashes an ear-to-ear grin. "And they're gonna let you take it. I'm gonna stay here a while and help them hunt skunk apes. Pervis's gonna teach me taxidermy. I got nothing to go back to at home and, well, I wanna shoot a big smelly monkey and stuff him, that's all."

"What about those college boys? How are they getting out of here?"

"That goofy one finally woke up. He's hung over and trying to rest it off out back. And I don't know about Spencer. He just kind of seems to have disappeared. We're gonna go out looking for him after you leave. But you gotta get going. Let us worry about him."

"Yeah," agrees Arnette, "kick-start that bad boy and head north. Just get it back to us at some point when you're done."

"Why are you helping me?" I ask. "I'm wanted by the law. You hardly know me. Why?"

"You seem like good people," says Pervis. Arnette nods in agreement. "And that exploding sombrero tower was the bull's nuts, man. You'll repay us, or someone else or some sort of good karma shit. You know, circle of life or whatever."

"Do you have a helmet for me?"

"Hell no," Arnette laughs. "Florida repealed the helmet law. You're riding bare back, brother. Now get out of here before we beat you senseless."

Pervis gives me a thumbnail of how to operate the all-terrain cycle. "Thumb operated throttle, six speed, manual clutch, shift with the feet. Lean into turns. No sharp turns at high speed. If you get throwed off, try to roll with it and don't let your head hit, you're not wearing a helmet ya damn fool. Now kick her in the ribs and ride that bitch out of here."

I kick the starter one, two, three times. It sputters on the third and catches. The three-wheeler roars. I shift into first gear and punch the thumb throttle. The front tire lifts off of the ground, dirt and gravel shoot from beneath the rear tires, and I hold on for dear life. I kick it into second gear and head out to the main road. All that remains of the Bratmobile is the motor home chassis that it sat on. Hurricane Angus picked up the broken wiener body and threw it somewhere in the swamp. I steer the ATC west on the Tamiami trail. I am on the road again.

**15**

Route 41 is littered with trees, torn-up billboards, portions of roofs that were ripped from houses, playground equipment and a general South Florida sampling of debris. Thank God for the ATC. I never could have traveled by car, and walking would have taken too long. The three-wheeler easily climbs over all road obstructions and handles great even in the swampy ditches. Instead of driving until I see the Gulf of Mexico and then turning right, I decide to head north at the first major crossroad I hit.

A convenience store sits at the southeast corner of the intersection of Route 29 and the Tamiami Trail. I should say that a convenience store used to sit at the corner. Now there is a building with no roof, one crumbled wall, and a large royal palm tree leaning out of the top of the structure. A flock of broken-up pink plastic flamingos is sprinkled about the parking lot, intermingled with random Budweiser cans from a scattered beer display. It looks like a bomb went off in the middle of a Jimmy Buffett concert. Gas pumps are on their sides; several are just ripped out of the ground and thrown somewhere else—perhaps dropped in the Everglades with the body of the Bratmobile.

I stop the ATC and take in the damage caused by the storm. *BLAM!* A shotgun blast booms from inside the store. "Go away!" somebody shouts. "No looting. Looters will be shot!" I kickstart the ATC and turn north on 29, waving at the store behind me as I leave. I feel the Luger sitting heavy in my waistband. I've never fired a gun before, but maybe it's good that I have it.

Just like the trail, Route 29 is cluttered with trees and debris. Once again I am thankful for the all-terrain cycle. The road is lined on both sides with ten-foot high chain link fence. I wonder if that is meant to keep man on the road or the animals off. The fences are not intact. In many areas they are toppled by palms and tall cypress trees. The highway goes on for miles with no crossroads, no buildings, no people. Occasionally I see an over-grown, unpaved access road off to one side or the other. Otherwise, Route 29 is a long, lonely, uninterrupted line of pavement through a big swamp.

Even with the three-wheeler, progress on the road is not fast. The obstacles, hurdles, and hindrances challenge the cycle, challenge me. At noon I stop the trike and snack on a rubbery piece of gator jerky that Arnette and Pervis packed for me. Overhead I see an enormous white-headed bird circling. His brownish-black body and wings making no effort. He glides on an air current above me. The wingspan is as impressive as I've ever seen on a bird. I'm no expert but I would guess that the majestic animal is a bald eagle. *This must be a good sign*, I think to myself. I finish up my salty gator meat and ride the ATC down a nice clear patch of road that is relatively free of hurricane damage.

Ahead I see large birds flocking at the side of the road. These birds too are enormous, but look more like wild turkeys. As I near them I realize that they are buzzards[20]. The reason for the congregating venue becomes clear to me. A bloated ten-foot alligator carcass has been torn into by the strange birds. I stop and shut down the ATC within fifteen feet of the feeding frenzy to watch. The birds all take flight at first due to my presence. Eventually, one returns and stares at me, sizing me up. I stare back, taking in the odd bird. He stands erect and spreads his wings to his full five-foot span. His wrinkled, featherless, red head is disproportionately small in comparison to his thick body. The gray lining of his inner wings contrasts with the dark brown feathers on the rest of his body. High above in the air, the circling kettle of his friends coasts drunkenly on the air currents. I think to myself that they are like many of the women I have ogled in my life: from afar they are beautiful and wonderful to look at; up close they can be hideous and smell like a regurgitated, partially-digested meal. The vulture decides that I am not a threat and returns to his lunch.

Taking their cue from the lone diner on the road, the rest of the birds swoop down on the road-kill alligator and resume their carrion feast. Horrified fascination grips me as the birds use their short horn-shaped bills to quickly rend the greenish

---

[20] After stepping on a carcass, turkey vultures frequently defecate on their own legs. The feces is white and fluid. The high uric acid content of the feces acts as a sanitizer, killing any of the bacteria the bird may have picked up from the dead animal.

flesh. The efficiency of their operation is impressive. More birds land and join in on the effort to strip the meat from the gator's frame. They tear at the dead lizard; they attack each other. I laugh to myself as one bird gets distracted by a smaller one and chases the runt away from the carcass. The little guy, half the size of any other birds in the melee, is so fucking ugly that he's cute. The immature bird's head is grey and his beak is black, instead of the ivory color of the beaks on the larger birds. He stands before me, cocks his head, and lets out a grunt.

I feel sorry for the ugly little fucker. The rest of his friends are dismantling the remains of the alligator in a workmanlike fashion while he's been banished. I pull more gator jerky from my backpack and throw it a couple of feet to the side of my vehicle. The lonely vulture creeps up, snatches the jerky and then skitters a safe distance away from me. When he is finished I throw out another piece. "There you go, little guy." I feel like Grizzly Adams communing with nature. I miss Idjit and crave some sort of affection from an animal. *Oh well*, I think to myself. *If you can't be with the one you love, love the one you're with.* "Come here, little guy," I urge, feeling a special bond with the bird. He creeps up slowly. I can feel his trust in me forming. "That's it, fella," I encourage him, holding out more jerky, thinking he might feed directly from my hand, "Come and get it." He inches closer, just out of reach, and lets out a little hiss. "Come to Daddy," I invite him closer. The little guy once again cocks his head and, just when I think he couldn't be any cuter, he lets loose with a stream of projectile vomit right in my face. Never in my life have I smelled anything so putrid and vile. It's like a zombie shat his insides out, right on my head. Rotted-flesh-vulture-vomit coats my front and burns my eyes like pepper spray. My stomach empties itself. I puke and puke more, until nothing is left, and then still continue with harsh dry-retching.

In the throes of my pukefest, my will leaves me. It just steals away into the swamp when I'm not looking and dissipates into the muggy air. I lay prostrate in the middle of the road, completely and totally overcome with exhaustion, lacking the spirit to move. Not sleeping, not awake, not caring, I stay face down in the road, wrapped in a wispy blanket of delirium. Images flash by in random fashion, lacking meaning and coherence. I am unable to hold a string of thoughts, one idea fades into the next and the last is lost. A vision of a large, tan panther appears before me. Without looking I sense it looming over me. It swipes at my head playfully, as if it were a large ball of yarn. The claws tear at my scalp. The cat growls and runs off. I smell something awful—different from the vulture puke but equally offensive, like a skunk gone rotten. I feel myself being lifted and carried. I don't care. I give up.

My back burns, my ribs ache, my ankle is swollen, my hair is sticky with blood and, for some reason, my asshole is sore. All of the drugs and alcohol have worn off and my body has regained its ability to feel pain. Aches, itches and injuries, contusions and lacerations, burns and broken bones; all of these check in with my brain through reopened neural pathways. Along with the renewed abilities of my pain receptors, my will has also returned after abandoning me and flitting about through the cypress swamps.

The return of my will to go on prompts me to open my eyes. Staring down at me are two wild-eyed, dirty, topless women. Usually I would view this as a good thing. Upon seeing my eyes open, one nudges the other and begins grunting. "Unghhh, *voulez-vous* grrrr *escargot.*"

The other answers in a series of clicks, grunts, and something reminiscent of the French I took for a semester in high school: "Glunggg... *C'est la vie* ... Ft-ft-ft ... *Oui Oui.*" The women are almost more simian than human in their mannerisms, but they are clearly Homo sapiens. They back away rapidly; one scratches the top of her head like a confused chimp and purses her lips.

I sit up and both of the feral women jump back further. I am on the ground in a clearing somewhere off of Route 29. It is later in the day, the same day (I think). The two women stand back, staring intensely at me. They are both naked, dirty and unruly looking. If I said *Boo!* they would probably run into the woods. I hold up my hands, palms out, to show them I mean no harm. These must be the French-Canadian broads that Arnette and Pervis were talking about.

I realize I am shirtless and the vulture vomit has been cleaned off of me. "Thank you. *Merci.*" I say to them. Although the puke is gone the smell sticks. I notice another odor, the same as I smelled in my stupor just before being picked off of the road. The rotted skunk smell. Around the campsite are impressive piles of greenish-brown scat. Black and white tufts of hair are strewn about the area and caught on branches. The ladies are tall and sturdy, but I think to myself that there is no way they generated these mounds of fecus. The piles look like something a cow would have dropped. Maybe a skunk ape?

Despite being wracked with pain, despite a nagging feeling that my batteries are somehow running low, despite the fact that there are two nude, nubile, feral females who are not running away from me, I feel the pull of the Galoot. I must get back to my dog. My drive has returned and I must return to my drive. "*Merci*," I tell the ladies. "*Merci beaucoup*." I wave to them as I back away; they waive back tentatively, with something like sadness in their eyes. I think to myself that I should come back someday and repay them for their kindness. But for now I must go.

Back on the road the alligator has been stripped clean by the turkey vultures. The only evidence of his existence is a perfectly intact skeleton on the berm, like something that should be in a museum. One lonely bird has remained, the runt of the group. He sits on my ATC, as if waiting just for me, maybe to apologize for his bad manners. "Peep," he squawks soft and sorrowful. The rest of his flock have abandoned him and are nowhere to be seen.

"Hey there, little guy," I answer. "It's alright. I forgive you. You were wound up from getting picked on. You struck out at me because I was there. Hey, I understand frustration." He tilts his head, listening, looking at me. Just like before, it seems like he might even trust me. Maybe I could go up and pet him. "Maybe I can come over there, without getting puked on?" I ask as I inch up toward him, fifteen feet, fourteen, slowly, thirteen, twelve.

"Peep," he says. I think he really likes me.

"Not this time buddy." I reach behind me and retrieve the Luger from my waistband. I bring it around and aim it at him. I've never fired a real gun, just bb guns at summer camp. But, I know how to aim. I train the sight on the buzzard and start pulling the trigger. *BLAM! BLAM! BLAM! BLAM!* Four shots, one after the other, shells ejecting from the side of the firearm, smoke from the barrel, deafening reports. Feathers and gore spray from the bird as he is thrown off of the handlebars. I see his fat body absorb the impact of the first shot as he is thrown off of the trike and then the later shots all slam him as he is flung backwards.

My ears ring and throb from the gunshots. It feels like front row seats at the Kiss concert. I limp over to the remains of the buzzard and look down at him. My heart is heavy. We could have been friends. I shared gator jerky with him. But the little fuck puked up some of the most vile shit I've ever smelled, right in my face. And I know deep down that he would have done it again. I kick his body off of the pavement and throw gravel over him, raking it from the side of the road with my bare hands. I cover him as well as I can with my bloodied hands in the hopes that his family and friends do not dine on him.

The ATC is covered with bird shit. Chalky droppings, runny, with gray speckles. Arnette and Pervis packed two t-shirts in the backpack for me, a 38-Special concert jersey and a World's Best Dad shirt. I put on the World's Best Dad shirt and wipe down the trike with the other. As night approaches I strap on the backpack, kickstart my ride, and head north again on Route 29.

**16**

The road becomes clearer as I continue northward, away from the hurricane's damage. Route 29 is desolate, as if everybody in this part of Florida collectively decided to pack up and move out. When I reach it, Interstate 75 will take me all of the way back up to Idjit. In the dark of the night I push the ATC further. I know it's not street legal and figure it's probably best that I'm driving it when nobody is out. I push north through towns with names like *Imokalee, Okeepokee,* and *Felda.* Only the lit streetlights give a clue that the towns are still inhabited. If I can find Gibsonton up along the coast I can stop at Uncle Doug's place to rest, wash up, and get some grub before leaving Florida.

I remember Gibsonton from my youth. One summer, when I was twelve or so, Mom sent me and Frank to stay with Uncle Doug. I guess you could call it white trash summer camp. We rode down on a greyhound without adult supervision. Me and Frank sat in the back of the bus, chain-smoking Winstons and sharing a bottle of crËme de menthe that we snagged from Mom's liquor cabinet. In those days you could smoke anywhere; heck, it was almost expected that you would light up on a cross-country bus. A chain-smoking twelve year old on the coach didn't even garner a second glance. The Greyhound seemed like it stopped to pick up more people every couple of hours and took forever to get us to Florida. For every one that got off, two more boarded, and they were mostly deviants, losers and transients. One passenger, an older man with a mess of greasy black hair, a crooked neck and squinty eyes, tried to come on to me. He told me that one in four hundred men could suck his own dick[21] and that the other three-hundred-and-ninety nine had all tried to, and, his theory went that if I was willing to put a dick in my mouth (albeit my own), I should be willing to do the same with his. "One is just the same as any other," he reasoned. Frank retorted with a punch in the throat and then continued his rebuttal by kicking the shit out of him in the back of the bus. I was impressed that my fifteen-year-old brother could deal out such a beating to a full-grown man. By the time we arrived at the bus station in Tampa my throat was raw from chain-smoking and my mouth tasted like ashes and diesel fumes. We both smelled like a forest fire. Doug picked us up at the station. "You boys smell like you been smoking," he said. "You might be able to fool your momma, but not me. Now hand over them cigarettes before I kick your asses." We did. Uncle Doug lit up one of the Winstons, put the pack in his t-shirt pocket, and told us he better not catch us smoking again.

The rest of the summer consisted of Frank, me and Cousin Denny running around and discovering the town. Gibsonton is the town for carnies, circus freaks, sideshow performers, and

---

[21] A disproportionately high percentage of this small minority is rumored to hail from Nantucket, Massachusetts.

the like. They all winter there when they're not on the road. The old ones retire to Gibsonton and are buried in the carnie grave-yard when they kick the bucket. All of Denny's friends had names like *Johnny the Elephant Headed Boy*, *Frankie the Pincush-ion*, or *Hairy Sherry the Monkey Girl*. Denny lost his virginity to Hairy Sherry. He said she had a big bush. Getting into the spirit, Frank and me gave Denny a sideshow name: Big Gay Wayne, the Burning Flame. It was immature, nonsensical, and maybe not all that funny of a name, but it infuriated Denny, and that made it fun. Denny would become enraged at the mention of his new name and I did receive several beatings from him as a result. Mostly, though, Frank was there to stop him.

Denny's step-mom, Bernice, was a nice lady who drank too much. Denny always seemed to have a new mom. I don't know if Uncle Doug actually married all of the different Moms but he seemed to change them out on an annual basis. When Bernice wasn't laid up in bed with a hangover, she would make us big greasy meals that would usually have a slab of something fried in butter that she called Scrapple. I once asked her what Scrapple was and she told me it was pork offal. I don't know about the pork, but it sure was awful. Otherwise she would give us money and send us to the Giant's Place Restaurant for lunch. The Giant's Place was fun, so when Bernice was hitting the bottle, we en-couraged her to hit it extra hard so as to induce a nasty next-day hangover, and, consequently, lunch for us at the Giant's Place.

The Giant's Place was a little restaurant right close to the Vagabond Village trailer park we lived in. It was run by a giant we called *Big Al*. Al stood 8-foot-four and often wore a cowboy hat, which made him seem even taller. He was the nicest man you'd ever seen. Al was the fire chief of the city at one point, probably because he could get cats out of the trees without much effort. Most of the time, though, he ran the restaurant along with his wife, Jeanie the Half-girl. The Giant's Place was a fun place to eat. You could always count on Three-Legged-Johnny being there, recounting tall tales of life on the road. On *All You Can Eat* nights it was fun to sit and watch Fat Cindy eat until somebody would tell her "that's all you can eat," and kick her out. The biscuits were warm and sublime and almost as big as your head. The crowd was a mixture of show folk and weary travelers. Waitresses would take your order for a well-done hamburger with fries and then shout at the cook something like *Alright angel, gimme a hockey puck, paint it red and drag it through the garden, and put some frog sticks in the alley.* Waitress talk is fun and we tried to become fluent in it that summer.

I continue north, take a left turn at a major road, head north again, take another left, and so on until I pass under I-75 and hit Route 41 again at a little town called Ruskin. Gibsonton is close, just up the road.

The sun peeks up over the horizon and winks at me as I pull off of the road in front of The Giant's Place. It looks just like I remember it. I am greeted at the door by the aroma of biscuits baking and a gum-snapping waitress named Brandy who calls me Darlin' and tells me to seat myself if I'm "hankerin' for some chow."

"Oh yeah," Brandy says, without missing a beat, "and don't bleed all over everything." Bloodied up folk are common

around here what with the high wires, knife throwers, elephants, stuntmen and whatnot. My condition doesn't shock her.

I sit down at the counter and tell the waitress "two please,
wreck 'em, sweep up the kitchen, draw one in the dark, and
give it shoes." The breakfast crowd collectively turns its head
toward me and gawks as I wait. I know that I probably look like
road rash draped over a skeleton. I'm sure I still smell like vulture puke. But none of that explains the staring. It takes a lot in
a community like this to draw the eyes that I'm getting. The
bearded lady is looking my way and whispering to the Mexican
dwarf beside her. A pinhead bobs his head up and down and
points at me. Even the Siamese twin busboys eyeball me like
some sort of hideous sideshow attraction.

A mule-faced waitress brings out a bag of food for me and leans
in close. Her waitress dress is unbuttoned several buttons down
from the neck, revealing impressive cleavage. She has what I like
to call *butter face*: her body is smoking, but'er face looks like a
constipated donkey. "Listen up," she tells me in a hushed voice. "I
know who you are. And so does everybody else around here. You
been all over the tee-vee. The police have been asking around
about you. We don't like the pigs nosing around our community,
especially after how they treated us with the investigation of the
Lobster Boy killing. Take your food..." she hands me my scrambled eggs with hash and coffee "...I ain't gonna charge you. Just
get out of here while the getting's good. We don't need no more
trouble around here." She was right, carnies and circus folk don't
like any kind of involvement with the police. Many of these
people probably have some sort of past that they want to leave
behind. The Fuzz coming around, asking questions, strong arming

people, picking open old scabs, well, it just wasn't good. I take the food and glance down once more at ugly-girl's beautiful breasts. It's like two perfect, ripe mangos hanging on a gnarled, blighted tree. What a waste. What a bra-full of trouble, enough to lead a man to do things he would later regret. I leave the Giant's Place, hop on the ATC, and retrace a map of memories.

Perpendicular to Route 41 is a road. On the road there is a trailer park. In the trailer park there is a doublewide. Behind the door is a man with bad teeth, whiskey breath, and a crumpled pack of Winstons in the pocket of his sweat-stained t-shirt. Inside, the man is angry at me for bringing him under the microscope of a law enforcement investigation. My hand reaches for the doorknob. The door flies open. A hand locks onto the loose skin of my neck and yanks. First my face flies forward. Second, my feet stay stuck to the ground, as if gravity is heavy today and doesn't want to release them. Third, my feet detach from the wooden steps and trail behind me in the air as I am pulled into the mobile home. Fourth, forceful open-handed slaps land about my head and shoulders.

"What the fuck you doin' around here, ya good-fer-nuttin'?" Uncle Doug slaps me a couple more times, a big smile on his face. "Man, you look like shit."

"Here, let me give him some too." And before I know it, Denny jumps out from the kitchen area and punches me in the nose.

"Ah, Jesus Christ! Enough!" I shout as Uncle Doug pulls his son back before he can flatten my nose any more. "What the fuck?"

"I'll tell you what the fuck," says Cousin Denny. "You fucking sold me out to that Pickles fucker. You told him I killed your

Daddy and butt-fucked his corpse. You know what those people do to corpse fuckers?" Denny shivers involuntarily. "Fuck, man!"

As Denny spews expletives I see him deflating, calming; the rage recedes. Uncle Doug blocks him until it's safe for me. The blow to my nose has popped an artery or something and loosed a flow of thick brown blood, which mostly oozes down my face and onto my World's Best Dad shirt. It seems like it should flow more, be thinner in consistency, less like used motor oil.

"Hey, I got out of there and called Mom," I tell Denny. A bloody bubble forms around the rim of my nostril and pops out into a spray as I explain myself. "She obviously called Uncle Doug and did something to help you out."

"Yeah. She got a hold of Dad and he called that lawyer you were talking about."

"Rhoton?"

"Yeah." Cousin Denny smiles. "He's good. Real good. But, uh . . . " Denny looks down at his feet. "I am gonna have to testify against you at trial. I told Pickles that you were into necrophilia and that you left a trail of dead molested bodies all along I-75. I hope you understand."

"Yeah, it's alright. I did the same thing to you. But I told him you had a refrigerator full of severed heads that you like to pleasure yourself with."

"Boy howdy, you two are sick. Listen up, my dear nephew. I'll do what I can to help you, but you're gonna have to beat it. It's too hot around here. The cops know that Denny came back here, and they have been keeping an eye out for you. The people around here aren't very happy with me and Denny. Your being here ain't helping. I'm gonna help you get out of here. You know, I'll do what I can, but you gotta go."

"Why do the cops have such a hard-on for me?" I ask.

"Well, I've been recording the news shows on you. Maybe you should watch this." Uncle Doug powers up the television and flips through the various menus as the digital video recorder makes sounds like electric bubbles popping. "Here we go. Check this out." He selects a program and then begins fast forwarding. "Ah, here we are. This is from this morning . . . "


" . . . Top o' the morning to you," says the news anchor. "Suchi Punani, filling in for Rusty Trombone. Coming up next: our top stories." Suchi's smile is unwavering as she reports on a grisly scene in Chicago involving ritual torture and dismemberment of residents in a retirement home. The smile stays set on *10* as Ms. Punani gives a lead-in to a story about the unprecedented strength of Hurricane Angus and the massive amounts of damage inflicted on South Florida. And then the smile disappears. "And now more disturbing news on the Sombrero Tower terrorists. Unconfirmed reports have filtered in that the terrorists have hijacked an American icon. It has been reported that the group has car-jacked the Albert Morgan Bratmobile in Sweetwater, Florida, and taken hostage the crew of the vehicle. It seems there is nothing these men will not do. We are working on confirming the reports. In the meantime, the FBI and the Florida Department of Law Enforcement have initiated a full scale man hunt for this man." My high school senior photo flashes onto the screen and Suchi Punnani mispronounces my name. Both Uncle Doug and Denny laugh at the indignity. "If you see this man, do not approach him. He is extremely dangerous. Head for a safe place and call 911. Please allow the professionals to bring this man in. In other news..." Suchi's smile returns as she segues into a story about a penis pump being found in the garbage of United States Ambassador to Italy, Melvin Sembler, and an attempt by the finder to auction the pump on Ebay.com.[22]

Uncle Doug shuts off the TV and laughs again. "Nice hair, douche-bag. Anyway, that should kind of give you an idea of what's going on and why you need to get out of here. I'm gonna see what I can do to arrange for some sort of transportation for you. You can't take that three-wheeler on the road. It ain't street legal and you're just asking to be pulled over. Let me see what I can do."

*B-r-r-ringg*. The phone rings. An honest-to-goodness ringing bell. Not a cell phone with some goofy ring-tone or the latest hip-hop song. Uncle Doug picks up the handset. It's actually attached to the base by a coiled phone cord. "Yeah... You don't say... You don't say... You don't say... Alright, thanks." Uncle Doug lets the handset hang in front of him by its cord. The handset spins and the kinks in the phone cord undo themselves. He sets the phone back down and looks at us.

"What did they want, Daddy?"

---

[22] STRANGE BUT TRUE. See http://thestraights.com for in-depth coverage of the incident. Richard Bradbury, upstanding young man and discoverer of the penis pump attempted to sell it on Ebay.com for $300,000.00.

"They didn't say." Uncle Doug pulls a half-smoked cigarette out of the ashtray and lights it up. "You guys sit tight and don't open the door for anyone. I'll be back soon. And then it's time for you to hit the road, my nephew."

Uncle Doug heads out the door. I sit down in his ragged recliner and start in on my eggs and hash. Cousin Denny rewinds the news report and pauses on my picture. He laughs at my haircut and calls me a douche. I'm with family for the moment. I relax. Before I even finish my eggs, my eyelids droop and I drift off into a deep sleep.

I dream that I'm with Daddy on the back porch of the Giant's Place. This is where the real showmen used to hang out and hold all night bullshit sessions. Idjit is curled up at his feet. "Shhh," Daddy hushes me as I open my mouth to speak, "the dog is sleeping. He really needs his rest."

"What's wrong with him?" I ask.

"He's old, he has halitosis, and he likes to hump people's legs. That's what's wrong with him," interjects a bearded lady on the porch.

"Hush, Fur-face," Daddy tells the hirsute hag and smacks her in the chest with his cane. She holds a hand to her (probably furry) teat and quiets down. "Now listen Boy, Idjit's been telling you what to do. He wanted me to remind you because sometimes your brain is like a sieve. You're smart but still a bit tetched. You remember what he told you to do?"

"Yeah, yeah. Get back to Tennessee and get my soul back

from Ramona. What a crock. I need to get back to the Galoot. He needs me."

"You'll do what we tell you. You better get back to Tennessee, Jed. Hear?" Daddy raises his cane at me, ready to strike.

"Yes sir." I look at Idjit and pat him on the head. He doesn't stir, he barely inhales and his breath hitches slightly when he does. He looks peaceful though, in the way that Daddy does sometimes. "What's wrong with my dog, Daddy? He looks like he's in a coma."

"Well he kind of is, boy. You're slowly sucking up his ch'i like a dome light can drain a car battery."

"His chee?" I ask. "What do you mean?"

"His ch'i boy! His soul energy, life force, aura. You're bleeding him dry."

"I don't get it. How can I be draining him?"

"You don't have a soul. You squandered it. Traded it away for beer and pussy like it was some kind of joke. You should've passed on to the other side shortly after you did that darn fool swap. But your dog, your best friend, has been giving you his ch'i, his energy, so that you can make things right. And you've just been a parasitoid, living in the belly of his soul like a tape worm, slowly killing his spirit. Now get cracking and do as I have told you. Get your own spirit back so that you don't kill this sweet hound."

"I will Daddy. I will. How long do I have?"

"Just go. Go now." He raises his cane at me again. "And you tell your Mama that I approve."

"Approve of what?"

"She'll know."

**17**

"Wake up, Sweety." I feel a hand applying light circular pressure on my crotch. Shaky fingers try to unbutton my jeans.

"Come on, Baby," the smoky voice urges as the button on my pants pops and the zipper opens willingly. There is a warm fleshy weight on my body and in my half-dazed waking condition my hips push forward, feeling a soft, receptive something through the fabric of my dirty underwear. Fumes of Scrapple and Canadian Club envelop me. I am roused and aroused.

"God!" It's Bernice. Her face is spackled with cheap makeup—rouge and aquamarine eye shadow. The fire engine red lipstick is worn away at the edges of her lips, revealing cracks and a crusted, healing cold sore. Her bare floppy titties swing pendulously, inches from my face, threatening contact between my forehead and her finger-like brown nipples. I hate my boner for what it is suggesting to me. Evil treacherous wiener. "Uggh. Get off!"

"Hey there, Guy." Bernice climbs off of me, not sad, not surprised at the rejection. "How'r'ya doin'? I haven't seen you since you were just getting ready to sprout your short 'n curlies. You're lookin' good." Bernice sits on the floor beside my chair. She roots in the ashtray on a coffee table that used to be a telephone cable spool. "Damn, yer lookin' good." Her tongue pokes at the chancre on the side of her mouth as she rubs her temples. She finds a promising butt in the ashtray and lights it up.

"Bernice, you and Uncle Doug are still together?" I try to button up my pants and tuck my erection away before she takes it as an invitation to jump on me again.

"Aw, hell no, Honey. We split up three dogs ago. Speaking of which, that man has all of the characteristics of a dog, except for loyalty. But I still live just two units down. Shit, most of this row is made up of your uncle's exes. Ain't none of us got a place to go after he's done with us. You know, a turd can only sink to the bottom of the outhouse." Her tongue flickers at the edge of the sore again, loosening some of the crust. "I seen you on the news. I seen Dougie runnin' outta here. I figured somethin' was up. I knew you must be around. I said to myself, 'girl, you ain't fucked a celebrity since Molly Hatchet last came through town.' I reckon I'll have to wait until the next state fair comes through before I get some more famous dick."

"Well, uh, Aunt Bernice, it's good to see you." I don't know what to say. I talk to stall her. She buttons up her Waffle Castle waitress shirt. The throbbing in my naughty bits recedes.

"You don't want my loving," she laughs, "then how about my cooking? I brought over some Scrapple cooked up in my famous mushroom gravy, just like old times."

"Well, I certainly can't pass on mashed up hog entrails cooked up on the griddle. Sure. Why not?"

Bernice hands me a plate of Scrapple and scrambled eggs, all swimming in gravy. As I eat, she fills me in on her life since the last time I saw her. A self-described star-fucker.[23] According to Bernice, she's been with somebody from every b-list rock band from 1980 on. "I'm kind of like the Plaster Casters in the 60's, but older and bolder," she explains. She likes to take trophies from each one of her conquests. "Shit in a ziplock. That's what I have 'em do. Most of those guys do a lot of smack and are so bound up. Some of 'em ain't shit in months. If I can urge a little bit of poo out of 'em, well, I'm doing them a service and they give me a little token of their appreciation in return. Hell, anybody can catch the clap from Lover Boy's bassist or crabs from a Flock of Seagulls (and so what if I did)," she gives me a sly wink, "but how many people do you know that have a love-nugget from Huey Lewis? I even have a perfectly round poo ball from Meatloaf. No kiddin', big as a baby's head and a perfect sphere. I call it my meatball."

"Ohh, God! Come on. I'm trying to eat Scrapple here. You're making my pork offal taste awful. Why couldn't you just get drumsticks or guitar picks? Hell, I'd want to see that."

"Oh listen to you, baby-boy. Don't go judging. It's just another way to collect celebrity memorabilia. I'll tell you what, if eBay would quit shutting my auctions down I could make a fortune." Bernice clears her throat; the bubbling phlegm does little to add to my dining experience. "Hey, name your favorite band. I bet I've got a trophy. I'll let you hold it."

"Oh come on now. You can't be serious."

---

[23] NASCAR groupies are frequently referred to as *pit lizards*. Professional wrestling groupies are known as *ring rats*.

"Name it . . . "

"Alright, do you have any Iron Maiden dooty?"

"Come on over to my unit. You're gonna view my Bruce Dickinson poo." She laughs a gurgling, mucous coated, laugh. "He even autographed the ziplock. A real class act, that man."

Stranded, eating Scrapple, waiting for a ride from who knows who. A chance to get close to my idol. What do I have to lose? "What the fuck. I don't believe you, but I want to see if you really keep poop in ziplocks."

Bernice gives me a swig of Canadian whiskey off of her pocket flask. She always liked to carry what she called an ass-pocket of whiskey. We check out the front door, the coast is clear. I put on one of Uncle Doug's baseball caps and a pair of Denny's aviator sunglasses and follow Bernice to her unit. The trailer is humid and warm, a swarm of little black bugs hovers above the kitchen sink. Air fresheners are plugged in all over the unit, mostly pumping out some sort of fruity smell. The air deodorizer barely masks something bad just underneath.

Bernice waives me over to a stand alone chest freezer that could easily hold a side of beef. "I keep all of my trophies in here." She pops the lid and a greenish haze mushrooms out. I hear soft chiming mystical Buddhist music or something.

"What the fuck?" I step back.

"Yeah, I just added the fog, music and lights for effect. Pretty cool huh?" She laughs her gurgle-chuckle.

"Okay, whatever. Let's see what you got from Bruce Dickinson." I lean over the freezer and see that it is packed three-fourths of the way full with plastic freezer bags of varying sizes: from little half-sandwich bags all the way up to the gallon freezer deals. And each one seems to contain a turd of an appropriate size for the respective bag.

"Calm down, Honey. Let me show you some of my favorites." Bernice digs around in the freezer and extracts a gallon bag with a round frozen turd the size of a grapefruit. "That's the meatball." She holds it out to me, expecting me to grab it. "Oh, go ahead and look at it. Don't be a pussy. It's frozen and in a bag. Ya ain't gonna get none on you. Hell, you can barely smell 'em when they's all freezed up." She holds the bag right up to her schnozz and inhales deeply. "Nothing."

I take the bag. I study it. Bernice claims that the sample came out just as I see it, a large perfect brown orb. But, I think I see fingerprints, like somebody (probably Bernice) molded it by hand. I tell Bernice my theory and she says that I'm seeing tracking marks, kind of like the marks a barrel will leave on a bullet that has been fired. She claims that each one of us leaves unique tracks on our excrement. According to Bernice, if I gave her five firm samples of my own, she could pick my sixth turd out of a lineup. I hand the meatball back to her before it can start to thaw in my hands. I still think that those were fingerprints. An image of Bernice molding the sphere enters my mind, followed by one of her cooking up my Scrapple.

"And look at this. From Kool and the entire Gang." She holds up another gallon bag that's chock full of different sized logs. "And here, Nitty Gritty Dirt Band...guano from a Flock of Seagulls...the drummer from Survivor...Brownsville Station...a roadie for Stryper...Foghat...some guy named Tommy Tutone...Kip Winger...most of the guys from Molly Hatchet..." I look at a bag of poo that supposedly came from

Gene Simmons. It looks like it has bits of hay in it. Before I know it, my arms are loaded up with frozen mookie stinks. Some of the bags are signed. Bernice is bent all of the way over in her freezer, digging down to the bottom. She hands me another gallon bag and says: "Hey, take a look at that one."

The bag is full and it looks like it has bits of mushroom and corn in it. "Gross. How'd somebody fill this thing all the way up? It looks like your mushroom gravy."

"It is. Look at the label." I flip the bag over and see that it's labeled *Mush Room Gravy*.

"Damn, woman! You keep food in there too?"

"Yeah, you still hungry?"

"Hey! Hey, enough! I thought I was going to see Bruce Dickinson's contribution to your collection. Hurry up. I'm not holding this shit much longer. I don't care what you say, I'm starting to smell it, frozen or not."

"Here we go!" She shouts up from inside the freezer. "I've got your golden nugget." A small Mylar zip-up bag dangles between Bernice's fingers, holding what looks like a chunk of dry dog food. A golden ray of light shines in from the window on the front door, directly on the blessed stool sample.

"Let me see that." I hold it in the lone ray of sunlight. I feel strongly about the sample. It radiates rock and roll. The back of my brain buzzes and I hear the guitar riff from *The Trooper*. My spidey-senses are tingling. On the front of the bag somebody wrote *Maiden Japan, Love Bruce*. I wrap my fingers around the bag, being careful not to squeeze too hard. "Why only such a little piece?"

"Well," says Bernice, "that was one classy man. Not into anything kinky. He didn't want to go dooty on my face or in my hair or anything, like some of those guys. He agreed to give me some, but he did it in the bathroom stall, without me watching. He said he can't go if somebody's watching. Anyway, that man left a big 'un in the bowl for me. I was gonna get it with my fish strainer that I use. But, out of habit, he flushed. I was devastated. But it was meant to be a double-flusher and he left just a little bit behind. That lone doo-doo ball was just a-bobbin' in the water waiting for me. It was meant to be. He signed the bag and gave it to me."

My body gains strength from the relic in the bag. The baggie vibrates softly, almost imperceptibly. I sniff gently. It smells like a Maiden show: beer, weed and sweat. "What do you want for this? I need it! It was meant for me. I don't know how or why, but I feel it."

Bernice smiles but her eyes are sad. "You're right. For some reason I've been holding on to that one for quite some time. And you know I've gotten offers on that little baby. But, I can see that it was meant for you. Take it, but take care of it. That one is special."

Bernice always was a nice lady. She just drank too much sometimes. She pours herself a whiskey and grapefruit juice drink and then offers to patch up my injuries as much as possible. I take her up on the offer and sip one of her mixed drinks myself while she works on me with gauze and band-aids and other absorbent pads. By the time she's done, I've finished several large drinks and I'm feeling less pain again. I look in the mirror and see a mummy with a feminine napkin taped across his forehead. We laugh.

And outside I hear thunder booming. But it doesn't stop. It's not thunder. It sounds like a herd of Harleys just outside the door.

"Get down." Bernice orders me as she peeks out her front window. "Aw shit, it's just your Uncle Doug and some of his weird friends. That must be your ride. You better get over there so that you can beat feet."

"Thanks for the poop," I say, thinking to myself *now there's a line you never expected to utter.*

"No problem, Sweety. Now give this old hag a hug and then get out of here." I tuck the turd in my front pocket and hug Bernice. Her hands slip down and squeeze my ass. I shudder and back away, thanking her for her help.

**18**

Sitting in front of Uncle Doug's trailer is the most pimped-out automotive aberration I've ever seen. A two-toned, maroon and tan, abomination of a two-door coupe with chrome running boards and side pipes running laterally on the car from just behind the front wheels. A spare tire sits squarely in the middle of the sloping trunk lid. The vehicle looks like an old model Monte Carlo that's been customized for a gay pimp. I stand gaping at the freakish car, studying the beast, trying to understand.

"Get inside, you dickhole!" Uncle Doug smacks me in the back of the head and Denny's aviator sunglasses launch from my face. "You want everybody in the park here to see you?"

Uncle Doug's gentle nudge brings me back to full alert. I duck into his trailer followed by Doug and two of the most peculiar looking characters I've ever encountered. "Alright, Buddy, I've got you a ride out of here, headed north as far as Atlanta. These are my close friends, so you treat them with respect. This is Dean, but we call him Fat Elvis."

Fat Elvis looks like ... well, he looks like a really fat Elvis. At least six-and-a-half feet tall and easily 400 pounds. Black greasy sideburns and a dirty, thick pompadour. Fat Elvis sticks out a puffy mitt and says "Ambulate over here and make my acquaintance," in a melodic southern tone.

I walk over and shake hands with Fat Elvis. His beefy hand dwarfs my average-size manus. "It's a pleasure. Should I call you Dean or Fat Elvis?"

"My mama calls me Dean. You call me Fat Elvis. That's my *nom de plume.* You try to call me Dean, well, I may have to defenestrate you."[24]

"You'll have to what?" I ask. It sounds threatening. I want to make sure I understand the man.

"Defenestrate you, Jack. I'll throw you out the window, man. Just don't call me Dean."

"Tha' man always using dem fitty-cent words, a-yow," says the ancient black fellow standing just behind Fat Elvis. "I ain't unnerstan a damn thing he say, a-yowww."

"Shut up, Clubfoot Jasper, or I'll wallop you." Fat Elvis shakes a balled up fist the size of a cantaloupe at the man.

"And, this ... " Uncle Doug interrupts and puts his hand on the black man's shoulder, is Clubfoot Jasper Moberly. Jasper shuffles up to meet me, dragging his right foot as he walks. The foot caps off one of his overly long, thin legs, points west to his north and drags on the ground. It looks as if he is walking on his ankle.

---

[24] Wikipedia.org, the online encyclopedia, gives a long list of movies and television shows that contain defenestration. It also provides examples of defenestration throughout history.

Clubfoot Jasper removes his weather-beaten fedora and extends a long thin arm that culminates in a wispy hand with long, spidery fingers. I shake Clubfoot Jasper's palsied hand; it shakes on its own. "It's a pleasure, sir," I tell him. The hunchbacked old man looks like he's in worse shape then me. If he could stand up straight he would probably amount to six-and-a-half to seven feet of man. In his present stooped state he stands five-foot-ten or so. One eye has an involuntary tick and the other looks to be clouded over with cataracts. The teeth that have decided to remain in his head have been woefully neglected and perhaps stay rooted just to spite the man who obviously ignored them most of his life. One front tooth is gold with a diamond set into it.

"A-yoww," replies Clubfoot Jasper. He mumbles something that I don't understand. Somewhere in the middle of his reply I think he says something about a guitar. Clubfoot Jasper turns around and walks out of the trailer.

"Don't try to understand him, Jack," says Fat Elvis. "You'll just drive yourself crazy. If he has something important to tell you, he'll articulate and enunciate like the dang Queen of England. Otherwise he's mostly just messing with you."

Denny pops his head out of the bathroom and wishes me good luck. I ask if he wants to come along but he says he's heading back to Utah to discuss the whole soul-binding arrangement with his girl, Marie. I tell him I think that's a good idea and wish him luck, too.

"Alright. You'se guys have to move, like now." Uncle Doug slaps the back of my head again. "See you later dickhole. Make sure to mention me when you're on Montel."

"Yeah. Let's make like a banana and split, Jack." Fat Elvis slaps me too. He pulls his hand back with blood on it. I think he popped something open on the back of my neck or hit a bloody bandage. "Aw shucks, fella. That's nasty. Don't go bleeding all over my car. Right?"

"Right on Fat Elvis. Let's roll." We get into the car and head north. I am on the road again.

Fat Elvis says that his car is a Stutz Blackhawk. His head touches the ceiling of the car. According to him, there are only about five hundred of these cars and at one point all of the celebrities wanted to own one. "Shucks, Frank Sinatra owned one, Elvis Presley, Evel Kneivel, Larry Holmes, Willie Nelson, Al Pacino, uh," Fat Elvis runs his fingers through his slick hair, "who else? Let's see. Hey, didn't Sammy Davis, Jr. have one of these cars, Jasper?"

Jasper is playing a three-stringed dobro in the back of the car, using a butter knife as a slide on the frets. Right in rhythm, he stops his guitar, grunts "a-yowww," and then jumps back into his song.

"A-yow is right, Jack." Fat Elvis laughs. He pushes the accelerator to the floor as we set tires on the entrance ramp to I-75 in a town called Brandon, just outside of Tampa. The Blackhawk roars, the tires mark the pavement with smoking rubber, and the g-force pins us back in our seats. All the while Clubfoot Jasper plays his metal guitar. "Feel that power man. Now that's a car, Jack." Fat Elvis tells me that power like that don't come cheap. "I get about 8 miles to the gallon in this baby, but damn, it do feel good."

"A-yoww," answers Clubfoot Jasper from the back seat, still picking away on the sweetest blues I've ever heard.

"I won this car off of Mr. T in an arm wrestling match. I darn near snapped his hand right off of his arm. You see that there." Fat Elvis points to a plaque on the dashboard engraved with the name Maximus Decimus. "That man was the first owner of the car. They engraved the original owner's name on that plaque when he bought it. And see there." Fat Elvis sets a plump index finger underneath the engraved name where somebody wrote the letter *T* with a permanent marker. "That's where Mr. T put his name. I pitied that fool when I had to take his car."

"So, like, this is the perfect car for you, being an Elvis impersonator and all, right?"

"Aw, jeez, kid. I ain't no Elvis Presley impersonator." Fat Elvis turns to me and the look he gives drains my blood and makes me cold. For a second I fear that he is going to thump me hard. "I'm a blues man, just like ole' Clubfoot Jasper back there. Elvis Presley stole from bluesmen like us. I ain't trying to be him. That man was trying to be like us?"

"But you look just like The King. I mean, don't you think that you are copying him, maybe just a little bit?"

"I ain't emulating that wannabe," Fat Elvis indignantly looks at me over the top of his gold-paint plated, rhinestone sunglasses. "This is just me. I've always looked like this. They been calling me Fat Elvis ever since I was a little baby. This mop of hair," he runs his fingers through the black hair, "it looks like this no matter what I do."

"What about the sunglasses? Those come standard with the Elvis Presley Halloween costume?"

"Clubfoot Jasper back there gave 'em to me for my birthday."

From behind us Clubfoot Jasper starts chuckling and mumbling over the penetrating soulful sounds exhaled by his guitar. "Hmmn, haw-haw, mn bin wearin' dem dare Presley spectacles, haw-haw, a-yoww."

"Dad-gum-it, Clubfoot Jasper, you prankster. You gave me Elvis Presley sunglasses and let me wear them for going on a month now. You know how I feel about being compared to that man." Fat Elvis goes to throw the glasses out of the window, but I convince him to give them to me instead. "That Clubfoot Jasper is always getting me with little stunts like that."

"Well," I ask, "why do you go by Fat Elvis if you can't stand the King? I mean, it's kind of weird."

"It's my name, my pseudonymous designation, my *nom de plume*. They been calling me that as long as I remember. It's got nothing to do with that white-boy, blues thieving, *poseur*. Besides, people see that Fat Elvis is playing in a bar, well, it helps to draw a crowd. People get curious. Then they hear our music and learn about the real thing."

Clubfoot Jasper's chuckles ring out in time and in tune with his guitar, just another part of his song. "Haw-haw. Crazy cracker, awmanaman-aw. Gib a man a vow-cab-oolarry book an' a-yow, da man get up wit' fitty-sent words. Haw-haw-haw. Soo-dough-magnimus detrimation. A-yow. Nam dee ploom. Haw-haw. Ayow."

"Shut up and play your guitar, Clubfoot Jasper. You keep it up and I'm gonna defenestrate you." At 90 miles per hour on the interstate Fat Elvis turns all the way around in his seat, taking his hands off of the wheel and tries to grab Jasper over the back of the front seat. "Dang boy, you the one gave me that vocabulary book for my edification. Now you want to make fun of my articulation, enunciation, and eloquence. I take umbrage at your affront. Keep it up and I will defenestrate you." I steer the car in and out of traffic while Fat Elvis and Clubfoot Jasper verbally thrust and parry.

"Ah-how." Clubfoot Jasper continues to laugh and taunt over the weepy blues strains of his guitar. "Da man g'win to depenestrate Ol' Clubfoot Jasper cuz Clubfoot Jasper copy dem words. A-yow. Always depenestrate. G'win to t'row Clubfoot Jasper out de window. Depenestrate. A-haw-haw-haw-haw."

"Stop echoing my words, you psittacine ignoramus." Fat Elvis turns around, regains control of the steering wheel and mumbles about defenestration.

Going north on I-75 we keep seeing signs for the Café Risqué. According to the girls on the sign, they bare all. Clubfoot Jasper wants to stop and eat lunch. "I'm a wanna geh me some tuner fish sammich and sniff around sum dem nekked girls."

"We ain't stopping at that den of iniquity to witness your depravity, Clubfoot Jasper." Fat Elvis ignores Jasper's pleas and drives past the Micanopy exit. "Dang it Jasper. You always spend all of our gig money and get in trouble in them places. What you didn't spend on the harlots in the last place, I spent on your bail after you got arrested for refusing to leave." Fat Elvis winks at me and smiles. "That old boy must be ninety years old but still has the libidinous aspirations of a fifteen year old boy. He leaves a trail of illegitimate children in his wake."

"I's hunnert-two, a-yow."

"You aren't a-hundred-and-two. Now shut up and play your guitar, Jasper." Clubfoot Jasper plays the guitar nonstop as we monopolize the passing lane, whizzing in and out of elderly tourists, Canadians, used school buses full of migrant Mexican field workers, and RV's with murals and the families' names painted on the back. Fat Elvis sings along to Clubfoot Jasper's guitar, a song about rolling and tumbling. Clubfoot Jasper croons a haunting song about shooting his woman because she cheated on him. I've never been so touched by a three string guitar and nearly incoherent grunts and utterances.

"Why is it," I ask, "that you bluesmen are always singing about shooting your woman? I mean, does that really happen or is it like these county stars that sing about prison but never did time?"[25]

Clubfoot Jasper sings back something barely decipherable about mean mistreaters doing their men wrong.

"That's the blues, man," answers Fat Elvis. "That man back there is the blues. He's nearly blind, nearly dead, crippled and lame as can be. Those long fingers used to play some of the most beautiful finger-picked blues guitar you ever heard. Now they can barely hold that butter knife that he plays slide with. But he still plays better and sweeter than anyone I know. And I ain't never known him to stop playing for more than ten or fifteen minutes. He plays while he eats. He plays on the toilet. In his sleep the man even plays. He just lays there supine, holds that guitar on his chest and drags that knife back and forth on

---

[25] Although he did several different stints in jail, Johnny Cash never served a term of incarceration in a prison.

the frets in time to his gentle snores. It's mighty moving to hear."

"Why's he play that guitar nonstop?" Not that it matters. It's just that his playing is so sweet it makes a grown man want to cry.

"That's a long story, Jack. But we have a long drive. This would be a long drive for someone with nothing to talk about, I guess. Sit back and I'll tell you the story of old Clubfoot Jasper Moberly."

**19**

"One night, sitting in a candle-lit piano bar in New Orleans, Old Clubfoot Jasper back there told me his story." Fat Elvis's voice goes down a notch in volume to make me listen closer, to draw me in. Behind me the guitar playing stops. I turn back to check on Clubfoot Jasper and see him with the rounded end of the butter knife digging into his nostril. Clubfoot Jasper pulls out the knife and studies a flat, dry booger stuck on the end. As if he doesn't care that I'm watching, he lifts the floor mat to the seat beside him, wipes the nose candy on the floor, and then resumes his guitar playing. Meanwhile, Fat Elvis continues with the tale of Clubfoot Jasper.

"We were sitting right at the piano and some white-bread couple requested *What a Wonderful World*. That piano man played a transcendent version that so warmed the crowd's cockles. The atmosphere was optimal for soul baring. The white-bread couple beside us were getting inebriated and chummy with the saltiest looking sea-dog you ever met. I mean, this old boy had dried up bird doo-doo on his shoulders. He should have had an eyepatch and a parrot. The man was ordering up drinks and talking loudly about his new pirate friend Dale. The lady looked like she had special sensations in her nether-regions for Dale. I wouldn't be surprised if that couple didn't take that crusty old man back in some alley and share sweet loving with him. I mean, there was a feeling in the air. And Old Jasper was feeling it too."

"A-yow," agrees Jasper.

"Jasper looked me straight in the eye and said, 'look, I've gotta talk to you, man.' I mean, he started speaking clear as day. I understood every word he said. We moved away from the piano and sat down at a table to talk. And the stuff Clubfoot Jasper told me, well, it made me shudder, gave me the heebie-jeebies, man." And so, to the musical accompaniment of a three-string slide guitar I learned Clubfoot Jasper's story.

Fat Elvis said that he didn't believe all of Jasper's tale, but enough of it to matter. According to Clubfoot Jasper, he was born somewhere in Mississippi, in 1904. And from the look of the deep dusty lines on his face, it just may be true. Clubfoot Jasper was born William Cleveland Roosevelt Marfan. His mother died during the birth and the father, a transient, was nowhere to be found by the time Little Bill Marfan entered this world. Baby Bill was long and light and spindly. As a child he was passed about between his many aunts and uncles, never really feeling like a part of any permanent family. The only constant in his existence was a beat up acoustic guitar given to him by his Uncle Jefferson Lincoln Washington Marfan. Little Bill was a natural on the guitar and took it with him from house to house, always clinging to it like a security blanket.

Early on in his teen years, tired of being shuffled from place to place, tired of never having a bed or a room of his own, and getting restless for something more than just plying a mule and scraping by, Bill took off and started riding the rails. Just Bill and his beat up old guitar seeing what this country had to offer a tall lanky black boy with no training or education. He picked up odd jobs along the way, slaughterhouses, dishwashing, shoveling manure, whatever could put some change in his pockets and a meal in his belly.

Bill meandered around the Mississippi Delta, from town to town, hitchhiking, riding buses, hopping trains. Along the way, he started playing his guitar on street corners for money. He played in juke joints and fish fries for free hooch and all of the women that his talent could draw. Fat Elvis tells me that "Clubfoot Jasper ain't never been pretty, but his guitar playing could make Mother Teresa brew a fondue in her panties. That old boy has had more dirty women than most men ever had."

Bill started hanging out with other guitar players in the region. He was often seen jamming on a street corner with his buddies Johnny and Robert. Around that time, Bill found the love of his life, a fifteen-year-old girl named Cleophus. Bill Marfan loved Cleo more than even his guitar. But his constant traveling left her unfulfilled. Once, upon returning to visit Cleo, Bill discovered her in an intimate entanglement with another young man. Bill shot Cleo dead on the spot, right between the eyes. A row ensued between Bill Marfan and the interloper. Bill came out of it with a badly damaged left hand. The interloper's life leaked out of the bullet hole in his chest.

As a result of Cleophus's death, Bill Marfan did a five-year stint in the Mississippi Big House. The prison doctors ignored his injured hand until it became rotten with infection. Only at that point was any treatment given, just in time to salvage the thumb, index, and middle fingers. The compulsion to play his guitar was undeniable. Bill gripped a butter knife in his mangled hand and changed his style, incorporating elements of blues picking for his healthy right hand and slide guitar for his mangled left hand. While in prison Bill wrote the first and original blues song about shooting down a cheating woman. One day, while playing his guitar in the exercise yard, Bill Marfan received a visitor, a genial white man from Texas who wanted to record his music. With nothing better to do and nowhere to go, Bill gave an impromptu performance with his blues-picking-butter-knife-slide-guitar and partially incoherent vocals about shooting down the mean-mistreatin', one time cheatin', woman he loved, the woman he killed.

Upon release from the penitentiary, Bill Marfan located his musician friend Robert. Robert told old Bankrupt Bill that he was "makin' music, rakin' money, and drawing in the honeys." One night, Robert sent Bill out into the country to meet a man who could help him make the most of his music career. The man, Mr. Eshu, helped Robert and could do the same for Bill.

Late that night, Bill went to the crossroads outside of Clarksdale and met up with Mr. Eshu. The man asked him what he wanted. *I want to be rich and famous and happy*, Bill replied. Eshu told him, *I will make you famous, but there are things I ex-*

*pect in return.* Assuming that Eshu meant he wanted a cut of his profits, Bill agreed. Eshu took Bill's guitar and tuned it for him. He then placed the tip of his pointer finger between Bill's eyes and began chanting, over and over, *Shama, Lama, Ding, Dong, Ewww, Mow, Mow, A-A-A-Ohhhh.* Jasper's vision clouded, his right foot cramped and contorted painfully. *From now on,* said Eshu, *you will be known as Clubfoot Jasper Moberly. And you will be famous, as long as you keep playing that guitar.*

*I don' like it. Why Clubfoot Jasper Moberly?* Bill asked Eshu. Eshu said that Clubfoot Jasper Moberly was a good blues name, whether Bill liked it or not. *That's fine,* said Clubfoot Jasper, *as long as I will be rich and famous and happy.* Eshu corrected Jasper, *I only agreed to make you famous.*

The next day, Clubfoot Jasper heard his songs on the radio, the songs that were recorded by that nice white man at the prison. Clubfoot Jasper was literally an overnight sensation. He began appearing on the King Biscuit Radio Show, recording records, playing shows in clubs. Everywhere he went, people wanted to hear his music.

Late one night, Robert approached Clubfoot Jasper. Robert was trembling and pale and shedding whiskey tears. *That Mr. Eshu,* said Robert, *done me wrong. I's famous, but I's got his hellhounds on my trail. I cain't get me no peace. That man must be the devil comin' to take my soul. He be af'er you next, Jasper. Don't stop movin' and don't stop playing that sweet guitar and maybe you be alright.*

Clubfoot Jasper never saw his friend Robert again. But he did start seeing the dogs, the hellhounds, as Robert called them. He saw them in his sleep. He saw them lurking behind trees and sensed them behind fences. Their faces, horrible. Lips turned up to bare pointy teeth. Long, droopy ears. Their bodies, long, thick and muscular, resting on disproportionately short legs. Clubfoot Jasper also sometimes spied a figure in the distance behind him, a presence like that of Mr. Eshu. The guitar playing never stopped. The more Clubfoot Jasper played, the less likely he was to see the hellhounds or Mr. Eshu. From the time of Robert's mysterious disappearance, Clubfoot Jasper kept his dobro with him, playing it in his sleep, on the toilet[26], and anywhere else he would go.

Throughout the years, Clubfoot Jasper found himself having to gun down his cheating women. Throughout the years Jasper also found himself serving time at Parchman Farm, the Mississippi Big House, for his misdeeds. Each time, he would receive a visit from that nice white man with the recording equipment. Each recording session would be a smash hit. Every time he was released from prison, Clubfoot Jasper would start touring the Chitlin' Circuit, playing major venues like the Apollo, the Cotton Club, the Fox Theater, and the Victory Grill. The hits kept coming and the crowds loved him. But Clubfoot Jasper was always looking behind him. Always seeing Mr. Eshu trying to come and collect on their deal. Always smelling those hellhounds on his trail. Eternal damnation following him like a piece of toilet paper stuck to his shoe.

---

[26] U.S. President Lyndon Baines Johnson also had interesting bathroom habits. He is known to have insisted that others accompany him in the bathroom to conduct official business (such as taking dictation) while he moved his bowels.

"That's the gist of it," says Fat Elvis. "I don't know if that old boy is 102 years old. I don't know if that Mr. Eshu is the devil incarnate. But I do know this—I've seen those hounds myself, slobbering, frothing, champing at the bit to get at Jasper. And intermittently, I will see a man behind us, maybe in a car, maybe walking, but he stands out, a tall man in a big yellow hat. Always in the distance. But I've seen that man all over the country. I never know where he's going to turn up. But he does. He never approaches us, but he watches. So I been hanging with Old Clubfoot Jasper now for decades. We are on the road. And that old boy, he don't stop playing that guitar for fear that if he does, well, Mr. Mephistopheles, or whoever he is, will come and put Old Jasper's soul in an empty whiskey bottle and lock it up in the devil's liquor cabinet. So Jasper keeps playing his guitar, and Mr. Eshu and his dogs keep their distance. Ain't that right, Clubfoot Jasper?"

"A-yoww."

Clubfoot Jasper's story is hard to top. We stop talking and listen as Jasper plays the guitar, providing the soundtrack to our trip north. We pass an old Cadillac and I notice that the driver is sporting a large yellow hat. The Cadillac fades into the distance behind us. Clubfoot Jasper's playing becomes more frenetic, a crazy flamenco-tinged slide guitar kind of blues. Just barely audible, I think I hear the howling of dogs.

**20**

Fat Elvis and Clubfoot Jasper are scheduled to play the lounge of The Paradise Inn for the next three weeks. The owner of the inn, Salvatore, is a blues aficionado. He managed to track down Fat Elvis and convinced him and Clubfoot Jasper to be the lounge band. Free food, free rooms and free booze are the perks. And Clubfoot Jasper and Fat Elvis can keep half of the door receipts. To clinch the deal, Jasper made Sal throw in free adult movies on the hotel television.

The Stutz Blackhawk shimmies and shudders. Fat Elvis pushes it faster, talking incessantly as we whizz past the other cars on the road. I kind of like that he talks so much, it makes it easier for me. I just smile, laugh and nod my head appropriately; he does all of the work. Behind me, Clubfoot Jasper continues to play the guitar. Sometimes he sings, sometimes he just plays. He plays a song called *Assfull of Whiskey* about having such a high tolerance to alcohol that he has to give himself whiskey enemas to get drunk. Then a little number he calls something like *The Gris Gris Mojo Bag Boogie-Woogie Blues*. Next comes a song called *Dust My*

*Broom*. I tell Clubfoot Jasper that that's the best version of a ZZ top song I've ever heard. For some reason, Fat Elvis smacks me in the back of the head and calls me a "*Blasphemer*."

Road signs, mile markers, and southern cities fade away behind us . . . *Valdosta* . . . Clubfoot Jasper plays his guitar . . . *Tifton* . . . Fat Elvis belts out a song called *Death Letter Blues* . . . *Cordele* . . . I tell the guys that I know how to play a little guitar. Clubfoot Jasper hands me his instrument and I kick out the opening riff to Smoke on the Water.[27] That's all I know is the opening riff. Fat Elvis and Clubfoot Jasper look at me expectantly so I play the beginning of Stairway to Heaven. All I know is the beginning. I only took a couple of guitar lessons and never really practiced. Mom told me she wasn't wasting money on lessons if I wasn't going to practice. Clubfoot Jasper bursts out in gravelly laughter, incoherent muttering that has a tone of mockery, and a healthy dose of *A-yows*. I hand the guitar back to Clubfoot Jasper and let him continue with his amazing songs . . . *Macon* . . . Fat Elvis continues to blabber. He tells me he once was in a relationship with a woman where they agreed to be completely honest with each other about any thoughts that came into their minds. True and utter frankness. No white lies, no shading the truth. *Does my butt look big in these pants?* Answer: *Hell yes, like two watermelons dancing under a blanket.* Just blatant, bald-faced, unmitigated candor. At first, said Elvis, it was refreshing and liberating to just

---

[27] It is an irrefutable, scientifically documented fact that the opening riff to *Smoke on the Water* will be played by any musically untrained person who picks up a guitar and tries to play it. This occurs regardless of race, religion, physical location of the player, or actual familiarity with the song. Tribesmen deep in the Amazon Rain Forests have been handed guitars and asked to play them. Immediately, and invariably, they break into the riff.

speak his mind completely and have his significant other do the same. But she asked far too many risky questions. The refreshing liberation lasted for three days and culminated in a red hand-mark on Fat Elvis's face and the consequent defenestration of his lady friend. Behind us Clubfoot Jasper is rocking to a song that is either called *Defenestration Blues* or *Deep Penetration Blues*, it's hard to tell...*Smarr*...Fat Elvis jabbers on. I am not good at conversing. One night in my basement, Idjit and I sat and watched a show on one of the travel channels about the death of native languages. There was an aboriginal guy in Australia who was one of the last two speakers of his language. Only one other speaker of his language in the entire world. That other person was his sister. And due to tribal customs or religious belief or something, the brother and sister were not allowed to speak with each other. I feel like that funny little pot bellied aborigine. Only Idjit and me really understand each other, and we're not together. When others talk, I just don't know what to say back. When I try to make a point, there is no meaty reply, no pithy re-tort, no reciprocation. I wish I could hold that old flea-bag on my lap and talk with him. He would understand...*Jackson*...Old Clubfoot Jasper taps me on the shoulder and says something about gree-gree. Fat Elvis explains that Clubfoot Jasper is going to make me a mojo bag, whatever that is. Jasper needs some-thing from my person that is most important to me. I give him the little turd that I got from Bernice. He needs something from my backpack, I tell him to dig through it and help himself. He for-ages through the pack that Arnette and Pervis gave me, grunting to himself, pulling things out and sniffing them, putting them back, and then says that he has to add something personal to him. I watch as Clubfoot Jasper scrapes a thimble full of dried boogers from beneath his floor mat and dumps it into a little red flannel bag along with the turd and something he pulled from the backpack, I think maybe a small scrap of gator-jerky or maybe some Florida Swamp Weed. Jasper ties a little string on the sack and sniffs it. *Whoo-eee, a-yow,* he says. Jasper sets the bag in his lap and lets his guitar scream out frenetic acoustic mayhem. Clubfoot Jasper passes the bag to me and says something about wee-wee or gree gree or something. I look at Fat Elvis and he says, *Clubfoot Jasper's just telling you to feed the mojo with a drop of urine once in a while.* I look at Fat Elvis, incredulous, *you mean he hands me a bagful of boogers, dooty, and gator meat, wants me to pee on it, and you don't think that's strange?* Clubfoot Jasper moans out *A-yow.* Fat Elvis nods in agreement. I'm supposed to keep the bag in my pocket and not let anybody else touch it or know about it. *Okay,* I say, *what have I got to lose?* I tuck the bag full of nasties in my pocket. There is something comforting about it. Small, almost imperceptible resonations . . . *Atlanta* . . . we pass on through and on the north side of the city Fat Elvis exits the highway, makes some right turns, some left turns, goes straight for a little bit here and there, and then parks his car in the handicapped spot in front of Sal's Paradise Inn.

Salvatore introduces himself to us as *Salvatore,* not *Sal* as his sign suggests. He sets us all up with rooms. Fat Elvis tells Sal (for that is what we called him and shall henceforth refer to him as) that I am the road manager.

It is always uncomfortable when a new person introduces himself with his full name. You never know from then on if you are offending him by being familiar. Oh, I am sorry James, please don't get upset if I just called you Jimmy. I don't take offense when you refer to me by my familiar name. I would rather call a David *Dave*. Robert should be *Bob*. Richard is *Rich* (and sometimes a Dick, depending on the particular Richard). And if you're a Theodore, please, just be *Ted*, or I will have to kick in your pecker-sucking face on principle. And Salvatore, well, he's Sal.

I am sorry if I seem testy. It's just that I am coming off of an extended drug binge, I now am fully sober and sore, most of my body has cuts, contusions, and cerebral hemorrhaging, I am wrapped up in bandages like a fucking mummy, I leak fluids that probably have some useful purpose for my continued livelihood, and I miss my dog. I really miss him and need to see him.

And we are at Sal's Paradise Inn. Sal is actually a pretty nice guy. He has a crooked smile and winks at us too much, probably is not trustworthy, but maybe I'm paranoid. When Sal leaves the front desk to check on our rooms, Fat Elvis says to me that Sal is "swarthy" and "unctuous." Although I don't have a dictionary with me, I would have to guess that these are good descriptions. Sal returns and takes us to our rooms.

Sal has set aside four rooms for us that are all connected by interior doors. It is disconcerting that the locks on our hotel doors are padlocks. The doors don't even have doorknobs. Just a latch on each one that is held shut by some generic padlock, probably bought at a flea market. Sal hands us little padlock keys and tells us to put them on our key chains. When inside the rooms, we are supposed to use the padlocks on the latches on the inside part of the door. He hands us another envelope full of little keys for the padlocks on the interior connecting doors in case we want to have a party. Clubfoot Jasper tucks the keys in his front pants pocket and gives a grunt/smile toward Salvatore.

We each take our own room. Mine has a bed with magic-fingers. That means if you feed it quarters the bed will vibrate and make your teeth chatter. Sal hands me a sandwich bag full of metal slugs that are the size of quarters so that I can enjoy the magic fingers all night if I wish. Without even pulling back the stained purple comforter, I lay down on my epileptic bed and feed it small metal disks. I need just a little bit of rest before I push on. Fat Elvis and Clubfoot Jasper will be performing in the lounge in a little bit. Later, Clubfoot Jasper's estranged wife, Beulah, will be stopping by. They tell me to stop down in the lounge before I leave. The magic fingers gently tickle me to sleep.

"It's good to see you again," says Idjit. "I've missed you, ya big dork." Idjit sits at the feet of a man in Daddy's chair. The man wears a big yellow hat with a red feather stuck in the band and has a curious looking little monkey in his lap. The man is flanked by the two biggest dogs I have ever seen. The hounds look like giant versions of Idjit but they have ridged backs and tusks like boars. "These are my friends. This is Mr. Eshu."

The man in the big yellow hat nods at me. "It's a pleasure. Mr. Galoot has told us much about you."

"It is nice to meet you too," I tell Mr. Eshu. "Um . . . that's my Daddy's chair you're sitting in. I don't mean to be rude, but I would like you to get out of it."

"No, no, it's okay," says Idjit. "Your Daddy gave him permission to sit there. Everybody's been in your Daddy's chair lately."

"I mean no offense," says Mr. Eshu. "If you wish for me to get up, I will."

"No . . . um . . . I guess it's okay if Daddy said so."

"Mmmm-hummm." One of the big dogs clears his throat to catch Idjit's attention and then rolls his eyes at his other doggy friend.

"Oh, I am sorry," says Idjit. "This is Haskel."

"It's a pleasure," says the dog on the left.

"And Cleaver . . . "

"Pleased to meet you," says the dog on the right.

"And the little guy there is Jorge."

"Hey, you're *muy interasante*," says the little monkey.

"I need to speak with you about your friend, Clubfoot Jasper," says Eshu. "He's been quite a challenge. Jasper has been on our accounts receivable list for some time now. It is well past the due date for Mr. Moberly and it really is time for him to shed his mortal shell and pass into another realm."

"So Clubfoot Jasper is right," I say. "He did sell his soul. And you're the Devil. And you and those hellhounds are going to drag him down into the bowels of Hell and put his soul in an empty whiskey bottle in your liquor cabinet if he ever stops playing his guitar long enough for you to grab him."

They all laugh at me, even Idjit. "Listen," chuckles Eshu. "You're right about the guitar thing, but you missed the mark on the rest. I'm not the devil. These are not hellhounds. There are no empty bottles in my liquor cabinet. And I wouldn't even consider driving Mr. Moberly into that neighborhood and dropping him off. Jasper never sold his soul to me; I am not in the acquisitions business. I am more of a guide, a psychopomp. I helped him because he was blessed with a talent that needed to be shared with the world. All that I wanted in return was for him to spread enlightenment and positive vibrations to his fellow man. He has more than met my wishes by making his gree-gree booger bags for others and through his music. He's also helped to rid the world of some evil mean-mistreaters. And now it is time for him to pass on to the next level."

"Why don't you just grab him by the ear and drag him into the afterlife?" I ask.

"It doesn't work that way," says Eshu. "Everybody has something in life that gives their spirit strength. With Jasper it's his guitar playing. It keeps him alive."

"You mean to tell me that your dogs couldn't grab Clubfoot Jasper by the scruff of his neck and carry him like a puppy to wherever it is that he's supposed to go."

"Well..." Eshu pauses. "They should be able to but...once again..." the dogs growl softly "...it's that guitar. As long as he's playing it, they won't go near him. Haskel and Cleaver are more refined. They prefer baroque music—lutes, harpsichords, oboes. They think blues music is crude, far too raw. Clubfoot Jasper's guitar makes them howl in pain, makes their ears bleed, some of that crazy slide guitar he was playing with you in the car would have ruptured a spleen if they would have been too close. You should see the vet bills I have for these beasts after they attempt to snatch Mr. Moberly. They just will not go close to him while he is playing that guitar. And he's always playing. Even in his sleep."

"You need to help Eshu to help Clubfoot Jasper," says Idjit Galoot. "This guy's on the level. You will be doing Mr. Moberly an enormous favor."

"What can I do?"

"I'm going to deputize you. You will be an assistant psychopomp. You'll know what to do when the time comes," says Eshu. "And as my employee, as a deputy soul guide, you will need a nametag. Here . . . " Eshu slaps a sticker on my chest. It's a nametag like they use at conventions that reads *HELLO. I'M . . .* and somebody hand-wrote *Gay* in the spot where you're supposed to write your name. Once again, everybody laughs at me, especially Haskel and Cleaver. "Now be gone."

I bend down to scratch Idjit behind the ear. His foot involuntarily thumps out a rapid rhythm on the floor. He licks my hand and looks at me with the saddest brown eyes I have ever seen. He lays down and falls asleep immediately.


I wake up face-down on my bed. I am groggy and my body is stuck to the bed sheets. My wounds have been leaking, draining me while I slept. I am crusted to the scratchy purple comforter on my bed, like a scab stuck to an enormous gauze bandage. I peel myself from the bed, leaving bits of flesh and coagulated blood adhered to the tacky bedspread. The digital clock beside the bed says that it's 11:00 a.m. I know that that can't be right because it would mean I have been sleeping over sixteen hours. It is daylight out. *Fuck, I've gotta get a move on.* It's like I am losing energy. I only wanted to sleep for an hour or so before getting back on the road.

My feet hit the floor and the haze of sleep begins to clear. I just have to take a shit before I go. I flip on the TV and turn to the cable news channel, turning up the volume so that I can hear it in the bathroom. With the bathroom door left open so that I can hear the latest, I cop a squat on an ice cold toilet seat. Most of the news is typical. Somebody somewhere in the Middle East blew something up and killed people. Some celebrities are having babies and some other ones are getting divorced. Some politician had some sort of a sexual scandal involving an employee and a bag of organic babycarrots. Some catholic priests didn't play in a nice way with some choir boys.

A reporter by the name of Cleveland Steamer mentions the Sombrero Tower Bombers. Steamer says that several possible co-conspirators were taken into custody in South Florida. I jam a wad of toilet paper between my butt cheeks, jump off of the toilet seat with my pants around my ankles, and shuffle-run out of the bathroom to catch the story. Standing in front of the TV with my pants down around my ankles, I watch as Steamer reports over video of Arnette and Pervis being handcuffed outside of their little house. Buddy does not seem to be anywhere around. "The two brothers seen in this video are suspected of harboring the bombers and helping them evade arrest," says Cleveland Steamer. "Also found in the brothers' house was an unconscious college student who had been an intern traveling the country in the Albert Morgan Bratmobile. It is believed that the suspects car-jacked the vehicle and took the driver and his coworker hostage. The other college student has not been found and may still be a hostage. The details are still unfolding here and we will keep you updated as we learn more. Back to you, Suchi."

I shuffle back to the toilet and sit down to finish my business. Just as I relax, gunshots slam my ears. Thunder booming in the room next to mine. *Blam Blam Blam.* Clubfoot Jasper's room. The door that joins my room to Jasper's flies open. Jasper bursts in with his guitar in one hand and my Luger, still smoking, in the other. He stands in the doorway of the bathroom, frantic, shaking, gore splattered on his face and chest. I stare back at him, in shock myself. There's not a more vulnerable feeling than sitting on the crapper and having somebody barge in on you. It's bad enough in normal circumstances when you're in a stall and the door is flung open. You're sitting there in your own funk, pants around the ankles and defenseless, your goodies just hanging out. The Pooper always blurts out something in a clipped tone like *occupied* or *in here*. The intruder, usually also shocked will respond *Sorry* or maybe a funny *Caught 'cha with your pants down*. Even worse, though I'm caught by surprise, mid-wipe, leaning over to my left, one butt cheek lifted off of the seat, when Clubfoot Jasper bursts in after some sort of shooting spree.

"AYOW!" Jasper drops the Luger. It cracks one of the bathroom floor tiles and rests between his feet, pointing right at me. "I done went to meet with Beulah after the show and found her in the room wit' 'nudder man. 'S good thing I done taked dis 'ere gun from yer pack. Dat mean mistreater. A-yow."

Before I have time to finish my clean-up down under, Jasper drops the guitar and yanks me off of the john. "We's gots to go. Come on boy." I yank up my pants, feeling only half clean. I think to myself that a warm white washcloth with a dab of lemon juice on it would be nice for freshening up. I drag Club-foot Jasper from the bathroom. We grab my backpack and the guitar and run out of my hotel room.

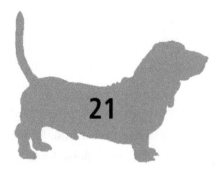

**21**

In the mad dash from the room, Clubfoot Jasper's guitar smashes on the door frame. The strings are connected to the head of the guitar. The head used to be connected to the neck. The neck and the head are now separated. Lonely, jagged wooden bits from the head and neck extend into the air, seeking out each other like desperate jigsaw puzzle pieces. The head dangles from six strings and drags on the ground. As I pull Jasper from the room, a metallic clanging chimes from the resonator of the steel bodied guitar. "It's time to go," I tell him.

Jasper grabs onto the handrail outside of the room and hooks his clubbed foot between the handrail posts. "A-yow. Gots to get another guitar. A-yow," he pleads as I tug on his arm. His speech is as clear as I've heard it yet. I pull again and hear a cracking noise, probably his ankle. As I drag Jasper away, his orthopedic shoe is wedged off by the posts.

"No time," I tell him. "You have to get out of here now."

Jasper's body goes limp in protest. I drag his rag doll body behind me as he pleads the whole time to go back and get another guitar. Jasper tells me that he thinks Sal might have a guitar in his office. "Please, mistuh, please. Lets me get me another guitar. I's gots to play or those devil dogs'll get me. A-yow."

I drag Jasper's limp body into the front office and tell him: "Okay, let's see what Sal can do for you. Maybe he has a guitar. Then we've gotta go. The cops'll be here any minute now." Clubfoot Jasper's body finds its muscle tone and he resumes an upright position. Jasper taps out a frantic rhythm on the bell on the front desk and Sal stumbles into the front office, rubbing his eyes and looking befuddled.

"What?"

"Gimme your guitar! A-yow."

"I don't have a guitar anymore. Some fool broke into my unit last week, stole my guitar, and left a giant turd in my toilet. Just a turd, and one little square of toilet paper," says Sal as he tightens the belt on his robe.

"How about a bass, a banjo, some sort of stringed instrument?" I ask.

"All I have is my niece's autoharp and a rhythm fish. I don't expect you'll be wanting either of those."

"Get the autoharp," I snap. "Please just get it."

"A-yow," agrees Jasper.

In the distance a single police siren approaches. I grab the autoharp in one hand and Jasper's wrist in the other. "Come on. It's time to go," I tell him. Jasper puts weight on his injured ankle and collapses. I hook one arm under his armpit and around his chest and drag Jasper outside. Fat Elvis comes running down the steps with a bath towel wrapped around his waist.

The towel is far too small, showing the most part of a fat hairy thigh, and barely covers *little elvis*.

"What the devil is all of this cacophony I'm hearing?" he asks as he sees me dragging Clubfoot Jasper down the sidewalk.

"Clubfoot Jasper shot Beulah," I tell him.

"Not again," Fat Elvis shakes his head. "That incorrigible, impetuous, buffoon. I'll get my keys and run interference. You get him in the car."

"I needs a guitar. A-yow," Clubfoot Jasper tells Fat Elvis.

"I don't have another one, Jasper. Just worry about getting out of here right now and we'll get you another guitar once we are clear of this."

I drag Clubfoot Jasper's floppy frame into the front seat of the car as he moans about not having a guitar. Fat Elvis, still wearing only a towel, throws me the keys to his Blackhawk and tells us: "Beat it. I'll slow down Johnny Law with obfuscation, prestidigitation, and pandemonium." Fat Elvis pulls off his towel and sets off the fire alarm. He grabs a fire extinguisher from the wall and sprays the parking lot with a powdery cloud from the canister.

I pull the Blackhawk out of the parking lot with Clubfoot Jasper strumming on the autoharp. "This ain't no autoharp," Clubfoot Jasper growls. "'S a gawdamm zither. A-yow. Howza man 'opposed to sing da blues wit' a gawdamm zither." A black and white police cruiser passes us on the street, its siren dopplering behind us. In the rearview mirror I see naked Fat Elvis smashing in the front window of the Paradise with a garbage can. The fog from the fire extinguisher clouds the parking lot and the cruiser's siren sings a warbling duet with the hotel's fire alarm. Obfuscation and pandemonium indeed.

I ease the car back out onto I-75 as Jasper continues to moan about the *gawdamm zither*. As we cross the state line going into Tennessee, Jasper opens his window, leans out and thrusts his good hand as far forward as he can. "Haw-haw-haw. I's the first one into Tennessee. A-yow," he laughs and then goes back to strumming his zither. It's hard to tell, but the driver of the truck behind me seems to be wearing a big yellow hat.

As we get closer to Erwin, I feel a sense of hope. This journey will be over soon and I will be back with Idjit Galoot.

The news on the radio reports that there is an all points bulletin out for a Stutz Blackhawk on I-75 in Tennessee. State troopers are keeping an eye out for Fat Elvis's car. We run out of gas just outside of Knoxville. I pull the car over on the shoulder of the road and curse my luck. Going south on 75 I see a trooper slowing down as he passes us. I grab Jasper and drag him from the car. His ankle is swollen to the size of a football and he is unable to walk. I haul him across the ditch and into the woods.

The trooper pulls across the median and parks just behind the Blackhawk. He did not see us get out. With Jasper slung over my shoulder, I run through the woods. Jasper continues to strum the zither and I continue to run. I continue to run, and Jasper continues to strum the zither. Zither and run, hither and yon, run and zither, yon and hither. I am going nowhere in particular, just as far away from the trooper as possible. I have not come this far just to fail because of a hungry gas-guzzler with an empty tank.

Overhead the whir of a police helicopter drones as I drag Jasper through the woods. As the sun sets I find myself dizzy from exhaustion. Jasper strums the zither and gently croons something unintelligible. We come to a ten-foot tall fence topped with razor wire. I walk the wood-planked barrier until I find a hole that has been dug under the fence, probably by some sort of a large animal. I climb under the fence and help Jasper under after me.

The woods stink of some awful rot. Sewage, decomposition, filth. The forest reeks of death. I drag Jasper, my right arm wrapped around his torso, like carrying a sack of flour. Under a giant oak tree I set Jasper down and collapse in exhaustion beside him. Jasper strums the zither and I fall hard onto my shoulder and into slumber. My weariness is so great that a knotty tree root suffices for a pillow.

"That was a good thing you did: giving him the zither," says Idjit. "Messieurs Haskell and Cleaver couldn't stand the blues dobro. But the zither. Well, Jasper's playing was close enough to the baroque music that those dogs love so much. They dragged that poor old man kicking and screaming to his final resting place. You'd think they were throwing him into the lake of fire by the way he fought."

"A-yow. It was time for me to go. Thank you kindly, sonny. A-yow." Clubfoot Jasper sits in Daddy's chair with Idjit on his lap. Jasper looks young and spry with a gleam in his eye, not a day over 20 or so it would seem. He appears vital, not like the twisted old blues-man I knew.

"Jasper, I'm sorry. I should have got another guitar for you. I wasn't thinking. Things got crazy and I just wanted to get you out of there. I didn't know it was going to kill you."

"It's aw-right." Jasper flashes a grin; the diamond in his gold tooth glimmers. "Dis where I done needed to be for long time. A-yow. I's jus' too dang stubborn and dumb to realize it." Jasper scratches Idjit's neck and then sniffs his fingers. "A-yow. Musky."

"So you're not mad at me?"

"Haw-haw-haw. A-yow," Jasper laughs. "Dis place even better den da Paradise Inn with its magic fingers and adult movies. All dem mistreaters I put out dey mis'ree. Dey ain't so bad now dat dey's rid of dem earthly bodies, A-yow. And dey's all waiting here for me. I done put dem where deys needed to be. Dey's better off. An' now you done da same for me, A-yow. Alls I does is eats country ham with red eyed gravy and plays da sweetest blues picking I's ever played. My hand works and my foot's like new. And I sexes up a diff'rent one a my ladies whenevers I's in da mood. A-yow. And we even gets HBO here."

"You've done a fine job." Mr. Eshu is now in Daddy's chair with Idjit at his feet. "Nobody else was able to help me with Jasper. Did you know that that stubborn old coot was 102 years old and would have kept on going if it hadn't been for your help."

"You shittin' me?" I ask.

"I wouldn't shit you, son, you're my favorite turd," says Mr. Eshu with a grin. "For your help, I am going to grant you a favor. You don't realize how close you are to joining your Daddy and Clubfoot Jasper. You don't have the life force to carry you through to getting back to Erwin. I'm gonna give you a little boost. Just enough juice to get you there ... if you don't fool around, that is. And do me a favor when you get there."

"What's that?"

"Get a rag and some Windex and clean the glass door on the front of the Brahman Bar."

"You got it."

"And don' forget yo' mojo boogie-bag," adds Jasper.

"It looks like it's time for you to wake up now," interrupts Idjit. "Otherwise you're going to get poked with a sharp stick."

"Huh . . . "

**22**

"Okay people, I want you to take a look at these two gentlemen over here." The pedagogical voice floats above me, like the background noise of a television or radio, not enough to wake me up, but enough to become part of my dream. I am too exhausted to move or even open my eyes. "These two must be new. One Caucasian, one Negroid. This old black gentleman appears to have mummified. And they are both clothed. This must be some of Richard Keith's research. He is studying how clothes affect the decomposition process. Does anybody want to take a guess at how long this unfortunate gentleman has been deceased?"

Another voice, male, younger, and less confident suggests: "Well, the Caucasian subject appears to have been in a nasty motorcycle accident and then chewed on by a pack of sharp-toothed wild animals. He's barely recognizable as a human. Just going by the smell, I'd say he's not fresh. And, hmm," the voice hesitates, mulling something over, "clearly putrefaction is right around the corner. He has a distended, taut belly, thoroughly bloated. Like it's about ready to tear open and drain."

"Why the bloat?" asks the pedagogue.

"The bacteria in his system that normally feeds on proteins... breaking down a steak dinner or whatever... well, they are now feeding on him. There's a ton of them. He's like a giant hamburger for the bacteria."

"And..." says the pedagogue.

"And the bacteria produce gas in the process. But his sphincter[28] doesn't work. His stomach muscles don't work. The small intestine has probably sealed itself off. The gas has nowhere to go. So his stomach bloats. And his is really bloated."

"What if we push on his stomach?" asks another voice, this one female.

"Give it a try," directs the teacher.

I feel a warm hand gently prodding my gut and I let out an enormous burst of flatulence. The kind that stays warm in your pants on a cold day. A chorus of *oooohs* and *uuugghs* follows, mixed with nervous laughter.

"Yes, people," says the pedagogue with a hint of humor, "cadavers can fart with a little prodding. Now somebody unbutton the pants and let's look at the genitals. The penis and the testicles are another area for high bacterial activity. Often the genitals will also suffer bloat and become overly enlarged... hmm..." I feel ventilation. "I would have guessed by the putrid smell of the intestinal gas that this one has been dead for three or four days.

---

[28] Contrary to popular understanding, a sphincter is not just a butthole. A sphincter is a circular muscle that usually controls a bodily orifice and can be constricted or relaxed as is necessary. The human body contains at least 42 different sphincters, some of them microscopic in size.

But, obviously no bloat has occurred in the penis and scrotal area. In fact, this unfortunate fellow's genitalia appear to be underdeveloped. I do note that there are insects and larvae gathering in that area though, which would indicate that he has been decomposing for perhaps a week. Given the lack of scrotal bloating, one would think he is very fresh. Quite interesting and perplexing."

"Can we prod the belly a little bit more?" asks the female. "I am curious about the apparent advanced stage of the bloating."

"Give it a good poke," says the pedagogue. "Let's see what happens."

"AHHHHHHHHHHHHH! AHHHHHHHHHHH!" I shoot into an upright position, screaming. A stabbing pain pierces my gut. I look down to see a stick . . .

*It looks like it's time for you to wake up now. Otherwise you're going to get poked with a sharp stick . . .*

. . . a sharp stick, parting the skin of my fleshy gut. "AHHHHHHHHH! AAAAAAAAAAH! SOMEBODY STABBED ME WITH A FUCKING STICK! AHHHHHHHHHHHH!"

A pale old man in a white jacket clutches at his chest and drops to the ground. A younger, tanner man, also in a white coat grabs the elder and quickly drags him away. Other younger white coated men and women run, one of them shrieking something about zombies and the undead. One man, dark skinned with a head of thick wiry black hair, stands in front of me and stares. The wide nostrils flare. One eye looks as if it had been stitched shut long ago. His face is badly scarred. He smiles in a way that makes me feel like his friend. "You're not dead," he says.

"I don't think so," I grimace as I pull the stick from my gut. My *Worlds Best Dad* shirt sops up my blood. "No thanks to whoever skewered me with this. Are you a doctor?"

"Not exactly," he smiles sheepishly.

"What about the white jacket?"

"Listen, let's get out of here," he says swiveling his head around suspiciously, like a bobble-head Jimmy "Superfly" Snooka, scanning the forest. "I will get you to a hospital. But you need to get out of here now. You're trespassing and I suspect that security will be here any minute. And I don't exactly need to be around when they start investigating this."

"Okay, help me up."

"What about your friend, the mummy?" The man nods at Jasper. "Is he still alive too?"

I look at Clubfoot Japsper. He looks much older. But the smile on his pruny face says it all. The man is finally at rest. "No, he's gone. Let's get out of here."

The man helps me to my feet and walks rapidly through the woods, obviously familiar with the territory. The woods still smell like death. When I was a kid we had a garbage disposal that broke when Mom was trying to grind up some rotten vegetables and a rainbow trout that sat in our fridge for too long. The disposer locked up and we had to wait a week for the repair man to show up. Mom wouldn't let anyone try to put their hands or anything else down in the disposal to try to clear the jam (*it'll cut your fingers right off, let a professional take care of this*). By the time the repair man arrived, the kitchen was so fouled up with the funk of dead fish and rotten vegetables that we couldn't even use the room. The repair man said that the smell would knock a buzzard off of a shit wagon. The odor of the woods reminds me of the garbage disposal, but worse.

As I run/stumble behind the man, I think I may still be dreaming. Out of my peripheral vision I think I see a bony hand reaching up from out of the ground. Further along I see a form slumped over the steering wheel of a rusted-out, abandoned car. I randomly think of a painting called *Waiting for AAA*. A dense cloud of flies buzzes in and out of the car's windows. "Hey, am I crazy, or am I seeing dead bodies all over the place out here?" I ask the man as I run behind him.

"Yeah. Yeah. You see dead people, alright Haley Joel Osment. You're seeing dead bodies. Just follow me and I'll explain later. We both need to get out of here right now."

We end up at a locked gate on the wooden fence that me and Jasper crawled under. The man ditches his white jacket and underneath he is wearing a pair of grey coveralls. The patch stitched on the coveralls says that his name is Chip. With his wide flat nose, kinky black hair and Polynesian features he looks as much like a Chip as much as I look like a DeShawn.

Chip pulls out a giant ring of keys and unlocks the gate. "Through here. Move it." Chip leads me to his car and tells me to get in. He wants to get away as badly as I do. "I'm going to take you to a hospital outside of this area. You're going to need medical treatment. But you don't want to stick around here."

"I don't want a hospital." I put my hand in my pocket and hold my mojo bag. Maybe it's all psychological. Maybe a bag full of boogers and poo doesn't give me good luck. Maybe it doesn't have healing powers. Maybe. But squeezing that smelly little bag sure as shit seems to make me feel stronger. "I need to get to Erwin. Do you know where that is?"

"Yeah, I live up in Lickskillet, just across the lake. I can get you to Erwin. Do you have any gas money?"

In the car Chip tells me that his real name is Mae Pake. He prefers to go by Chip. I don't blame him. I understand what it's like not to like your name. Chip says he's from the Hawaii. I notice fingers missing on his right hand as he steers the car. Chip notices me looking towards his hand. "Yeah, I know. The hand looks kind of fucked up, huh?"

"No. I wasn't looking at … "

"Hey. It's alright. You look worse than me. I'm only a little scarred up and missing some fingers. What the heck happened to you?"

"It's a long story. I doubt the ride to Erwin is long enough." I ask about the corpses in the woods.

Chip tells me that the woods are owned by the university there. The bodies in the forest are part of a government-funded study on the decomposition process of the human body. It's supposed to aid law enforcement agencies in determining the time of death for dead bodies they find. "It's like, hundreds of cadavers strewn about in all different positions and predicaments. They bury them in shallow graves, hang 'em from trees, put 'em in garbage cans. I've seen them dismembered and scattered about. Once they painted one green to see how paint would affect the decomposition process. I'm not really sure why that would be a concern, but they did it … "

"No shit."

"No shit, *Brah*. And they used to do shit that didn't seem so scientific to me. One *Kalohe* used to work here, he used to set them cadavers up around a picnic table when he was eating lunch. He'd just sit there munching on his submarine sandwich and carrying on conversations, laughing like those cadavers was the funniest people he ever heard."

"A forest full of dead people." I ponder it. "So that explains the smell."

"Yep."

"What are you, like a scientist or something?"

"No," smiles Chip. "I'm a maintenance man. That's why I have keys to the woods."

"Well, what's up with the white jacket?"

It turns out that Chip has worked as a maintenance man for the university for the past twenty years. During that time he has taken almost every class the university had to offer. Chip's cousin works for the registrar's office and has managed to insert his name into the roster for whatever classes he wanted to take, free of charge. Although never officially a student, Chip has managed to sneak into enough classes to have a PhD in science and hygiene, a master's in popular culture, a bachelor's degree of liberal studies, and an associate's in interior decoration. "All of it was possible because I kept things low key. Never any incidents, never any attention. Your little stunt may put me smack dab in the middle of an investigation. I mean, everybody thought you were a zombie. You were supposed to be dead and then you started screaming like you'd just been stabbed in the gut."

"I was stabbed in the gut."

"Regardless. I can't be around when they start asking questions about this. I'm this close ... " Chip holds his forefinger an inch away from his thumb " ... to becoming a certified crime scene investigator. I'm not going to let your little display ruin things for me."

As we drive Chip tells me about his degrees. He's the smartest custodian I have ever met. I ask about Hawaii. I've always thought it sounded cool with luaus and volcanoes and topless girls in grass skirts. Chip tells me he used to live on an island called Molokai.

"Molokai." I say it out loud and mull it over. "It sounds beautiful. Tell me about it."

"Okay," says Chip. "Molokai was the island where the government imprisoned people who had leprosy.[29] I was one of those people. Imagine a community full of sick people with lesions, bloody noses, loss of vision and general physical deterioration..."

"Sounds like Pittsburgh."

"Yeah, well, that's the upscale area of my village."

"So that's why your fingers fell off? You're a leper?" I ask as I make an attempt at inconspicuously sliding further away from Chip.

"I prefer to call myself a person affected by Hansen's disease. I don't like the negative connotation of being called a leper. And by the way, my fingers didn't fall off. It doesn't happen that way. It's not like you just fall apart. You don't sneeze and your face falls off. Your hands don't just drop off of your arms. You don't jump into a whirlpool and turn into oatmeal." Chip chuckles softly, bitterly. "And you don't have to hug your door like that. Relax, I'm not contagious. Most people can't even contract the disease anyway."

---

[29] Kalaupapa was the village on Molokai where lepers were forcibly isolated. The mandatory isolation law was repealed in 1969. A handful of people suffering from leprosy still reside there.

"So what happened to your fingers, then?"

"I cut them off with a hatchet while chopping wood. Couldn't feel a damn thing. Just kept on chopping. And then I saw my fingers scattered about on the ground. Did the same thing with my toes, and I didn't feel a thing. That's what happens. You're shit doesn't just fall off. You usually end up lopping it off while chopping wood or food or something."

"So, you're, like, cured?"

"Yeah, I'm cured. You're more likely to catch leprosy from an armadillo than from a person nowadays."

At the mention of armadillos my mouth begins to water. Arnette's possum on the half shell was damn tasty. "Are you serious? You can get leprosy from armadillos."

"Damn straight, *Brah*." Chip laughs. "You know them fools down in Texas, always having armadillo barbeques, eating the Hoover Hogs. They're feeding their faces with meat that has been known to carry one nasty bacterium."

"Hmm. I bet a lot of people don't even realize that, huh?" I say. My ear starts to feel funny, like it's going to fall off.

Chip keeps on driving. I hold one hand to my ear and grip my mojo bag in the other. Chip tells me that he read a story in the newspaper about a high school football player in Texas who would practice his tackling by diving on wild armadillos. "He caught an armadillo social disease," says Chip. "The fool ended up infected with lepromatous leprosy." Chip chuckles to himself and shakes his head. "Well, we're passing through Lickskillet now. I'll have you in Erwin in no time."

**23**

Just after Lickskillet, Chip turns left onto Electric Avenue and tells me we're taking the ferry across Norris Lake. He says it'll be quicker that way. The old cable ferry looks to be barely seaworthy. Chip eases the car up onto the rusted-out punt and it feels as if it's sinking. We are the only ones on the boat besides the ferryman.

"Halloo there boys," says the ferryman. "Name's Charon. I'll be ferrying you across the lake. We're gonna wait around a little bit to see if anybody else wants to come along."

The ferryman is immediately likeable. With his black Greek fisherman's cap, wind-chapped cheeks and closely trimmed white beard, Charon looks like he may have been a model for one of those fisherman-head ceramic mugs. He looks us over, me looking like the walking dead, and Chip with his missing digits and sewn-up eye. "Well dang it, as my granddaughter would say, 'you two are tore up from the floor up'. Are you boys alright?"

"We're fine, *Brah*," Chip flashes that friendly grin and the cloud of concern hovering above Charon's head dissipates.

"Yeah," I agree, "I look a lot worse than I feel." I squeeze my mojo bag and actually feel much better than I have in days despite my obviously worsening condition. My ear still feels like it's going to fall off if I sneeze or something though.

We chat with Charon and wait for other passengers, making the kind of small talk that strangers make while waiting in line or for a bus: weather; the water; hey, how about that local sports team. But the feeling underneath the talk goes much deeper than the superficial conversation. Charon is comfortable for me, familiar, like a kindly grandfather type. When it appears that no other passengers will be joining us, Charon clangs the gates on the end of the boat shut and we shove off, still gabbing, still enjoying the company.

"This is a beautiful, lake," I say as I take in my surroundings. The water is clear and looks cold. I look over a side-rail and see a school of large brown fish swimming beside the boat, escorting us to the other side of the lake.

"Yeah," grunts Charon. "It is beautiful. I love it like a child. I love to look at it, listen to it, smell it. I learn from the water. One can learn much from water."

The thick diesel fumes from the boat gag me and make it hard to breathe. I try to hold my breath until the wind blows the fumes away from me. I breathe deep and quick whenever the wind shifts and diverts the exhaust. I start to feel nauseous and dizzy, either from the fumes or the alternating hyperventilation and holding of my breath. My vision starts to tunnel and Charon's face blurs. As I begin to consider either fainting or hurling over the side of the boat, we approach the opposite shore. The wind blows the fumes away from me again and I breathe fresh cool air in, deeply, slowly. The oxygen clears my head. The school of fish breaks away from the boat, maybe waiting just offshore to escort Charon back to the other side.

"Um," Chip pats at his pockets and shrugs his shoulders at Charon, "I left my wallet at work. I'm afraid I don't have anything to pay you with."

"That's okay," Charon smiles at us, "I kind of had a feeling. I didn't really expect any payment from you. You will pay me back sometime."

"Really?" Chip smiles again at Charon. It seems that the two men also sense the newly established friendship.

"Really. I have learned from the lake. Everything comes back. You fellows will come back through, one way or the other. For now, may your friendship be my payment." Charon laughs as he pats me on the back. "Now, farewell. May you think of me when you sacrifice to the gods."

Me and Chip step into his car and pull onto land from the front of the ferry. "I don't wanna talk no stink, but, uhh . . . that was kind of weird, *Brah*." Chip shakes his head.

"What?"

"You know, that whole *think of me when you sacrifice to the gods* thing. He was a pretty cool old dude, but, I mean, what the heck was that?"

"I don't know. But I kind of liked him." Parting from Charon, I found myself smiling at his friendliness. He is like Idjit Galoot. Many of these people that I am meeting are like Idjit. All seem to be grateful, although they are the ones who deserve my thanks. All are subservient and wish to be my friends. They are like children who wish to obey and think very little. "I hope that he is right and I do see him again."

Chip talks to me the whole time he drives, not even seeming to pay attention to where he's going. Before I know it, we are almost to Erwin.

**24**

We pull into Erwin and I'm feeling about half past dead. Several vacant black and white police cruisers sit outside of the Egg Hut. I look the other way. The last thing I want at this point is to be made by Major Pickles. Gravel crunches under the tires in the Brahman's parking lot. The building is still; the neon bull is sleeping. The lights are off. It's still early afternoon. Ramona hasn't even opened up for her nightly business yet. I tell Chip that I need to go inside.

"Looks like a nice place, *Brah.*" I open the door and step out. Chip doesn't. "You go ahead. I'll just wait out here for you. Once you're done with whatever you have to do, I can still take you to the hospital to get your gut looked at."

The front door of the Brahman is locked and no lights are on inside. I cup my hands around my eyes and try to look through the glass. All I can see is heartbreaking darkness and swirling forms in the smudged up glass, forms that look like screaming faces. The faces trapped in the door are not readily apparent. They're more like the image of Mother Mary that some might see on the windows of an office building or a rust spot that resembles Jesus on the side of a water tower.[30] But those faces are there, clear as day if you're willing to stare intently and let your eyes go out of focus, kind of like looking at one of those magic eye pictures. Standing slack-jawed in front of the door, I study the images and remember Eshu's request that I clean the glass. And then I see my own face, reflected back at me as if the door is some sort of fun-house mirror. The distorted reflection is weeping.

I pull hard on the glass door. It moves a little more, like it wants to open. I pull harder in rhythmic jerks. On the forth or fifth tug the door opens for me. "Ramona?" I call out as I walk into the darkness. No one answers my call. I look out the front door and waive to Chip, asking him to come in. While he gets out of the car and heads toward the building I go behind the bar and pop open a couple of Pabst Blue Ribbons for us.

"What are you doing, *Brah*?" asks Chip as he enters the bar.

"Waiting," I answer. "I need to speak with the owner of this place. She should be in any time now."

"Aren't we kind of, you know, trespassing here?"

"She's a friend, it's okay." I hand Chip the bottle of beer I opened for him and he seems more comfortable with hanging out.

"Go ahead and help yourself to the drinks if you want." I grab a bar rag and a spray bottle of glass cleaner from under the bar. "I've got something I gotta do." The front door is even dirtier

---

[30] In 1978 a woman in New Mexico was making burritos and noticed a strange skillet burn on one of the tortillas. She believed the burn to be the image of the face of Jesus Christ. A priest reluctantly blessed the tortilla and the woman built a shrine for it. Thousands of people flocked to the shrine from around the United States to witness the blessed tortilla and pray for cures for their ailments.

from the inside, smudged with smoke residue and spit and beer, mingled with the body oils from the hands of the patrons and years worth of dust. I spray half of the bottle on the glass, starting at the top of the door. The cleaning solvent drips down the window, cutting clear moist paths in the smudge. I wipe at the window and in no time the rag is a dripping, dirty black swatch of cloth. All I accomplish with the rag is smearing the blackness around on the glass and it looks no better than when I began. I return to the bar and grab a box of clean bar rags and several bottles of cleaning solvent to use on the door. Rag after rag becomes a muddy black mess. I empty bottle after bottle of cleaning fluid. With each rag I begin to see improvement in the window. The pile of rags beside the door bleeds out onto the floor. I clean the door both inside and out. I wipe the last smudges from the glass and stand back to appreciate my efforts. The glass is clear, almost invisible. I look out onto the parking lot and recognize a group of patrons from before when me and Denny were here. I recognize Crash and Peaches in the slow-moving congregation as it approaches.

And then, without saying a word to each other, the motley looking group stops. They look at each other. Crash slaps himself in the head, turns and walks away, shadowed by Peaches. The rest of the crowd breaks apart and walks away from the bar. I am reminded of thoughtless lumbering zombies from the movies.[31] When they get further from the bar I see them begin to appear human again in their movements and actions. The happy hour crowd makes a group decision to forego the Brahman for the eve-

---

[31] See *Shaun of the Dead* for one of the best zombie movies ever. It has identical twin zombies.

evening. I go to sit at the bar with Chip. We open two more beers and just sit. No talking. No laughing. Nothing. Chip picks little bits of dead skin from around his remaining fingers and piles it up in a little mound on the bar. I decide to look for Ramona upstairs in her apartment. Chip decides to stay at the bar.

Around the side of the building and up the stairs to Ramona's apartment. Hand knocking on door. The sharp raps ring out unanswered: lonely, pregnant question marks dangling impotently from Ramona's doorknob. Uncooperative doorknob, refusing to turn. Where is she?

"I don't usually do this," I hear Ramona's voice, "but you seem so nice." She rounds the corner of the building with her hands looped around the elbow of a young man. The man holds a full paper bag that says *Egg Hut* on the front. They stop at the bottom of the stairs. "My God!" says Ramona when she sees me leaning against her door. "I knew you were going to be in bad shape but I didn't expect this." She takes the bag of food and sends the young man away.

Ramona opens the door to her place and a whoosh of warm smoke and cat urine air washes over me. I follow Ramona into her place. She sets the bag of food on her table and begins pulling out Styrofoam containers of Egg Hut grub. Somewhere a bell rings and I salivate as the smell of the greasy food hits me.

"We have a bucket of griddle taters that have been smashed, squashed, splattered, chewed, chunked and spewed," Ramona says as she sets a steaming paper bucket onto the table. The grease from the food has already begun to soak through the bucket. I pick up the container, leaving an oily stain on the table. Inside is the tastiest, greasiest looking glop of potato mess I have ever seen—a glistening oily clusterfuck of hash browns, ham, cheese, onions, peppers, some sort of brown stuff and little bits of crispy fried gristle. "I also have a mess of scrambled eggs. I know you like eggs," she says. "I hope you like them swimming in butter. They use two sticks of butter to cook up each order. Guaranteed to clog up the arteries." She licks her lips and smiles at me.

I load up griddle taters and buttery eggs onto my plate. I tell Ramona about a man in a yellow hat and an abandoned basset hound and my dead Daddy relaxing in a chair. I tell her about category five hurricanes and exploding Mexican headwear. I speak of injuries and visions and epiphanies. I tell of adventure and loss. Ramona sits and listens as I tell her, through a mouthful of masticated breakfast food, about turkey vultures and skunk apes and giant RV's shaped like wieners. And, I tell her that I need to cancel our contract.

"Well, I don't usually void my transactions," she says, "but, I'll make an exception in your case." She looks me straight in the eyes and says: "I can't have the daddy of my baby being a soulless monster, now, can I?"

"*Phhst-t-t-pyow!*" I almost choke on my eggs and then manage to spit-spray them out onto my plate. "Baby?" The one word is all I can manage. "Baby?"

Ramona comes up behind me and rubs my shoulders. "Calm down, you big wuss. There ain't no need to bust a grape over this. I don't expect nothin' from you. God knows we don't need to get married. I don't want child support or anything like that. I just want to make sure you're around for this little man."

"How do you know it's a boy? How do you even know you're pregnant? It's only been a few days, a week, I don't know. It's too short of a time to even know. How do you know it's mine? Can you prove it? What do you want from me? How can I be responsible for this? What? Do you want me to take it home and take care of it? Oh yeah! Mom's just gonna love that. Is it healthy? What do we name it? How's Idjit gonna feel about this?" I am unable to stop the frothy diarrhea of questions bubbling from my mouth.

"Calm down." Ramona rubs my head like she's petting a dog. My foot thumps on the floor. "I just know. But let's worry about all of this later. We have more pressing business right now." She comes around to my side and sits down and mutters to herself while digging through a handbag the size of a small suitcase. "Now where did I put that?" She makes a mountain on the table out of the contents of her purse. The pile in the middle of the table grows as she adds on half-full cigarette packs, containers of breath mints, a tube of something called *Gyno-Vagiclean*, a Kiss Alive 8-track tape, a pair of swimming goggles. Ramona continues to dig through the purse and extracts crumpled receipts and battery powered whatzits and pandoodles. She stacks up popguns, pamponas, pantookas and drums, checkerboards, bizzledinks, popcorn and plums. With the purse near empty and a precarious pile of teetering handbag debris on the table, she looks up and says, "Ah, here it is," and hands me a wadded up piece of napkin. I try to uncrumple the tissue and part of the napkin sticks together.

"Ugghhh. Did you blow your nose on my soul?"

"I blew my nose on the contract," she says. "I sneezed and had stuff dribbling down my lip. I needed to wipe it off with something. But it ain't like I wiped a booger on your soul. Just on the stupid contract. And I'm giving it back to you now so don't bitch about it." She empties an ashtray and hands me an antique brass cigarette lighter. "Go ahead, burn that thing up, before I change my mind."

The napkin sits on the table in front of me. I peel the boogered-up portions of the napkin apart. She blew her nose right on my name. The ink is smeared beyond readability. I study the napkin that caused me so much trouble. Something scratches at the door and Ramona opens it up, letting in a mangy old German Shepherd. The dog approaches me and curls up at my feet.

"What's up with the fleabag?" I ask and instinctively reach down to scratch his head.

"Oh, that's Crazy Chester's dog, Jack. He fixed a little boat I have. I like to get out on the lake once in a while. It was strange, he didn't ask me to pay him for the repair work. He just asked that in return I take old Jack." Ramona grins as she looks down at the dog. "He's sweet but he's a lot of work to take care of and he stinks like a grease trap. If you're gonna renege on that con-tract we had, well, I also want you to take the load off of me and take that old dog when you go."

Jack whines a little bit and stares me down with bloodshot eyes. He's no Idjit Galoot, but he seems like a good dog. What the hell, he can be my travel buddy for the rest of my journey. And if Idjit approves, maybe Jack will come down to Florida with us. "Alright," I agree, "I'll take Jack your dog."

"Well, then, quit yanking your crank and let's get on with it," says Ramona. "Let's torch that stupid napkin."

I turn the wheel on the antique lighter. The flint throws a spray of sparks and fires up the wick. I hold the napkin over the blue tip of the flame and it goes up in a poof like a big sheet of flash paper, larger than you would expect from a small bar napkin. Without thinking I yank my hand back and throw the flaming paper across the room. The fiery ball lands on the cat. Earnest takes the flame on like an oily rag and runs about the room, setting fire to furniture, dirty clothes, curtains and paneled walls. Ramona screams. Jack howls. Earnest shrieks in a way that is almost human until his still flaming body drops on its side and sets fire to the carpeting.

"Get out of here!" I shout at Ramona. We run for the door and Jack follows us. At the top of the stairs Jack gets caught up under my feet and I fall forward onto Ramona. We roll down the stairs, a mass of flailing limbs and dog parts, each of us hitting something hard on each step on the way down. At the bottom of the stairs I pull myself out of the heap and wipe blood from my eyes. I look up to see black smoke pouring from the door of Ramona's apartment. Jack pulls himself away from the building with his front legs, the back legs dragging uselessly behind him. Ramona is unconscious, her arms and legs bent at painful angles away from her torso. I try to stand so that I can pull us away from the burning building. My left leg buckles under me and shoots a flow of burning pain all of the way up to the back of my head. A hand grasps the back of my shirt and pulls. Me and Ramona are being dragged backwards away from the bar. Chip has one hand on my shirt and is gripping Ramona's hair in the other hand. He drags us all of the way back to his car and then carries Jack over to us. I hold Ramona by the head and talk to her. She doesn't answer. My mind goes fuzzy. I hear footsteps and sirens above me just before I pass out.

25

The ambulance smells like dog. I come to and my vision clears. I look to my left and see Jack the dog in a gurney beside me. The EMT's are working feverishly on him while I lay in my own gurney, neglected and in pain. "Good God!" I say. "Are you transporting a dog in your ambulance."

One of the paramedics gasps at the sound of my voice and turns in my direction. "Oh! Oh! Max! He's alive!" the man says to his coworker, and they both turn to look at me.

"Of course I'm alive. Why wouldn't I be? I feel pain in places I didn't even know I had. I'm oozing fluids out of every pore in my body and for some reason, my asshole hurts. But I'm alive."

The other emergency medical worker, Max, stares at me. "You were dead. You had no heartbeat, no breathing, nothing. This is a miracle." Max rubs the back of his left hand against the hair on his head and makes a confused circle with his mouth.

"You guys were working on that dog instead of me, weren't you?"

"Yeah, he was my dog and I gave him to your friend, Annie. We figured that since you were a goner, we would work on saving Jack," says the man. I realize that he is Crazy Chester. "But none of that matters. You were dead and now you're alive again. You're in bad shape and you need to not get worked up." Chester turns to look at Jack once more then turns back at me with watery eyes. "Listen buddy, I think you broke your back when you tumbled down those stairs. I'm going to see to it that you recover. I'll make sure they fix your back, if you'll take Jack my dog. Agreed?"

"Agreed." It seems like the right thing to do, taking the dog. "But I'm in a shitload of pain right now. Can you do something for me?"

"We're way ahead of you." Max tries to hand Chester a syringe, fumbles it, and drops it on the ground. "Uh-oh, I dropped it," says Max as retrieves the syringe and hands it to Chester. Max steps away and rubs the back of his hand on his hair again.

"What's in that?" I ask.

"Morphine," answers Chester as he jabs the needle into my arm and pushes the plunger. "That should take care of the pain." Warmth spreads throughout my body. The pain recedes and I begin to sweat. The urge to vomit builds. Everything looks as if I am viewing it under water. I mutter something about Idjit Galoot. A muted clicking sound ticks off, *di-di-di-di-di-di-di-di*, as Chester and Max do a slow-motion turn away from me and go back to work on the dog. I sink into opiate soaked delirium.

In a dimly lit room, sitting cross-legged on a tattered Turkish rug is Idjit. He holds the bowl of a long bamboo pipe over the flame of a small lamp and takes a pull. Idjit exhales slowly, the white smoke envelopes his head. He passes me the pipe, saying nothing. All around on the floor are men sucking on long pipes like the one Idjit hands to me. Some are sleeping. Some stare off into the darkness. One hums softly to a sparse arrangement of bass and saxophone playing somewhere above us. I hit on the pipe and choke a little on the fruit-like, not unpleasant, smoky taste.

"Sit back," says Idjit. He hands me a long tubular pillow. "We can talk while you enjoy the pipe. As Albert Einstein said, 'I believe that pipe smoking contributes to a somewhat calm and objective judgment in all human affairs.'"

I hold the pipe over the flame of the lamp and take a long pull until the glowing glob in the bowl goes black and turns to ash. Smoke sluggishly exits from my mouth and nostrils, as if it has no better place to go, leaving in its place a vagueness of mind. "Yeah," I laugh, "these guys in here look as if they have a calm and objective judgment in their affairs."

The men lounge about on the floor, staring at the ceiling, humming to the infectious mellow soundtrack of bass and saxophone. One digs in his bellybutton and then holds an index finger under his nose, sniffing it as if it were a flower.[32]

"These men are seeking answers, as you should too," says Idjit. "There are opium dens where one can buy oblivion, dens of horror where the memory of old sins can be destroyed by the

---

[32] Graham Barker, of Perth, Western Australia, is the world record holder for collecting navel lint. Barker has been collecting the lint since 1984 and keeps it in jars. See www.feargod.net/fluff.html for Barker's story.

madness of sins that are new. This is not such a place. That is not opium you smoke. That is life. That is my body. That is my blood. That is my essence." Idjit rolls a tarry black ball between his paws and places the goo in the bowl of his pipe. He holds the bowl over the lamp to warm the contents and then hands the pipe to me. "Take a long pull and hold it. Hold on to me as long as you can."

Holding the bowl over the flame of the lamp, I inhale as deeply as possible and hold the vapors. Idjit smiles and tells me "it's real good that you done that, getting the contract back from Ramona. Now just keep holding your breath." I hold the smoke in with all of my will until everything goes black and I deflate. Waves of tranquility wash over me.

In my darkness I hear random noises: beeping, respiration, growls, barks, voices, elevator music, the voice of Rod Roddy telling somebody that they've won a *Newwwwwwwww CARRRRRRRR*, Mom crying, babies crying, me crying, the buzzing of insects. In the silent lulls between the noises I return to a catatonic state, which is quite restful. I am occasionally visited by Idjit.

My arms and legs refuse to move, no better than hunks of wood nailed to my torso. My eyes don't open when I ask them to. My lips won't speak. I know I am in a hospital. Sometimes it seems that I am awake and can hear what is happening. Sometimes I can't tell sleep from dreams. In my gut I feel a wiggling, a gnawing, a buzzing. In my dreams, or maybe in reality, it feels as if something, a large rat or maybe a dog, is chewing on the open wound in my belly. Unable to scream at the pain, I try to direct my dreams away from the gnawing sensation. Most of the time, though, there isn't pain. Just blackness.

I have learned to measure days by the voices of Bob Barker and Rod Roddy. If I am not dreaming, demented, or delusional, then somebody watches The Price is Right every day at 11:00. *Come On Down!* It seems that after The Price is Right, somebody pulls a tube out of my dick and reinserts it. There may also be some sort of suppository application happening too. It's hard to say. My ass is always sore. I sleep. I wake. I sleep. I wake. I sleep. I wake. I don't know which is which. Sometimes I visit Idjit; sometimes he visits me.

The elevator zips upward and I melt into an iridescent oil slick of a puddle on the floor. Elevator doors open to a white waiting room. I regain solidity and pull myself out of the puddle that has become me on the floor of the elevator. The waiting room is completely white. The furniture is white. Ceiling and floor, white. Cold, antiseptic white. Idjit sits at the receptionist desk, his ears rolled up in a bun on top of his head and snapping on his gum. "Welcome," he says, "to the waiting room. Have a seat. Read a magazine. Make yourself comfortable. You may be here for a while." On the tables I see out of date Readers' Digests and Highlights magazines. I am reminded of Goofus and Gallant and find myself smirking. Goofus is cool.

"The waiting room for what?"

"The waiting room. Waiting to go wherever it is you're supposed to go."

"Like purgatory or something?"

"Yeah, kind of," says Idjit. "But purgatory is a Catholic invention. And they got the whole thing wrong. Purgatory is all about punishment for venial sins and obtaining purification so that you get to go to heaven. That's all a bunch of hooey. Those in the waiting room are incomplete for some reason or another. Usually it's not even their fault. And here is where they wait until they reach whatever state it is that is deemed necessary to become. And then they go wherever it is that they are supposed to end up."

"Who are they and what state is necessary and for what purpose?"

"Hey, I'm on a need to know basis. I'm working this job through a temp agency. I'm just taking this all in and speculating to a certain extent."

The room is filled with long-legged beautiful women. Some wear skimpy swimsuits and others evening gowns. Just waiting. They strike perfect poses and look bored. Every once in a while a primitive looking man or woman wanders through the room looking confused.

"What's up with the babes?" I ask, checking out the women.

"They're supermodels," says Idjit.

"No duh. Why so many models in the waiting room?"

"You remember some of those documentaries we would watch where the African tribes wouldn't let people take their pictures because they were afraid it would capture their souls?"

"Yeah."

"Remember how you laughed at how stupid those, what did you call them . . . cavemen . . . were?"

"Yeah."

"Well, they were right. At least partially."

"No shit."

"No shit," Idjit laughs. I laugh. "But it's not like you take one picture and you have somebody's soul. It's more like each picture chips away at you just a little bit. A tiny fragment of your being is flaked off. For most of us it's insignificant. But, if your picture is taken over and over and over . . . "

"Like if your career is having your picture taken . . . "

"Exactly," Idjit taps his nose and points at me. "If your picture is taken all of the time, then eventually your soul just kind of flakes away."

"And it's totally gone?"

"Not totally. There's always a little kernel left. But all of those little flakes have to catch up with you. They have to find you. Sometimes it takes a long time. And in the meantime you have to wait."

"In the waiting room. I get it." I look around and notice that not everybody in the room is physically beautiful. "But not all of these people were super-models though, huh? I mean look at that woman over there. Who'd want her picture?" In the corner sits a spry looking creature, contemptible and insignificant.

"Yeah," says Idjit. "She was a meter maid. She probably deserves to wait for a long time. I don't even see her on the list. I suspect she probably is waiting to be sent to her own personal hell. And the skeezy bitch probably deserves it."

"And what about those primitives over there?" I point to a small tribe of practically naked dark-skinned people in the corner who look like something straight out of a National Geographic special. "I thought that those people wouldn't let their pictures be taken for fear that they would lose their souls."

"It's not all a bunch of people who had their souls photographically eroded," explains Idjit. "I was just giving you an example. All of these beings here, for one reason or another, are incomplete. They have to wait. And once the waiting is done, they go through the door."

"Give me another example then."

"Um . . ." Idjit looks around the room and points to a young man sitting and reading a torn up magazine. "That fellow over there is an identical twin. He's waiting around for his brother. Turns out that there is only one soul for identical twins. The soul enters the embryo at the time of conception. When the embryo splits, half of the soul goes with one twin and half with the other. When one identical twin predeceases the other, he has to wait around for the sibling's demise so that the essence can once again become one."

"I always knew there was something weird about identicals."

Behind Idjit's desk is a wooden door on cast-iron hinges that looks like a door to a castle or something. Above the door is a sign that reads: THE DOOR.

"What's behind THE DOOR?" I ask.

"Oh it's beautiful," raves Idjit. "There's a long hall with a bright light at the end. You float down the hall and when you get to the light you feel complete serenity and love. Beings made of light greet you there. All of your loved ones will be waiting on you to have a big party. And the air tastes sweet, like cotton candy. Once you get your wings, halo, and harp, they open the gates of heaven and let you in where you will live a life of persistent peace, happiness and contentment."

"Wow! Really?"

"Wow! Really?" Idjit mocks me and laughs. "No, not really. I have no idea. I told you, I'm on a need to know basis. For all I know, that's the executive washroom. I haven't seen anybody go in or out."

"What do they need you here for then?" I ask.

"Don't know," says Idjit.

"Well what do you do most of the day?"

"I play spider solitaire on the computer mostly. They don't have any good games on here and won't give me access to the Internet."

"That sucks!"

"Tell me about it."

"Hey," I say to Idjit. "I have to go. Something is gnawing on my gut."

"Baby, please don't go," he pleads.

"I must."

"Don't. Don't."

"Must. Must." I go.


I often return to the waiting room but Idjit is never working when I visit. The new receptionist is gruff and unlikable. She refuses to give me any information about Idjit. She's watching me, she says, always watching. I check back regularly, only to be rudely ignored and deprived of answers to my questions about Idjit.

Days pass. Weeks. Months. Each new day starts when I hear a voice telling me to *Come on Down*. The gnawing in my gut never goes away, although most of the other pains seem to have died down. Sometimes I hear a baby. Sometimes I smell barbeque ribs. Unconnected events flow into each other and I lack the ability to tie them together or even know if they are real or not. What is real? What's a dream? They merge into one for me. Random images and sounds come to me with no apparent connections. Smells, sensations, sounds, colors. I welcome the dreams. The thought that I will see Idjit again keeps my heart beating and my blood pumping. I have dreamed of Idjit. I will see him again.

After what seems like years Idjit comes to me again. He stands before me in the yellow robe of the ascetic. He looks sad and asks "why did you leave me?" I embrace Idjit, put my arm around him, he says, "call me Govinda." I draw him close to me and kiss him. He is Govinda no longer. He is Idjit no longer. Idjit is gone and I know this. He is now a woman. And out of the woman's gown emerges a full, firm breast, and I lay there and drink; sweet and strong is the milk from the teat. It tastes of woman. It tastes of man. It tastes of newly bloomed flower and the forest. It tastes of fresh air and morning dew, of sun and of forest, of every fruit and every pleasure. It is good. It is intoxicating. I feel fine, but I'm going to miss my best friend.

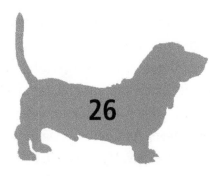

**26**

"Come on down!" shouts Rod Roddy, sending electric, spastic, synaptic transmissions flowing through my brain and spinal column, lighting up each and every nerve. Fire shoots through my veins. Almost to the point of explosion, the ghost of John Bonham pounds out Moby Dick on my heart with massive fucking baseball bats. I'm alive. Lightening bolts shoot from the sky directly into the top of my head. A thousand suns shine on my face and my whole being lights up. It's a fucking epiphany. For one moment, one nanosecond, it all comes to me. My journey makes sense. My travels were not random, meandering, empty experiences. My encounters were not unconnected and meaningless. I had purpose. I realize that for just a blink in my timeline I served some sort of a higher purpose. Maybe even a divine, spiritual purpose. Angels sing. The sky splits open and a giant bearded face that looks like Kenny Rogers floats above me.[33] Its finger lowers itself down slowly and pokes me in the

---

[33] See www.menwholooklikekennyrogers.com.

stomach. My belly tingles at the touch and I giggle like a doughboy. And then everything is normal.

I open my eyes. Beside my bed is Jack the dog, comfortably curled up into a big black and tan ball. He looks up at me and thumps his tail on the floor. I send a message to my feet. They wiggle under the sheets. Another message to my arms. My fingers twitch. I roll my wrists. My arms lift. I sit up, feeling weak. My atrophied muscles are tired from the little test.

I sit back and feel content. There's a feeling I get sometimes after I take a huge blow-out of a shit. Like my body is cleansed. The act of voiding the bowels releases endorphins or something and the result is a general feeling of contentment and satisfaction. There's a sense that everything is going to be okay. That's the kind of feeling I have right now. I jam a hand down between the mattress and my bare ass to check if I shit myself. I haven't. I just feel good. Jack rises and stands beside me at the bed. I scratch his head and relish the feeling of post-shit tranquility. Jack's eyes lock with mine. I know him. I know him well.

I've been in a coma for the past three years. This is what my nurse, Mildred[34], tells me. She says that my body sustained too much abuse and damage in such a short period of time that my system just shut down. Mildred shoos Jack away from the bedside and says: "It's like a coma *slash* post-traumatic syndrome

---

[34] Nurse Mildred Ratched, portrayed by Louise Fletcher, from *One Flew Over the Cuckoo's Nest* was voted as the fifth greatest villain in film history by the American Film Institute in 2003.

*slash* catatonic stupor that you suffered. You were out of it for a long time."

"What all was wrong with me?" I ask.

"Let's see," she says as she flips through the thick three-ring binder that is my medical chart. "Multiple contusions and lacerations, lepromatous leprosy, liver failure, broken ribs, bovine spongiform encephalitis, treponema pallidum, cracked skull, fractured wrist, gingivitis, halitosis, broken nose, acne conglobata, infectious carbuncles, priapism, Lyme disease, anal fissures, tinea cruris, toxic shock syndrome, Pneumonoultramicroscopicovolcaniosis."

"Sounds bad," I say. "How am I doing now?"

"Well, earlier this morning you were covered with bedsores and you smelled like you were well past your sell-by date. But you seem to be just fine now." She lifts my medical gown and looks at my stomach. "Well waddayaknow. It looks like your stomach wound has healed up too. We've left that gash open for three years. It looked like it was turning gangrenous so we recently decided to administer MDT. And it looks like it worked."

"What's MDT?"

"Maggot Debridement Therapy. Your injury wasn't healing, we just left it open and tried to keep it clean, but gangrene was setting in. So Dr. Zacharias started a regimen of MDT. He placed a small quantity of sterile maggots in your wound and allowed them to eat the dying flesh. He just retrieved the maggots from your wound earlier this morning. I'll tell you what, those bad boys really fattened up on your necrotic flesh. And," she shakes her head, "well, I've never seen this before, but your wound has already healed over just this morning."

I feel a buzzing in my stomach. "I think he left some in there. My belly feels funny."

"That's just the healing process. You'll be fine." She pats me on the shoulder and sighs. "We thought you were never going to come back to us though."

"Really?"

"Yep. We thought you were in a permanent vegetative state. One of your relatives was even trying to have you euthanized."

"Who?"

"You have a cousin, Denny, right?" She watches for recognition and continues when I nod yes. "He has been claiming that you told him if you ever were in a coma that you wanted no life-saving procedures. He says he was one of the last people to speak with you and you told him that. He's been trying to get the doctors to pull you off all machines. Once you were off almost all of the machines he was trying to convince the doctors to pull your feeding tube. Lately, you've actually been accepting spoon-feeding. So Denny's been petitioning the courts to just allow him to smother you with a pillow. The courts have rejected his petitions. But your cousin has garnered quite a bit of support from some of the different right to die groups. It's a good thing you woke up when you did."

"Yeah, that sounds like Denny," I sigh. It makes sense. Denny was obsessed with Dr. Kevorkian and his death machines. He used to say that Dr. Kevorkian was the world's greatest serial killer. He even bought Dr. Death's jazz-flute album. For a while it was all that Denny would play in his car. "Has anybody else been concerned about me or come to visit while I was out?"

"Well your parents will probably be in for their regular visit in just a little while."

"You mean my mom."

"No," Nurse Mildred shakes her head. "Both your mom and dad. They come up as much as they can. They are nice. And your dad looks so young."

"My dad is dead."

"Well he certainly looks alive to me," she says as she rolls me on my side and wipes my butt crack with a cold rag.

The cool, soothing wipe feels nice on my sore asshole. I realize I am hungry and ask for deviled eggs. Nurse Mildred tells me that she will see what she can do as she double-bags the wipe and throws it in a biohazard bin. She scrubs her hands in the sink until I can hear them squeaking against each other, wipes them dry, and tells me she'll be back later. She chases Jack away from my bed again before leaving.

"Oh, my baby." Mom runs into my room with tears streaming down her face. "My baby. My baby." She smashes my face into her bosom. The soft weight of her breasts on my face gives me the heebie-jeebies and with every little bit of muscle fiber left in my weakened limbs I fight to push my face away from her not-insubstantial boobage. "Baby, I knew you would be back. I knew it. I even made you one of my linty pillows so that you would be comfortable when you regained consciousness." Mom has always collected dryer lint. For as long as I remember the laundry room has been full of coffee tins, cat litter buckets, garbage bags and various containers packed with the fuzz collected from the lint trap of our clothes dryer. Mom used to put a ziplock bag full of lint in our school bags *for just in case*, she would say. She would brag about the versatility of dryer lint and claimed it could be used as fire kindling in an emergency. She said it absorbed bad odors in the refrigerator. Once, in a hushed tone, she claimed that lint was the secret to longevity. She would cram pillowcases with the fluff she scraped from the lint trap. Most of my life I have rested my head at night on a linty pillow. One time Frank told me that you could get high off of the stuff. I rolled up a tiny little dryer lint joint and tried to smoke it. The smoke gave me a headache and made me vomit.

Mom cries herself out and I gaze around the room. Behind her is a wooden cigar store Indian that says: "Hey there, Son. We wondered if we would ever speak with you again." It's not a cigar store Indian, it's Totem.

"Son?" I ask.

"Oh Baby," Mom sighs. "It got so lonely without you around the house. Ad it was so tough on me dealing with Idjit's failing health. Oh ... " she gasps and covers her open mouth with her hand. "I didn't want to tell you this yet. But ... "

"I know Mom, Idjit's gone."

"Oh, Baby. I didn't want to tell you just yet, but ... "

"Mom, I got to say goodbye to him. And it was beautiful." Mom's lips curve up into a relieved smile. "Now tell me why Totem is calling me Son."

"Well, Baby. You've been gone. Idjit's been sick. And Barney keeps getting denied parole. I started realizing that things were not going to work out with him. The prison wouldn't give us conjugal visits and my weekly visit with him in the visiting park was really starting to hurt my wrists. And meanwhile, I let this fine young man stay with me after you went crazy and took off from the new house." Totem sidles up and wraps an arm around Mom's waist. "Well. You just dropped this perfect little man in my lap and you know, things happened. I needed a man around the house and you weren't there. Anyway, we went on a casino cruise one night and had a few too many Appletinis. Next thing you know," she snaps her fingers, "the captain of the ship performs a ceremony and we're married. And it's been wonderful. Hasn't it, Totem Pole?"

"It has," Totem flashes a shit-eating grin at me. "Unadulterated bliss."

"It's just Totem, Mom. Just Totem."

"I call him Totem Pole," she says.

A queasy feeling grips my stomach as I look at Mom and Totem standing with their arms around each other. My stepfather is half my age. He'll probably try to tell me what to do around the house. No way I'm calling him Dad. Vague images of them in the bedroom try to creep into my head. Inside I am screaming. In order to avoid vomiting I change the subject and ask about the specifics of Idjit's demise.

Mom says that on the same day that I was brought to the hospital, Idjit was taken to a veterinary clinic by a woman who ran over him with her car. Idjit darted into the street right in front of her. Both the left front and rear tires thumped over him. Idjit was taken to the veterinary hospital and tended to. The vet removed Idjit's collar and called animal control to try to locate his owner. Both Mom and that nice boy, Kevin Emery[35], had checked with animal control on a daily basis so they knew how to get in touch with Mom. Mom told the doctor to do everything he could to save Idjit. And save him he did. Idjit recovered as well as an old dog can from such a thing. Kevin Emery took that dog and drove him all the way down to Mom in Sweetwater. Mom took care of the Galoot for me, trying to keep him hanging around until I came back. She says that every day he seemed to sleep more and move around less. They would have to coax him out of the house with deviled eggs. Mom would dump a beer in his bowl outside just to motivate him to get up and go out. Totem gave Idjit regular belly rubs to stimulate bowel movements. Over the past couple of weeks Idjit has slept almost continually, he has turned his nose up at both food and beer, like he just lost his will to go on. "Baby," Mom says. "I hate to tell you this, but Idjit Galoot passed away in the middle of the evening just last night. You just missed him. He's probably curled up at the feet of the Lord right now."

"What did you do with him?" I ask.

"I filled up the bathtub in the hotel room with ice and put him in there," says Totem. "We were going to put him in a freezer for you until you came back."

"But," says Mom, "now that you're back, we'll let you decide what to do with him."

"Keep him on ice and bring me his collar."

---

[35] He's such a nice boy. He used to mow the lawn.

Idjit's collar fits Jack perfectly. He wears it with pride, as if it were a three-karat cubic zirconia necklace with a matching butterfly pendant. Jack has stayed by my side since I came to this hospital, despite Nurse Mildred's efforts to kick him out of my room. Every day at eleven in the morning he would bark and howl until somebody would turn on The Price is Right. Eventually, they just made sure to turn the TV on each day a little before eleven o'clock. Jack was Chester's dog. Chester's father is on the board of directors for the hospital. Chester lives with his parents. Chester's father was tired of Jack chewing up his newspapers, humping the furniture, and barking in the middle of the night. Chester's father told Chester to get rid of the dog long ago. Chester's father was happy to hear that I agreed to take custody of Jack the dog. Chester's father made it so that Jack could stay in my room. Chester's father made it so that I could keep Jack, even in a coma. Chester helped to care for Jack during my downtime. Jack stayed in my room, by my side, for three years. Jack is my friend. My hospital room smells like Jack. Jack smells like Idjit. My room smells nice.

The day has been amazing, regaining consciousness and control. I become aware of new things and sensations every moment. I realize that I have an ankle bracelet locked onto my right leg. Mom tells me that I'm on house arrest. "I hired that big-city Tampa attorney you told me about," she says. "You were right. He is the best around. And a handsome devil to boot. I'll tell you what. If I weren't a kept woman . . . "

"Mom..." I stop her. "What do you mean I'm on house arrest? I haven't done anything."

"There were so many criminal charges against you." She shakes her head. "That prosecutor down in Clearwater, he hit you with every charge in the book: federal arson and property damage charges, DUI, aggravated battery, grand theft auto, possession of marijuana, kidnapping, accessory to murder, manslaughter, felony littering, trespassing..."

"Mom, none of that makes sense. Even if I was guilty of them things, how can they prosecute all of those different offenses, both state and federal, that occurred in different states, in one Florida state court?"

"I told you," she says, "I hired that Tampa lawyer that you said was so good. And he was. He managed to somehow get all of the charges consolidated. He pleaded you out to all of them and got you house arrest with adjudication withheld. That means you don't have a record as long as you can stay out of trouble."

"But, how could he plead me out when I'm in a coma. Don't you kind of, like, have to be conscious for something like that to happen. It just doesn't seem right to me. I'm in a coma, different charges from different states, all dealt with in one court that probably doesn't even have jurisdiction. Shit, I was never even in Clearwater. What kind of judge is going to allow that to happen?"

"It's Pinellas County, Florida," Mom laughs. "They don't care about jurisdiction, justice or any of that. Lighten up. You've got three years out of your sentence behind you. One year to go and you're done. Otherwise you could have ended up in the can just like Barney. You want to be in prison, getting traded for a pack of cigarettes? I don't think so." She raises one eyebrow at me. "I don't know how that attorney finagled it, but you got the deal of a lifetime for all of the charges they slapped you with. Now don't worry about that. You've got other things to take care of."

"Like what?"

"Like your son."

"My son?"

"Yeah. The little boy you had with that Ramona girl."

"I have a kid?"

Mom purses her lips, hands on hips, and nods, matter-of-factly.

"Why can't his mom take care of him? I can visit him on summer vacations or something."

"His momma's dead. She was hurt pretty bad falling down the stairs at her place. They said she should have made a full recovery, but she didn't. Just didn't have it in her to go on. She hung around until she brought the little guy into this world, held him for a couple of minutes, gave him a kiss, and then handed him to a nurse. After it was all over and the baby was taken care of that girl laid back in her bed and bled to death. Nobody even realized there were complications until it was too late. And she didn't say a word about it."

Mom and Totem have been raising the boy. They haven't given him a name. "That's your job," says Mom. She also says that he's the sweetest little boy that she's seen since I was his age.

Through my doorway walks a little redheaded boy, gripping onto Totem's hand and smiling. His blue eyes beam. He grips a rubber ball in his other hand. A good-looking boy, he looks just like me, minus two hundred pounds and three and a half decades of self-abuse. He radiates love. He is bursting with potential. Just looking at him I can see what a smart kid he is. *Oh my God*, I think, *I am going to fuck that kid up so bad*. I can't even take care of myself, let alone a two-year-old.

The boy climbs up on a chair next to my bed and locks his big blue eyes with mine. He's incredible, maybe a little dorky looking in the clothes that Mom dressed him in, but incredible. He holds the ball up to show it to me with a beatific look on his face and says "Ball-doo-Ball," as if he's sharing the meaning of life with me.

"What's he saying? Is he talking in French?" I ask Mom.

"He's showing you his ball. That's just the way he talks. Mostly it's about his balls and he says *doo* a lot. We're having him tested for that. It's a little bit weird. But he's a sweet boy."

"He looks like an Angus with that crazy red hair. Put a kilt on him and hand him a battle-axe and he could be an extra from a Braveheart battle scene. He's definitely an Angus." Yeah, Angus, just like the hurricane. Plus, Angus Young is the fucking man. Who doesn't love AC-DC? Whoever doesn't like AC-DC should be pushed down to the floor and kicked in the jaw with steel-toed boots until their face looks like a bloody bowl of oatmeal. My boy is an Angus. If you don't like AC-DC, Angus will split your skull with a Scottish Claymore broadsword.

"Angus it is, then," agrees Mom.

The days pass quickly now, more so than I would expect in a hospital room. Angus spends most of the time in the room with me now, talking to me about his *ball-doo-ball.* I am almost never alone. Mom stays with me sometimes. Other times Totem sneaks me some Pabst Blue Ribbons. We hide the dead soldiers in the dresser drawers. One morning Nurse Mildred chastised us when she opened a drawer and found it to be full of empties. Also much to Mildred's displeasure, Jack stays at the foot of my bed and we watch The Price is Right every day promptly at 11. I am surprised to see that the announcer on the show is not Rod Roddy, but instead some guy named Rich. I learn that Rod Roddy has been dead since 2003, before I went on vacation in vegetable-land. *How could I have been hearing him in my coma?* I wonder to myself.

On the day of my discharge, Mom wheels me out of the hospital in a wheelchair. I can walk just fine but it's hospital policy that I have to be taken out in the chair. The drive to Florida is calm and uneventful. I-75 stretches out before me and my family. The Georgia roadside is cluttered with billboards for Japanese spas where truckers can soak in murky hot tubs and obtain release from slant-eyed women of low moral standards. From the road we can see that one city has a water tower with a round top that is painted like a peach. The crack painted down the front makes it look like a giant ass. Angus laughs at the enormous butt. He is a good kid. We stop to get cheap gas before crossing the state line into Florida.

In Florida we pass RV's towing economy cars and pickup trucks with rebel flag bumper stickers. Tourist traps beckon. Every fruit stand off of every exit seems to have the cheapest tickets for the happiest theme parks. I tell Mom that I saw a sign for an Indian restaurant named the *Armpit Palace* and she tells me that it's just my mind playing tricks on me, that it's my pain pills making me loopy, that I'm still recovering. Memories of Fat Elvis and Clubfoot Jasper visit me, as if I was driving up I-75 with them the opposite way just yesterday. It all seems so fresh. We pass through Tampa, through Bradenton, through Sarasota. We stop at an Egg Hut. Me and Angus share a double order of griddle taters and a plateful of scrambled eggs. Mom says that it looks like I'm thinking real hard. She asks me what I'm thinking. I tell her that "I'm thinking I'll have me another plate of those fried taters, um-hmmm." Angus laughs. He's a smart boy. With our bloated grease-soaked bellies full of eggs and griddle taters, we sluggishly head out to the highway.

And we are on the road again. I give Jack a cardboard container full of carryout scrambled eggs. He eats it all, including the container. For the rest of the trip, Jack burps up sulfur belches. I nod off for a while without dreaming. Near the southern tip of the state Totem suggests that we take Alligator Alley across to the other coast. I tell him to take us across on the Tamiami trail. Angus agrees and tells Totem, "ball-doo-ball."

"Ball-doo-ball, it is," Mom agrees and tells Totem to take us through on the Tamiami trail.

The area outside of Arnette and Pervis's compound is still torn up from the hurricane. A mess of palmettos, palm trees and mangroves rises up around the cinder block building like a bird's nest. Hundreds of broken and faded plastic pink flamingos are tangled in the brush along with traffic cones, newspapers, beer bottles and random auto parts. A narrow path is cut out of the debris all of the way to the building. The fiberglass bun from the Bratmobile sits in front of their house.

The front door creaks open and out walks Pervis. He invites me in. "Come on in and have a sit down for a while." I tell him that I can't. I'm not even supposed to be stopping off anywhere that is not approved by my probation officer. Rest areas, gas stations, and restaurants are approved. Demented redneck backwoods party shacks with tin roofs and rust are not. If I stay too long I may be in violation of my house arrest. Pervis tells me that Buddy has taken to living in the swamps and says he's real secretive. Every couple of weeks Buddy will stop back in for supplies and "fellowship on the mellowship," as Pervis puts it. Arnette has been out for the past couple of days hunting the skunk ape. Pervis says that he thinks Arnette is closer than he's ever been to proving the big monkey's existence. Pervis shakes my hand and says that he will tell Buddy and Arnette that I'm doing fine. His strong grip makes my hand throb. Pervis helps me carry the heavy camping cooler into his building. I thank my friend for everything and tell him I'll be in touch soon. And we are on the road again.

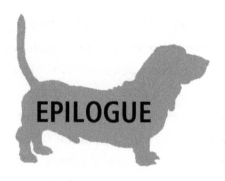

# EPILOGUE

House arrest is supposed to be brutal. They say that most people end up violating the conditions of their supervision and going to prison. Prosecutors call it the layaway plan because they know that usually their guy will screw up the probation for one reason or another and end up in prison. House arrest is supposed to be brutal. I thought it was awesome. I didn't have to look for work because my attorney also ended up qualifying me for disability payments due to my condition. The only thing my probation officer required of me was to get more schooling. First it was my GED, which I didn't even need because I already graduated from high school. And then, what with online college courses and correspondence schools, I'd managed to accumulate an ass-load of degrees. I got an Associates degree in paralegal studies and a Bachelor's in sociology. My Master's thesis was on the history of the Mississippi Delta Blues, and in particular, Clubfoot Jasper Moberly and his influence on popular music. I'm a licensed chiropractor and an ordained minister with the Universal Worldwide Spiritual Humanist Order of the Monasterial

Brotherhood. Through the Monasterial Brotherhood I have acquired impressive certificates that show that I have official Doctor of Divinity and Doctor of Metaphysics degrees. It took me all of about ten minutes online and Mom's credit card number to become ordained and receive my certificates. Now I can legally perform weddings, funerals, affirmation of love ceremonies, I can take confession, and I can do something called hand fasting, although I'm unsure exactly what that is. I can even start up my own church if I want to. I am mulling over the possibility of starting up the Ministry of the Monastery of the Flatulent Gastropod. But that seems like a lot of work and a lot of planning. For now I just want to hang with Angus and Jack.

The house is full. Mostly it's me, Angus, and Jack hanging around. And we are bums together. Mom cooks for us, lots of eggs, coffee cakes and breakfast foods. She squeezes us fresh orange juice from the wild orange trees in our back yard. It's so damn sour you can't drink it without loading it up with sugar. Angus makes his juice a sugary sludge before he'll take it. Totem hangs out and doesn't try to be my dad. And it's a good thing because Daddy has top billing in the house.

Daddy sits in his favorite chair in front of the TV. He still visits me in my dreams. Last night he told me to whack Totem in the head with a ball peen hammer while he was sleeping. Usually Daddy gives me good advice. I disregarded it last night. I kind of like Totem. I don't think I'd be as fond of him if he had a gooping head-wound. Right now Daddy is dressed in a Cleveland Browns jersey and souvenir helmet. He's getting geared up for football season. At his feet sits a perfectly preserved, stuffed Idjit. Pervis fixed him up real nice and lifelike. He even tricked out the Galoot a little bit with sparkling green glass eyes and a rack of antlers, just like on a jackalope. He looks tough, like he would disembowel you if you got too close to his food bowl. I move Idjit around the room just to give him a little variety. He likes it when I set him in front of the window and let him stare out at the egrets feeding in our front yard. Other times he likes to sit on the front porch to greet visitors. Sometimes Jack or Angus cuddles with him on the couch. Usually he's at Daddy's feet. They've become very close.

For the most part we watch TV. Jack likes deviled eggs and beer. Just like Idjit. Everything he does, every action, every bark, even the smell of his farts, is just like Idjit. It's eerie and comforting at the same time. Angus loves Jack. The big mutt absorbs the abuse from my boy like he took lessons from Rodney King. Angus loves Jack, and Idjit, and peanut butter and jelly sandwiches. The messy sandwiches with the crusts cut off are almost all he eats. The boy turns his nose up at most kinds of eggs. It concerns me but I tell myself that he'll learn to love them as he gets older.

Frank is now driving a tractor-trailer around the country for a living. His trucker name is Pigpen. Frank lives out of his rig and stays with us when he's not on the road. He hauls all kinds of meat and is always pulling a load of beef, pork or chicken. Sometimes he ends up with something exotic. When he does, he skims a box or two of the good stuff and brings it to us. Last time he stopped in he brought us a freezer full of giant tiger prawn. Each shrimp is over a foot long and weighs more than a pound. We go through gallons of cocktail sauce.

I try to keep up with the lives of the people I know. Arnette and Pervis visit us on a regular basis. Arnette says that he caught the skunk ape on video but was forced to destroy the tape by government agents in a black car. Arnette has been slowly approaching and befriending a band of the giant monkeys, trying to work his way into their group. Kind of like the Diane Fossey of Skunk Apes. Arnette's video supposedly caught images of him shaking hands with the troop leader. Even though the tape was confiscated, Arnette says that he still has proof of his encounter. He makes me sniff his hand. It smells like someone ate vomit and then shit it out onto a rotting skunk carcass. "That's the scent of a silverback male skunk ape," he beams. "That ain't never coming off."

Pervis always brings me a new creature to decorate the house. Last time he visited he gave me something he called a globster. It was just a squishy brown unidentifiable glob of mottled flesh with a kinked, hairless tail, teeth in random places, furry patches and twisted antennae jutting out awkwardly. According to Pervis, he found it one day when he visited the beach. I have to admit that it doesn't look manufactured. Either it's for real or Pervis is a master. He says that a ranger unsuccessfully tried to take the globster away from him. The ranger must have seen something in the old boy's eyes that made him back off and let him keep it. Pervis took it home, taxidermied it, and now it sits on in the middle of our kitchen table, a wonderfully horrid centerpiece.

Arnette says that Buddy has gone off of the deep end; Buddy now insists on being called *Bufo Bufo Gargarizans* and says that he is part of a skunk ape cluster. Although he can't confirm it, and Buddy won't say one way or the other, Arnette believes that Buddy may have fallen in with the French-Canadian broads that are still running around out in the swamp. Pervis says that they're probably licking psychoactive Cuban tree frogs out there and "trippin' balls." Buddy stops by Arnette and Pervis's place less and less, looking more disheveled, more like a madman with each visit. They show me a picture they snapped of Buddy the last time he stopped in. His hair is long and dirty, his beard unruly, matted and tangled. Buddy stands tall with his chin jutting out. He is nude, thin and muscular, and looks as if his beer belly just fell off and sunk to the bottom of the swamp. The shaggy body hair obscures his genitals, making him look a bit Sasquatch-like. Despite his physical appearance, the gleam in his eyes and the smile on his face indicate that he is not mad. Instead, Buddy has a look of utter bliss. He seems to me to have matured into a swamp-dwelling mystic, a holy man who has found answers to all of his questions. I wish him well and hope to see him again.

Denny is doing great. After giving up on his campaign to euthanize me, he went to Utah and retrieved his true love, Marie, sneaking her out of her little fundamentalist Mormon village in the middle of the night. Marie gladly went along with the abduction and let Denny bring her to Florida with him. As an ordained member of the clergy, I performed the marriage cere-mony and counseled the couple on the soul binding nonsense that had so worried Denny. Marie had no powers over Denny's spirit and just wanted to keep him around so she made up the story about getting him into heaven. After the ceremony we all sat around in the back yard, drank fruity punch spiked with pure grain alcohol and shot off fireworks.

Now and again I see people on TV that I met in the course of the Idjit rescue mission. Last night, on a national talent show, I saw Peaches singing the Safety Dance. Peaches, from the Brahman. And she was fucking awesome. The panel of judges just about came all over her with how good she was. Even "Hot Carl" Blumpkin, the show's host, couldn't stop raving. In the background, for just a second, I saw Crash, the dent in his head grown larger and softer, clapping his hands out of time and flashing a moronic smile that says *I'm in love and I have brain damage, I may have just smudged my pants, but I'm happy.* Occasionally I see someone on the news or some reality show that looks familiar. I get the sense that I know them. The cloying, smoky scent of the Brahman comes back to me. Were these people somehow imprisoned by the Brahman? Was it like quicksand for lost souls? Did I somehow free them from their chains by setting the bar on fire? Maybe Ramona was some sort of soul-sucking vampire, a succubus who enslaved the bar patrons with cheap booze and karaoke while she sapped their wills to live. I don't know. Maybe. Or maybe it's just the holes in my brain getting bigger, eating away at what little I have left up there.

Private investigators have come to see me lately about Kyle, the Bratmobile kid. He seems to have just disappeared into the swamps. He reappears spasmodically, taking a job at a pizza shop or car wash for a week or so and then disappears after his first paycheck is issued. It's the same every time. His boss will give him a paycheck and Kyle says that it's "like, so glorious and random." He cashes the check and then is not seen for weeks or months. The investigators say that his coworkers usually report that Kyle reeks of decomposition and stale malt liquor. With each reported sighting he has more body-piercings and tattoos. I always say that I'll keep an eye out for the kid. I can understand his parents' feelings. I know what it's like to have an errant loved one. I suggest to the investigators that they might want to check with Kyle's friend, Spencer. They say that they have. Spencer is still driving around the country in one of the Bratmobiles, handing out meat-whistles. All he does is smirk when they ask about Kyle and say that "what he did was glorious."

I still have the mojo bag that Clubfoot Jasper made for me. It brings me luck and serenity. It gives me guidance. It soothes aching joints, removes plantar's warts, and fights gingivitis. As part of my thesis work I lobbied the Rock and Roll Hall of Fame to induct Jasper. He was *THE* quintessential Mississippi Delta Bluesman. He was the blues. Jasper lived the music he played. He slept, ate and shit the blues. I mean, the man invented the *I-shot-my-cheatin'-woman-down* blues format, for Christ's sake. "It's crap," I told them, "that Muddy Waters and Bo Diddley and B.B. King are inductees, but not Clubfoot Jasper Moberly." Hell, even Jasper's friend Robert was inducted into the Hall of Fame. Don't get me wrong, those guys were all good, but they couldn't hold a candle to Jasper and his influence on rock music. My campaign on behalf of Jasper has thus far been disregarded. But I swear it on my mojo bag, the man will get his due.

Fat Elvis has settled down in Gibsonton. He rents a room from Denny and Marie and is dating my former aunt, Bernice. She wants him to move into the trailer with her. Fat Elvis says he loves Bernice but needs his space. "And I just cannot visualize myself cohabitating in a trailer with a feculent freezer loaded chockablock with doo-doo," he says. "You know what kind of an olfactory onslaught I would suffer in that manufactured home if we got walloped by a hurricane and the electricity went on the fritz." Every couple of months Fat Elvis will come and stay with us when he gets a gig playing on one of the gambling ships or cruises going out of Miami. It's good to see him. When he goes out to work a cruise he leaves me with the Stutz Blackhawk. Angus loves that freaky old car. Fat Elvis is out to sea right now, oozing the blues to a boatload of pasty Midwesterners and Canadians on their way to the Bahamas. When he gets back he will have loads of cheap t-shirts, hemp necklaces, Jamaican coffee, and duty-free booze to hand out. But while he's gone, we have the car.

Me and Angus and Jack are on the road again. We're driving the Atlantic coast, straight up A1A. Jack hangs his head out the window and his tongue dangles from the side of his mouth, flapping in the wind. Angus laughs at him. I sit on an inflatable hemorrhoid pillow as I drive because my asshole is sore. We have a cooler stocked with Pabst Blue Ribbon, deviled eggs and PB&J. It'll be a couple of days before Fat Elvis returns. I'm thinking Angus will like the Golf of Mexico. We should be back in time to pick Fat Elvis up at the port, as long as nothing weird happens to us.

## ABOUT
## THE AUTHOR

The Dr. Reverend Lance Carbuncle was born sometime during the last millennium and he's been getting bigger, older and uglier ever since. Carbuncle is an ordained minister with the Church of Spiritual Humanism. Carbuncle doesn't eat deviled eggs, and he doesn't drink cheap beer. Carbuncle doesn't wear sock garters. Carbuncle does tell stories. And he likes to hear what his readers think. You can let him know how you feel about his books at Bonesbarbuncle@Lancecarbuncle.com.

## ALSO BY LANCE CARBUNCLE

**GRUNDISH AND ASKEW**—Strap on your athletic cup and grab a barf bag. The Dr. Reverend Lance Carbuncle is going to kick you square in the balls and send you on a wild ride that may or may not answer the following questions: what happens when two white trash, trailer park-dwelling, platonic life partners go on a moronic and misdirected crime spree?; can their manly love for each other endure when one of them suffers a psychological bitch-slap that renders him a homicidal maniac?; will a snaggletoothed teenage prostitute tear them apart?; what is the best way to use a dead illegal alien to your advantage in a hostage situation?; what's that smell?; and, what the hell is Alf the Sacred Burro coughing up? *Grundish and Askew* ponders these troubling questions and more. So sit down, put on some protective goggles, and get ready for Carbuncle to blast you in the face with a warm load of fictitious sickness.

**SLOUGHING OFF THE ROT**—John the Revelator awakens in a cave with no memory of his prior life. Guided along El Camino de la Muerte by a demented madman and a philosophical giant, John sets out on a quest to fill in his blank slate and slough off the rot of his soul. Part dark comedy road trip, part spiritual quest, and part horror story, *Sloughing Off the Rot* is literary alchemy about John's transformation from repugnant wretch to reluctant hero. To be released in 2012.

CPSIA information can be obtained
at www.ICGtesting.com
Printed in the USA
LVHW03s1827110718
583385LV00002B/287/P